RIVALS IN FURY

Mason and Walker had been in the Marines together. But they were never what you'd call buddies. They were the toughest men in their outfit, and between them was a rivalry every bit as tough. Along with that rivalry went a deep respect, for each knew that the other would never take the easy way out—in *anything*.

So when Mason and Walker faced each other, years later, on opposite sides of the law, they knew what had to happen . . . a brutal struggle from which only one man would emerge alive!

A CLEANER BREED

NICHOLAS J. COREA

AVON
PUBLISHERS OF BARD, CAMELOT, DISCUS, EQUINOX AND FLARE BOOKS

A CLEANER BREED is an original publication of Avon Books.
This work has never before appeared in any form. The details,
the names and the characters are not intended to, and do not,
relate to any real persons, living or dead.

AVON BOOKS
A division of
The Hearst Corporation
959 Eighth Avenue
New York, New York 10019

Copyright © 1974 by Nicholas J. Corea.
Published by arrangement with the author.
Library of Congress Catalog Number: 74-20623.

ISBN: 0-380-00167-5

All rights reserved, which includes the right
to reproduce this book or portions thereof in
any form whatsoever. For information address
Avon Books.

First Avon Printing, November, 1974.

AVON TRADEMARK REG. U.S. PAT. OFF. AND
FOREIGN COUNTRIES, REGISTERED TRADEMARK—
MARCA REGISTRADA, HECHO EN CHICAGO, U.S.A.

Printed in the U.S.A.

Author's Note

This book is a work of fiction. There is no thirteenth district within the command structure of the St. Louis Police Department, and in most cases the names of streets and businesses have been changed to avoid comparisons with actual persons or incidents. The book's characters and their names are also fictitious, and any resemblance to living persons is purely accidental.

N. J. C.

La Bret.
Alone, yes! But why stand against the world?
What devil has possessed you now, to go
Everywhere making yourself enemies?

Cyrano.
Watching you other people making friends
Everywhere . . . as a dog makes friends! I mark
The manner of these canine courtesies
And think: "My friends are of a cleaner breed;
Here comes, thank God! another enemy!"

    Rostand's *CYRANO DE BERGERAC*

Chapter One

JOE MASON pulled the old Chevy to the curb in front of Frank's Fireball Lounge. He flicked the ignition off and, bending forward, rested his head on the steering wheel. After a moment he straightened to stare down the cold and nearly deserted expanse of Olive Boulevard. He was thinking that he should just keep going down Olive and make it home. All the way home. But he knew, even as the thought came to him, that he wouldn't do that. He was not going to spend his only night off this week in the cluttered four rooms of his apartment. Not alone, he told himself. Not alone.

He rubbed at his face, rousing himself. He opened the car door and stood up into the cold wind, taking several deep breaths, before walking slowly around the back of the Chevy—weaving only slightly—across the cracked and pitted sidewalk, and through the door into the lounge.

The room was crowded with black men and women, and Mason hesitated at the door, feeling his whiteness like a brand. He leaned back into the shadows and stripped off his gloves. He jammed them into his jacket's big pockets and felt the heavy weight of the .45 automatic in its shoulder holster under his left arm, bumping his ribs. His eyes, squinting into the near darkness, swept the interior of the bar with the calculating look of a general surveying a proposed battlefield.

Solid soul from wall to wall. Not another white face in the place. Music from a brightly lit jukebox, pounding the walls, and shapes moving on the small dance floor—dipping, shadow-elongated bodies—flailing, snaking arms and legs. Smoke like a gray fog over bending heads; the men wore slouched Applehats and Broadbrims; the women with elaborate hairdos, bobbing wigs, or blown-out Naturals. Soul. Pure black soul.

Behind the bar two girls in sequined mini-skirts bobbed back and forth like puppets. Drinks were lifted and set down, ice rattling against glass. The bartop—a puddled length of mahogany, intersected by dozens of black arms—was crowned at its far end by an ornate gold cash register. The register's bell sounded counterbeat to the ceiling-vibrating jukebox. A rippling mirror, behind the working girls, reflected the dark faces of the Fireball's patrons and the whirling figures of the frenetic dancers.

Mason straightened up from his crouching slump. He squared his shoulders and moved carefully down a barely distinguishable path between the round tables. The tables were all, every damned one, jammed with customers. They stared up at Mason as he passed. Eyes hardened at the sight of a white man, but then softened with recognition. He was soon being greeted from both sides.

"Joe baby! What's happening, man?"
"Hey, Mason!"
"What's to it, ice-man?"
"Who is watching my crib, police?"

He nodded and waved at the ones with the grins. He glared at the few who glared. He felt strangely shy, having to cross the short distance from the door to the bar, being inspected. Some of them, Mason knew, were genuinely glad to see him. But he was aware that if rock-bottom trouble started they would not stand with him against their friends. It was not so much that he was white as it was the blue he wore on duty. It was his job they resented. His blue suit, his badge, and shiny, leather-covered service revolver. His motherhumping job. Because you don't stand with a cop against blood.

Mason reached the bar and smiled crookedly as a very small Negro, a birdlike young man wearing a shabby beret and black-leather jacket, slid down from his stool and tried to move past him. Joe touched the black man's arm lightly.

"Where you going, Little Bit? You don't have to leave just because I'm here."

"What?" A quick spin to face Mason, and Little Bit repeated: "What?"

"I said, you don't have to run off, man."

"I'm not running anywhere, police," Little Bit said, swallowing nervously. His pinched little face bunched itself into belligerent planes. "This a bust?"

"Com' on, Stanton. I'll buy you a drink. Stay put."

"Keep your fucking drink. Is this a bust, or not, Mason?"

"No bust." Joe Mason's grin widened, but there was no laughter in the stretching of his thin lips. "I'm off duty tonight."

"You are never off duty, man. If this isn't a bust, then I'm leaving."

"Hold on, bad-ass," Mason said, and his fingers tightened on Little Bit Stanton's skinny arm. "When you see Walker tonight, I want you to tell him something for me."

The record died in the jukebox. Another disc flipped out, crashing more music into the air. The dancers, halted for a moment, leaped into the beat, and Little Bit jerked his arm away from Mason. The black men and women on either side watched them with white-edged eyes.

"I won't be seeing Walker tonight," Little Bit said, but Mason ignored the remark and tightened his grin.

"You just tell Walker that you, and the rest of his little group, won't be staying on my beat very long."

"I ain't seeing Walker. I'm goin home to my aunty's crib and watch the late flick on TV. I hear it's a fucking Dracula movie. I really dig on vampires, man. They remind me of police."

"You just tell him that he don't have long on my beat."

"I'll tell my aunty, Mason. I'll tell Bela Lugosi!"

"A comedian, huh?"

"One of my life-long ambitions."

"You're not funny. You're not making me laugh at all, Little Bit. Maybe we ought to take a walk outside, and you can maybe make me laugh where the air's fresher."

"I'm leaving all right, but not with your ass." The nervous tension had slipped back into Little Bit's face. The tip of his pink tongue flicked out and disappeared behind crooked teeth. "If this isn't a bust, I'm leaving."

"Leave then, Stanton." Mason turned away, resting his elbows on the bar. "It wouldn't be worth it to kick your ass. Just tell Walker what I said."

Little Bit snorted an obscenity. He stalked through the crowd and pushed the door open. It shut behind his hunched figure with a clearly audible whoosh of cold air. Mason looked down from the bar mirror. He felt the patrons on his right and left staring at him. He felt the bar's curled edge pressing into his clenched stomach, and he didn't see Frank Brown, the Fireball's owner, until the huge black man stood at his side. Mason met Brown's hard stare and nodded with mock formality.

"Evening, Mr. Brown," he said, and indicated the empty space in front of him on the bartop. "Seems I can't get a drink around here."

"Is that right?" A flash of gold winked between Brown's thick lips. He gestured to the far end of the room. "Com' on down here with me, Mason. You won't be so fucking visible. People come in and see you they might just turn right around and split."

"Prejudice, Mr. Brown . . . is always with us."

The club owner rolled his eyes at the closed front door.

"So I noticed. Why you running my customers out of here, Mason?"

"I'm not running anyone anywhere. Little Bit had a late show to catch. He's wild about vampire movies."

Brown displayed more of his gold teeth in a snarling grimace that was as close as he ever came to grinning. He had a mouthful of gold teeth, but the two front teeth were minor masterpieces of dental artistry. Each flashed a tiny diamond star set into the gold, and Mason could never look at Brown without seeing an enormous black-and-gold crocodile.

The impression sharpened in Mason's imagination as Brown jerked his head toward the rear of the crowded room. It was a movement of bestial power.

"Com' on, Mason. You can get a drink at the other end."

"After you," Joe said, and followed the other man down the length of the bar, holding on to his grin as they passed the dance floor and its burden of wildly gyrating couples.

"Johnny Walker over ice?" Brown asked, and seated himself with ponderous difficulty on the last stool. Though not tall, Brown was very heavily built in the neck and shoulders, with a massive chest and long arms.

"Johnny Red over ice is fine," Mason said, standing next to Brown and lighting a cigarette. One of the barmaids set his drink down and he handed over a crumpled dollar, covering her reaching fingers as he did so. "Mona here?"

The girl looked at Brown, then jerked her hand and the dollar away and moved to another customer.

"This is beginning to groove into a routine with you, Mason. Two, three nights a week." Brown leaned around the end of the bar and took a Coke out of the cooler below the cash register. "A fucking routine."

"I live near here." There was a tremor of tense anger in Mason's voice.

"Mona's not around right now." Brown pried open the Coke cap and took a long pull from the streaming bottle. He belched loudly. "Besides, man ... she ain't your type, anyway. She ain't your type at all, Mason."

"That right?"

"That's gospel truth."

Mason toyed with the ice in his drink. The smile that had begun with Little Bit faded.

"You shouldn't underestimate that girl," he said quietly; just audible above the blaring music. "Mona's the only reason I don't try and close you up, Mr. Brown."

13

The black man pulled out a handkerchief and swabbed his thick neck. He pocketed the square of monogramed white silk and gave Mason a long look. His gold teeth were completely hidden.

"She's not around."

"Isn't she?" Mason glanced at the flight of narrow stairs behind the bar owner's broad back. "Guess I'll go up and see if I can locate her."

"You don't want to do that, Mason," Brown said, and the two men stared at each other. Mason's face twitched back into its mask of smiling anger. The smile was painful, and he thought it would reach a point where it couldn't stretch any further, but would break off his face and go sailing into the mirror on his left. The thought amused him and he turned away from Brown's sweating face to sip his Scotch, puff at his cigarette, and, finally, lift his glass and drain it. The tension eased; Brown told the barmaid to get Mason another drink. When the empty glass had been refilled, Brown said, "This one's on the house."

"Accepted with thanks," replied Mason, and once again glanced at the flight of dusty stairs.

Brown shook his bullet-shaped head.

"Okay, man. She's upstairs. But you still ain't going up there. You're not that dumb. You can wait."

"She got a customer?"

"She's a hostess."

"Is that what you call it now?"

"It's on her W-2 form. Hostess."

The jukebox thumped electric guitars, hard brass, and wild drums. The dancers snaked and shook. The seated customers snapped their mouths open and shut, heads bobbing, rolling, and jerking.

"I'll wait," Mason said. "I just didn't want us to be bullshitting each other, Brown. Anybody can see I'm Custer, and you guys are the Sioux. It's no big deal that Mona's upstairs. I just didn't want bullshit."

"You wouldn't have got to the first step," Brown said, evenly taking in the room with a revolving sweep of his eyes. "All these brothers and sisters'd be my witnesses."

Mason hissed out a stream of blue smoke.

"You know Brown, you must be watching a lot of TV lately. You're beginning to sound like a very bad, old time hoodlum movie."

"And you're acting bulletproof, knifeproof, and fistproof! Com' on in here all the time!" Brown shook his head. "You know, Officer Mason ... there are people in the district who are not too fucking fond of you. You are the Man, you know! Even if you were a blood, you'd still be the damned Man!"

"The only ones in this district who aren't fond of me," Mason murmured, "are the thieves, shitbums, and pimps. The thieves I try and lock up. The shitbums I hassle until it becomes too much of a problem for them to hang around. And the pimps"—Mason stared at Brown—"the pimps I drink with and make nervous."

Brown's square face tightened. His chin pulled in toward his neck, creating a second, softer chin. His forehead gleamed with tiny droplets of sweat, and his beady eyes stared without blinking. "What about Vernon Walker? What do you do about Vernon Walker, Mr. Police?"

"I don't worry about that dude," Mason said lightly, but his face suddenly clenched shut, like a closing fist, and Brown rumbled a deep laugh.

"Well, now. I wouldn't have thought so, but I believe it at last! The ice-man's got a weak spot!"

Mason signaled to the barmaid closest to him, placing a five-dollar bill on the stained mahogany.

"Give me another, Shirl."

"They say," Brown rumbled, "that you and Walker were in Vietnam together. That right, Mason?"

The white man said nothing, and Brown's big hands clutched at the bar's curled edge as Mason's drink arrived and the cop counted his change, placing coins atop damp dollar bills. When there was no response, Brown, inching closer and closer to danger, said, "Is that why you turned down plainclothes, Mason? Is it because you wanted to stay in this district where you could keep an eye on your old buddy?"

15

"Get off it," Mason finally said. "You're fishing for something that isn't there."

"Am I? But all us niggers love to fish. You know that, Mason. We are the fishingest motherfuckers in the world."

"I'm impressed," Mason said. "I never knew you were an outdoorsman. And all this time I've been going around thinking you were just a plain old ordinary crook-pimp."

Brown stared. Anger washed over his features, but he broke into loud laughter. Heads turned and stared at the two men as Brown roared his way into a fit of coughing, and had to drain his Coke before he could stop. He inhaled deeply and leaned close to Mason's shoulder.

"I wouldn't have believed you had a warm spot in your cold, white heart for us black folks, Mason. But I should've figured it. The way you've been coming in here to see Mona and all. And now I find out that Vernon Walker was in the marines with you—an old buddy! The biggest fucking militant in St. Louis!"

Mason was trying very hard to control himself. He knew that a burst of violence in the Fireball could very well climax in his instant departure from the land of the living. He forced a short laugh and said, "What's Mona doing up there, trying to convince that John to marry her?"

But Brown wasn't to be sidetracked so easily. He gripped Mason's arm and once again was convulsed with barely controlled laughter.

"What you goin to do 'bout Walker, ice-man? You told me what you do with thieves, shitbums, and pimps—but what you goin to do 'bout your old marine buddy?"

Mason twisted away from the other man's hold, and cold Scotch sloshed over his hand. For a moment he seemed to be thinking, just staring at his wet hand, thinking. But his head came up and his eyes fixed on Brown's oily, grinning face, and the black man's laughter faltered. Mason's eyes were pale blue, glazed, in their dark sockets. His nostrils flared out and a muscle twitched along his jaw-line with spastic anger.

"Get off it, you black son of a bitch! You get off it, or I'll get your big ass alone one night and break you up with an ax handle. I'll break every bone in your fucking body, and then I'll see to it that you never run another girl, or another bar, for as long as you manage to stay alive!"

Frank Brown drew himself upright on the stool. He breathed through his flat nose in sharp, slow gasps. His thick hands, resting on either side of his empty Coke bottle, contracted into bigger fists. Mason watched and did not move, but stood glaring at Brown and ready to fight. He suddenly wanted very much to fight—and to hell with the odds—but Brown took visible control of himself and let out another deep breath. He fumbled with the inside pocket of his suit coat and took out a cigar. After lighting the long cigar he mopped his face with the silk handkerchief.

The threat of violence receded. For the moment both men had felt isolated, but now the music and the noise of the bar flooded back around them. A trembling tic at the corner of Brown's slit mouth and liver-colored lips turned into a faint smile.

"You been in business as long as I have," he said, "You see all kinds of cops. Even cops like you, Mason. I've seen your kind before. I know where you are, man, and that's why you're not eating this floor right now."

Mason wiped his wet hand dry on the small napkin inscribed with the circled impression of his glass. He was suddenly sorry for blowing his cool, and his next words pushed out through clenched teeth in a low monotone.

"You pushed too far, Brown. Let's leave it at that."

"Okay, Officer Mason, it's left." He puffed on the tapered cigar. "Mona will be down any time, now. She can leave early tonight if she wants."

"Okay."

"Fine. Have another drink on the house, Officer Mason. You're not that bad for business. You can stand here and guard the fucking cash register."

17

"I'll buy my own drink," Mason said, and didn't look up from his hands, the crumpled napkin, and his glass of Scotch and ice, as Brown heaved himself off the stool and pushed into the crowd of customers.

"Suit yourself, ice-man."

Little Bit Stanton hurried down the dark alley—a tiny figure illuminated periodically in pools of dirty yellow light from the tall poles lining the cobblestone passage. Icy wind blew down the concrete canyon formed by squat buildings to either side of him and made the small man bend ever deeper into his too-large jacket. Little Bit had no gloves, and his hands were tucked into beltless jeans. White puffs blew from his puckered mouth.

He crossed a small parking area on his right, skirting piles of trash, and moved between a parked Lincoln Continental and a green Ford pickup. He stopped at a gray steel door in the chipped, red brick of the building's rear. The words FREEDOM NOW! were scratched onto its surface. He knocked twice. He waited, then knocked twice more. He waited a full double count, then knocked just once. He cursed at the pain in his knuckles and blew warm air on his knobby hands as a voice asked from behind the gray steel, "Who's that fool out in the Hawk?"

"Little Bit," he answered. "Open up, man! It's fucking freezing out here!"

Metal rasped on stone as the door creaked open. Stanton slipped inside to a dimly lit corridor. He nodded at the fat black man who had admitted him.

"Hi ya' Walleye, old rap. Vernon here?"

"In there." Walleye Jones, twice as tall as Little Bit, and at least twice as wide, indicated the closed door on their right. The two young men, so different, yet somehow very much alike in the way they gestured, moved, and talked, stood in the hallway and grinned at each other. They were old partners. They could read each other's minds after more than twenty years in St. Louis's roughest streets and dirtiest jails, hacking it all together. A skinny, dwarfed Mutt, and a fat, popeyed

Jeff. And the times were too damned many to count when they'd saved each other's ass, or hid out from the cops or other motherhumping niggers looking to waste them, or pushed smack in the deserted dawns of bus terminals and graveyards, or trimmed the same chick in the same room and paid her out of both pockets (then maybe rolled her pimp and got a hurried return on their investment). Being tight was the word for it. Tight dudes, ol' Walleye and Little Bit. Tight fuckin' partners.

"He must be with that Jew lawyer," Stanton said. "I seen the Lincoln outside."

"Chuck's in there, too, with Vernon and the Jew. Terry T. went and got himself busted again."

Little Bit nodded, as if this was only to be expected. His emaciated little sparrow's face twisted into pained resignation. "You ready to make it to the East Side tonight?"

"I'm here, ain't I?" Walleye's bulging eyes flickered with quick indignation, and even quicker fear. "But do you really think Vernon's serious, man? Is he, do you think?"

Little Bit cocked his head at his friend, and Walleye nodded, then shook his head. He suddenly wanted to change the subject.

"Where you been, man? I checked the crib out, but you weren't there."

"Fireball Lounge," Little Bit said. "I saw that cop, Mason."

"That fuckin' pig!" Walleye rubbed a thick finger across an equally thick nose, and followed Little Bit to the tiny bathroom across from Vernon Walker's closed door. Little Bit stood, legs braced, and relieved himself, as Walleye leaned against the cubicle's doorframe. Pipes rattled insanely as Stanton washed his hands under the ancient faucets. He rubbed his hands across his jacket's front, drying them. He hadn't turned on the hanging bulb, and in the Lysol-smelling half dark, he stared up at Walleye.

"Mason was acting a little high, but he could've been trying to fake me out. So I walked around in circles after I left, checking to see if he was on me, or not. I froze my black ass off, but I don't think he left the Fireball."

"What's a white cop doing there anyway, man ... if he ain't looking to make a bust?"

"Mason's been going there a lot." Little Bit grinned. "He's trimming a sister who works for big Brown."

"A sister!" Walleye's voice was incredulous and loud. He glanced over his shoulder at the closed door, where the murmur of voices could be faintly heard. He looked at Little Bit, his gaping eyes gleaming wet and round. "You going to tell Vernon? He'd want to know. If it's about Mason, he'd want to know."

"Vernon's already been informed," Little Bit said, and laughed softly. He motioned Walleye into the front office. They stepped into the big room from the hallway, and for a moment Little Bit stared at the sandbags stacked against the boarded-up windows, feeling the way he always felt when he saw them. There was an answer to why things were the way they were in his world. But that answer always fled too quickly for him, and he was left empty. To hell with it, he thought, and jerked off his beret. He sat down on a folding chair behind a large metal desk, the only pieces of genuine furniture in the room. Just back from the wall of sandbags, a table of sorts had been made from an old door laid across two carpenter's horses, and there was a bench for the mimeograph machine, but nothing else. The room was stripped for war.

Walleye lowered his bulk onto the desktop. He asked his friend: "What do you mean, 'Vernon's been informed'?"

"He just knows Mason's seeing this Mona chick."

"How does he feel about it, man?"

"He just knows, is all. He thinks it might be valuable someday."

"Huh?" Walleye arranged his soft face into what, for Walleye Jones, passed for anger. "That honky motherfucker trimming a sister is *valuable?*"

"Correct, Fatman. And we are her brothers, dig?

And maybe the fact that we are her brothers could be bad for ol' Mason."

Walleye considered this and a sudden smile lit his cherubic face. "I get it, yeah! I can dig it!" He dropped his voice then. "Has the chief got to her, yet? Is she with us?"

"Vernon just knows about it," Little Bit repeated, growing tired of explaining every goddamned thing, like he always had to when he talked to Walleye. "Stop straining your brain, bro. Be quiet. The Little Bit's got to figure out a good route for tonight's buying trip." And he spread the map out, his fingers moving across the creases and wrinkles like a blind man reading Braille. The old Shell Oil map had come from inside Little Bit's jacket, and Walleye caught a fleeting glimpse of a pint's brown glass bottle.

"You got a sniff of something there, man?"

"Forgot that," Little Bit said, and passed Walleye the bottle of cheap bourbon. "Oil yourself, man. But not too much. We got to be very cool tonight."

"I wish we weren't going," Walleye said, and took a pull of the whiskey. His teeth clicked against the bottle's mouth. He swallowed and gasped a curse. Tears stood out along the reddened rims of his dark eyes. "East St. Louis ain't the bad part. There's lots of bloods in East St. Louis. The east side is crawling with us niggers, but we have to make it all the way north to redneck country, Little Bit. We got to go into them lynchin' cops' territory."

Little Bit looked up from his study of the map. His sepia-brown face had lost its usual expression of wry humor and sarcasm. When he spoke, he surprised himself at how serious he really was.

"But it's something we both believe in, ain't it, Walleye? Ain't it the first goddamned thing we've ever really believed in?"

Walleye nodded slowly. He clenched his pudgy fingers around the bottle. "You're right, Brother Stanton. I got to dig down inside of me and find some fucking guts!" Then, realizing what he'd just said, Walleye stared at Little Bit and at his bulging stomach

21

and started laughing. He slapped the rolls of fat hanging over his belt and squealed.

"Guts? I got so much guts now I could start a fuckin' tripe factory!"

Vernon Walker lay on the army cot in his office-bedroom and clasped his hands behind his neck. He listened to Chuck Williams and Henry Lehr, the group's lawyer arguing, but he made no comment. He lay very still, staring up at the ceiling, and tried to concentrate on a course of action that would free Terry T. and satisfy Lehr at the same time. He was slowly coming to the realization, lying there and listening to his Prime Minister and legal advisor, that he could do only what was right for the organization . . . and to hell with anything else.

Walker's body covered the cot and his legs hung off the end. He was broad-shouldered, but not very heavy in the chest and arms. He had a very wide upper lip, clean-shaven, and an almost Caucasian nose, though his complexion was as dark as his eyes.

For almost an hour Walker had listened to Williams and Lehr debating, and he was tired of trying to concentrate on what they were saying. Instead, he turned his head and stared at Lehr, noticing that despite the chill of the small room, the attorney sweated. Walker decided that Lehr was afraid almost all of the time, and he wondered what it must be like to have that kind of fear.

Feeling Vernon's eyes on him, Lehr held up a pudgy, well-manicured hand to silence Chuck Williams's angry words. He turned in his chair to face the supine Walker.

"Vernon, you know how I feel. And it's obvious how Chuck feels. But you've said nothing, Vernon, and we're right back to where we started."

Williams stood up so fast that his metal folding chair collapsed. He kicked it out of the way and paced back and forth, talking in staccato bursts, his hands chopping an accompanying beat.

"You want us to leave a member to rot in jail, Lehr!

We can't do that! It goes against everything we've been telling our people! How're we going to give them that kind of shit? How're they going to take it when we lay on them the fact that just because we want to kiss some political butt, Terry T.'s got to stay behind the Man's bars?"

Lehr licked his lips and smoothed down his drooping mustache. He was a once-handsome man, fading into his forties, and trying to look young. His neatly razored hair and mod clothes were unsuccessful tactics. Nothing could hide Henry's fat belly, his rapidly diminishing hairline, or the fine tracery of wrinkles beginning to pattern his round, sunlamp-tanned face.

"Terry T.," he said now, looking up as Chuck stopped his furious pacing to stand and glower down at him, "was arrested in the act of beating an old man and attempting to rob him of thirteen dollars. To cap it all, the victim was black! And this is the animal you want out of jail in the name of the Party, using Party funds!"

"He is still a member!" Chuck gritted his teeth, looking very fierce with his goatee and high Afro haircut. But the anger in Williams's words, the obvious threat behind his stance, failed to silence the lawyer. Lehr felt himself unable to slow the stream of words rushing from him. He gave Vernon a despairing look, but saw that Walker was content—for the moment—to be silent.

"I'm not talking about membership," Lehr said, turning back to face Williams. "What I'm trying to get across to both of you is the importance of maintaining a certain image—what the public, black and white both, think of the Party. If you continue to associate yourselves with obvious criminals like Terry T. Logan, then all you do is undermine the trust built up in the black community, and the support we've been able to develop in the white!"

"Fuck our image!" Chuck slammed his fist down on Vernon's desk. He turned to face Walker's calm eyes. "Man, tell this white mother what he can do with his image!"

Walker looked at both men, then lurched off the bunk and made his way to the hall door. He opened the door and spoke quietly, "Walleye?"

The answer came at once: "Out front, Vernon."

"Little Bit here?"

"I'm here, Vernon."

"We'll be finished in a minute. You both ready to go?"

Little Bit answered: "Ready, great black father!"

Vernon could not help grinning as he stepped back into the room and closed the door behind him. He kept his smile when he looked up and saw the two anxious faces waiting for him to speak.

"Henry," he said to the lawyer, "I want you to pop Terry out when, and if, they set bail. Have warrants been issued yet?"

Lehr's shoulders slumped down and forward. He stood up and closed his briefcase. He shook his head. "No, Vernon. That won't be until tomorrow morning. Vernon, isn't there someway I can convince you? This is not going to read well in the papers. We know how the *Globe* will play it; they've been against you from the beginning. But, Vernon, even the *Post* will blast us for this kind of thing. And the people who've contributed to our bail bond fund. They'll want to know why their money's—"

"No more talking," Walker said. "We've talked it into the ground. Right now, I need Terry T. much more than I need the papers, or the approval of suburbia liberals."

"That's it, man! That's—" Chuck Willliams cut his own sentence in half at Walker's look. He held up his hands and smiled. "I'll just shut up, Chief."

"And I'll be leaving, Lehr said, and walked to the door. He stopped next to Walker and met the tall black man's look with his own faltering stare. "Why do you suddenly need a man like Terry Logan? I thought we were progressing past that kind of thing, Vernon?"

"You never 'progress past' needing men like Logan. This kind of man is used by every city administration in the country. Most of them wear police uniforms. And don't be so quick to say 'we,' when you talk about the Party. You aren't 'we' any more than I'm white. Your talents are bought and paid for, and you do a good job. Stop worrying about anything else."

Lehr's face paled under his artificial tan. He bent his head and buttoned his overcoat with one hand, while clutching the briefcase with the other. "You're as bad as the men you fight, Vernon," he said, "if you exclude someone who wants to help because of ... what he is ... by accident of birth."

Walker didn't answer. He led the way into the hall and opened the steel door. Cold wind bathed his face with the chill stench of the alley.

"Get in your shiny car, Mr. Lehr, and go home to Ladue Hills." And as the attorney moved past him, Walker added, "Forget about trying to grow a pair of balls, Henry. I like you much better without any."

Lehr said nothing. He unlocked his car and got in quickly. The Lincoln's engine roared into life as he backed out of the alley, spun his tires in the frozen cobblestones, and drove west.

Vernon turned away and walked down the hall to the front room as Chuck closed and locked the steel door. He stood behind Little Bit and glanced down at the map. He looked up and saw Walleye staring at him like a condemned man waiting for his reprieve.

"Take it easy, fatman."

"I'm all right, Chief."

"I know you are." Walker put his hand on Little Bit's bony shoulder. "You got the streets marked on that map?"

"No way, boss."

"The location where you'll make the pickup?"

"I ain't that stupid, Vernon."

"Good." Walker grinned and stretched. "Who's got a square?"

Little Bit offered him a pack of Kools and Vernon shook a cigarette free and lit it. He handed the pack back to Stanton and Little Bit said, "I saw Mason tonight at the Fireball. He gave me a message to deliver."

"For me?"

"Yeah. He said that I should tell you that you're not going to stay on his beat, that he'd get all of us off his beat."

Walker laughed loudly. His laughter sounded very strange, and he stopped short. "We'll have to see about that. We'll just have to see about that."

Little Bit stared up at him, and Vernon gave him a playful punch in the arm.

"Isn't that right, little soldier?"

"Anything you say, Vernon. Anything you say."

Chapter Two

PAIN RUNNING to numbness. Shock turning to despair. Black night. Monsoon clouds. No stars, a sky of slate gray and black. They've left you, Mason. You're alone. You're lying in the mud, and in your own blood, and the blood that pumped from Johnson before he died. And you're alone.

Maybe Johnson's better off. He won't have to wait anymore. It won't be sitting just off to the side for Jimmy Johnson any longer. He's tasting it now. And it's your turn to wait, Mason. Johnson's done his.

But at least the squad made it out. They lost track of you, or they wouldn't have left you, Mason. You know they wouldn't have left you. They're Mason's Raiders, and they wouldn't leave Sergeant Mason himself.

Would they?

Can't feel your legs. Too afraid to look at them. Couldn't see them if I wanted to, but I don't want to. Don't want to see them!

So damned dark. So cold lying in this paddy. And you know the Cong are all over the place. Waiting, too. Only different. They're waiting to kill you, Mason. Sergeant Mason, of Mason's Raiders. That's a joke! The squad made it out and left you. Be happy, man! Your squad made it out....

But it is so lonely. It is so hard to wait until the sun starts burning the night away: until he sees Jimmy Johnson's dead, black face, the eyes opaque and staring; until he sees the figure rising up out of the far treeline and jogging through the watery mud toward him.

Gook or marine? Roll over on your stomach, Mason. It could be a marine. It could be life. Through the fog-gripped paddy the man splashes closer.

A marine: and life. Mason sees him, blurred through tears of relief. He croaks something and the man kneels next to him.

"Walker ... Vernon ... you—"

"Shut up, Sarge. Put your arms around my neck. Com' on!"

He lifts you up. He cradles you in his arms like a child. The tears cut through the dried blood on your face. You hold on as he jogs into the trees. He runs, his rifle slamming his back, and his breath panting down on you, and all the time he's grinning and talking. So fuckin' proud of himself. So goddamned proud!

"Seen Jimmy," he says. "Knew he was zapped, but I wasn't sure about you. Didn't want to go out there if you were zapped, too. But I seen you move. I knew they couldn't waste a mean bastard like you, and I had to come out and say hello. Now you owe me one, Sarge. You really fuckin' owe me one!"

"Don't owe ... nothing!" And your blood's running down his flapping green trouser legs. How far to the company? You pray for the VC to spot you and kill you both. You don't want to owe Vernon Walker anything.

"We always were pretty even," he gasps, stopping to kneel and get a better grip on you. And the pain returns, reviving fast. "But I got one on you now, Mason! Damn, you're heavier than I thought!" And he lunges to his feet. "They said you were zapped. But I knew you weren't dead. Hold on, man! We're off to the races again!"

And the pain leaps in you. Vision blurs till all you can see is Vernon Walker's gleaming black face, bobbing above you.

Joe Mason swam slowly out of the dream, rising through terror like a diver struggling away from the ocean's floor. He fought through successive depths of fear until he knew the dream had been left behind. Still, he would not open his eyes. He allowed the sounds of the new morning to penetrate his brain until he was positive he was back—all the way back, and safe.

In that instant of awakening, acutely aware of the murmuring traffic outside the frosted bedroom windows, and the rapid hammer beat of his own heart, Mason knew a voice whispered insistently, "You must face Vernon Walker." He came totally awake then, charging head-on into the most painful of hangovers.

He felt the smooth brush of someone else's skin against his naked thigh. Still tasting the chill flavor of the dream, he saw pieces of the night before, like a shattered mirror restored in slow motion, fall into place. He remembered the duel-like conversation with Frank Brown, but not the drive home with Mona in tow. And he remembered the drunken climb up leaning stairs to upzip trousers, unzip her dress, unsnap bra—stand weaving above her on the bed—fall into her dark arms, breasts crushed beneath his weight, a gleam of white teeth, wet tongues.

As usual, the realization that he'd made love to a black woman, a woman who gave herself to other men for money, produced its momentary twinges of shame and anger. But he cast aside any feelings of guilt. Fuck it. Mona's a whore. But Mona's real, too. She never turns her head away from me, Mason thought, and she never pretends to feel what she isn't feeling. I paid for her to begin with, but now we like each other enough so that money doesn't matter. I ball her. I trim her. And I can laugh with her while we're making love— trapped between her long legs, panting. What more does a man want in his woman? Nothing more.

Mason opened his eyes then. He turned his head carefully, trying to contain the pain pulsing inside his skull. He saw that Mona was awake. She was twisted onto her side and smiling at him. Her smile was a combination of sarcasm and sensuousness, as if she had been discovered suddenly with her guard down. Her large brown eyes were very wide, and opened for him a view of herself she kept hidden from almost everyone else. He felt, for the first time with any woman, that this time, with this woman, he was aware of everything she was. He stared at her, in this understanding, and saw the short black hair etched against the white of the pillow, the nipple of an exposed breast poking up through the tangle of sheets and blankets like the nose of a curious puppy. He attempted to smile, but the effort only nauseated him, and brought back a flashing view of the dream and Vernon Walker.

"Jesus," he murmured.

"The tough cop awakens," she said. "I don't know whether or not to kiss you good morning, Mason. You look like you're ready to puke."

"Very possible," he agreed. He felt her touching him between the legs, her hand trying to soothe but only stirring an itching irritation. He rolled away and sat up. The bedroom tilted. He dropped his legs over the side of the bed and sat with elbows on bent knees, his hands dropping like strangled birds. The headache rushed to that place, sending its stabbing messages to every part of his crouched body. He stood up, hoping he could escape suffering through movement, and pulled the shade away from the window.

"Custer's last stand," Mona said, not bothering to hide the mirth in her voice, "and you are General C. himself."

"Then you must be Crazy Horse," he said, and his tone of voice, the empty growling from his compressed lips, discouraged further conversation. Mason didn't mind the silence at all. He pressed his hand against the cold glass of the window and stared out at a northern sky so hard and slick it appeared to be sprayed-on enamel. On the street below moved a continuous line of cars. Blinking eyes that felt filled with gritty sand, Mason wondered where the hell they were all going in such a hurry. From nowhere to nowhere, he decided. From Point A to Point B . . . and back again.

Decide about Walker. You must decide about Walker!

The words resounded through Joe's mind and he rested his forehead on the icy windowpane, watched intently as his breath made spreading designs on the glass, blinked at the strange blue sky showing between the trees and buildings on the other side of the street, and asked himself again: Could you have made it out of that paddy without Walker's help? Could you have made it back to the company without him?

He thought that perhaps he could have, but it still didn't alter the fact that Vernon Walker had been there, when no one else had come looking; that Vernon Walker had lifted him and run with him, like a black crane, loping through mud and water and tangled brush, grinning down at him, grinning down at him. . . .

"You were sweating," Mona said. "You were talking in your sleep."

"Was I?" Mason let the shade fall back and shook a cigarette from the crushed pack on the nightstand. He clicked open the beat-up Zippo and puffed from its wavering flame. His thumb caressed the rough steel of the Third Marine Division insignia welded into the lighter's scratched front. How did everything get to where it is now? he wondered. How did everything come to the point where I'm thinking, "Get Walker before he gets you!" ? And the word "get" didn't fool him for a minute. He knew what his head meant when it said, "Get Vernon Walker." Mason knew damn well.

"Joe?"

"What?" He turned and faced her.

"Are you okay?"

She stared at him from the bed and pulled aside the sheet and covers as he turned. Mason realized he was holding his breath. He released a sigh of frustration and anger.

"I've had enough bed," he murmured, and moved on bare feet to the bedroom door, big-boned, six feet tall, and with the beginnings of a paunch swelling out over his dangling manhood. The dark-blue uniforms were hung behind the door on an aluminum extension. His faded green robe was draped over the door's edge.

Mason pulled it down and wrapped his hairy nakedness. Mona sat up on the rumpled bed, her small brown breasts bobbing as she moved, and Mason found himself examining her with an objectivity he had seldom experienced. He felt disoriented, as if he'd never been in his own bedroom before, as if he'd never seen Mona naked before. He licked dry lips as his eyes focused on her breasts. He noticed how dark her nipples were against the cocoa-brown skin.

"You look bad, Mason," Mona said, and grinned at him, and the moment of feeling adrift and lost was gone. Mason knotted the cord around his waist and once again reminded himself to start a fitness program before he ended up fat-assed and sloppy.

"Thanks a lot. That's just what I need on this lousy Saturday morning. Something to boost the old ego." He held out his hand, standing at the end of the bed and looking down at her, and she knelt up, grasping his outstretched fingers. Her small hand was warm and dry. An overwhelming sense of her took him, and he said, "Stand up, baby."

Without asking why, Mona very gracefully stepped from the bed and stood in front of him, naked. Mason motioned for her to turn around, feeling it all in his throat and knowing that he would have to cough before he could speak. She cocked her head at him and a fleeting look of surprise crossed her face. Then she did as he indicated. She held her arms out and performed a lazy pirouette. The circle completed, she stopped and let her hands fall to her sides. "Pervert," she said, and smiled at him.

"It's like I'm just seeing you," he said thoughtfully. "And one of the things I've decided I really dig about you is the way your breasts stand out, and the way your neck slants down to your shoulders. You have a long swan's neck. Did you know that?"

"A black swan's neck," she said, trying to maintain the bantering tone of their conversation. But her smile turned to a slight frown as Mason ignored her remark and talked on, touching her gently as he itemized.

"I like your short hair. Most guys like long hair. But

yours makes you look strong and young. And I really like your waist, here where it wraps around to your back, and this deep groove over your spine. A groovy groove." He turned her around again, and his fingers pressed into the places his words described. "And your ass. You have a fantastic ass, Mona. And good legs, too." She faced him once more, and Mason's hands were on her shoulders. She stared up at him without smiling. Her head was back and her eyes were very wide, and she had lost all of her earlier sarcasm.

"What's all this for, Mason?"

"I'm just trying to tell you that I think you're a very good-looking chick."

"I got that part of it. But there's something else. This isn't your kind of scene, Joe. You're talking love-talk, now, baby. Real, honest-to-God love-talk."

"I am?" He shrugged, and turned his head to stare at the shade over the cold window. His cigarette, which he'd lit and left in the ashtray near the window, smoked itself, blue smoke wavering toward the ceiling. "Maybe I'm getting soft."

She unfastened his robe and pressed herself to him. He looked down at her slanted profile and the smooth curve of her naked back, and closed the robe around her and held her to his chest. She murmured, "I could give you a rub-down with some extra added attractions. It'd make you feel better, Mason. They say it's good for a hangover."

"No rubdowns, lady." He felt himself grinning against her hair. "But I am offering breakfast ... if you cook it."

She didn't answer immediately, but gave one of her quick shrugs instead. He felt it ripple through his arms: a complete washing away of now and a beginning of what will be. "Okay," she said, and pulled away from him, grabbing at her strewn underwear, and heading for the bathroom. "Bacon and eggs instead of a rubdown!"

"Mona."

She stopped in her tracks and blinked at him, but Mason only shook his head. His dark hair had fallen down over his forehead and into his eyes, and she thought he looked very young now with his robe dangling open, his hair mussed, and his eyes sleepy with bad dreams.

"Nothing," he said. "Go on. I'll start the coffee."

"You're nuts, Mason!" she said brightly.

He nodded. "I know that, kid. Go on."

When the door to the bathroom closed behind her, Mona turned on the shower but didn't get in. She leaned on the basin and stared at her reflection in the small mirror. Tears welled up and spilled from her eyes. After a moment, she gained control of herself, stepped into the tub, and bent under the slashing spray, adjusting the water as hot as she could stand it.

Little Bit and Walleye, side by side in the cab of the green pickup, drove west through the flattened-looking jumble of closed and boarded-up stores, filling stations with rusted car skeletons in their lots, litter-filled streets, and the hopeless alleys that were East St. Louis, Illinois. They were heading back, rolling down the pockmarked surface of Collinsville Avenue. Ahead lay the cloverleafed roadway leading to the new free bridge that spanned the Mississippi's sluggish brown waters. The toll-free bridge would take them to the heart of downtown St. Louis, on the Missouri side of the river, and back to the red-brick building on Delmar Avenue.

The sun was high up behind them, but gave off little warmth, and the truck's heater wheezed loudly above the clatter of the Ford's engine. Despite the noise, Walleye felt like talking—shouting really—as they passed railroad yards, vacant packing houses and slaughter pens, slum shanties—all lining the clean concrete approaches to the bridge. He interrupted himself several times to glance back nervously through the pickup cab's small window. The truckbed itself was covered by a brown-canvas tarp that undulated frantically in the cold wind.

"If we get stopped with those guns in the back, we have had the fucking cock, man!"

Little Bit grunted a choice obscenity. He gripped the large steering wheel with his too-small hands.

"That's why I've been driving like an old maid! Let me do the worrying, will ya'? I'm better at worrying than you are! And besides, when you get all shook up 'bout something you start quivering like a bowlful of black jello!"

"Wash your mouth with soap!" Walleye snapped, looking back through the rear window for the thousandth time. "You can be as wise-ass as you want, but I feel like we're pushing it too fuckin' close this time!" He turned back to glaring at the road in front of them, and hunched his shoulders. He wore a thin nylon windbreaker. Bright red, it had a Budweiser Beer label sewn on the back. The jacket made Walleye look even fatter. And as they started up the ramps leading to the wide concrete-and-steel bridge, he moaned, "Jesus fucking Christ! Across the state line! Little Bit do you realize we are crossing the motherfucking state line? Now we can get it on a federal rap!"

"The fed's got better prisons, fat man! Relax!" Little Bit couldn't help smiling at his friend's fear. His cigarette clamped between crooked teeth by its smashed flat filter, Stanton felt downright cocky. The feeling was getting better and better now that they were actually en route back to headquarters. They had had to make the buy from a white man, in a white neighborhood, and Little Bit was only just now beginning to relax as they neared the other side of the river.

A product of almost continuous street combat, Little Bit Stanton (whose legal first name was Harlan) was conditioned to stand up under pressure. His twenty-six years of living were a chronicle of disaster, survival, and the development of extraordinary resilience in the face of odds that, particularly to a man of his stature, were always very great. Little Bit could never remember a time when he wasn't fighting: for his share of food in a family of seven, against bullies in his ten years of schooling, and with cops from then on. In between lay a nightmare of hustling to earn what it took to carve out a place of your own in the ghetto.

With Walleye's bulk and his craft, the two of them had managed to make it, day by day, and week by week, never being stupid enough to plan ahead farther than a month. Stanton barely remembered his mother, who had died when he was five years old, and didn't want to remember the succession of aunts and so-called uncles who had tried to hold the family together when his old man had left for parts unknown. And for his brothers and sisters, Little Bit had only a passing interest. They had come into this fucking life with much more height and muscle than he had, and as far as he was concerned they could look out for themselves.

"Fuck!" Walleye twisted around and stared through the rectangle of yellowed glass. "The tarp's popping loose!"

"I can hear it, man. Take it easy!"

"You can see the damned cases!"

"What do you want me to do, Walleye? You want me to stop on the fuckin' bridge? You want me to stop and fix the tarp in the middle of this fuckin' bridge? Is that what you want?"

"Lord Jesus Christ—Go! Fucking! Damn!"

"That's telling him!" Little Bit laughed, and the laugh rose to a series of high-pitched giggles. "You tell the Man upstairs about that damned ol' tarp!"

"Buying rifles!" Walleye said, and moaned. "Buying rifles and carrying them across state lines! This is getting too deep, man! This is turning into something else! It's too damned heavy, Little Bit! Too damned heavy!"

"It is, isn't it?" Little Bit gripped the steering wheel of the old truck as though he would wrench it from its column. His wiry arms hurt from the pressure on them, but he couldn't seem to let down an inch. He tasted the wire-taut tension in him and decided it was good. It was better to run at danger than to live waiting for it to come get you.

The laughter swelled out of him as the tall arch of the Gateway to the West monument appeared on the west bank of the river. The truck began the long curving roll toward St. Louis. "You're right, Walleye, old rap! This is heavy! It is living at its heaviest!"

Vernon Walker spit into the basin and turned on the water. The pipes clattered behind thin walls. Vernon could hear the mimeograph machine cranking away outside the bathroom. He decided it was going to be a busy, noisy, screwed-up Saturday.

Soaping his face and armpits, Walker tried to control the shaking that made his teeth chatter uncontrollably. The heat's never working right, he thought. Damned Jew landlord! But Walker had to laugh out loud at that—sputtering into the soap and splashed water. He wasn't even sure that the landlord of the building was Jewish, and he wondered if he were becoming a victim of his own propaganda.

He toweled off, rubbing his chest and arms vigorously, then threw the coarse towel over his shoulder and crossed the hall to his office. He opened the door and nodded at Chuck Williams, who sat on the cot and drank coffee from a styrofoam cup. Williams smiled at Vernon's look and handed up a cupful of hot coffee.

"Let's get some real cups," Vernon said, and set the restaurant container down on his cluttered desk. "Start making this place feel a little more permanent."

"We could get 'em painted with our names." Williams's handsome face was inscrutable. "And hang 'em on the wall, and when one of us got busted, or wasted, we'd take the dude's cup down and smash it in the fireplace."

Vernon dressed quickly, trying to kill the cold that seemed to grow with each minute. He smiled to himself at Chuck's words and muttered, not wanting to give up the impression of a bad mood, "Yeah. If we only had a fireplace, that'd be all right."

Williams nodded his head, Afro bobbing, and giggled soundlessly, spasms of laughter moving his shoulders and chest. "Yeah, Chief. Yeah, that is right."

Sunlight pierced the back window and illuminated the floating dust motes. Finished dressing, in worn black corduroy trousers, black jersey, and black boots, Vernon stood for a moment and stared over Williams's head at the alley. He turned away and sat at his small desk.

He'd seen alleys before. All his life seemed an endless progression of alleys.

"Who do you have on that loud-ass machine out there?" he asked Chuck, and sipped from his steaming cup.

"Spider." Williams had a small hand mirror out and was combing his goatee. He seemed impressed by what he saw in the mirror and preened himself like a peacock, long fingers pressing and patting at mustache, chin whiskers, and blown-out hair. "And Spider is kicking that ol' mimeograph's ass!"

"How long's he been with us now?" Vernon decided the coffee was miserable. He could taste the styrofoam.

"Two weeks," Williams answered, "and still in Basic Training."

"Is he starting to growl?"

"A little. He considers himself a bad dude and he wants action."

Vernon Walker's big hand reached down and covered a thin red volume lying on top of a haphazard stack of books. Mao. Beneath that were others like it: Vo Nguyen Giap, the North Vietnamese General, Van Thai, Bayo, Che, and even the sage Lin Piao. "Spider'll get his action," he said, and met Williams's suddenly serious eyes. The Prime Minister put away his comb and pocket mirror. He leaned forward, his dark hands intertwined around the white cup. His eyes left Walker's and blinked at the stack of books.

"The army carried me to Nam, Vernon. The marines sent you." He took a gulp of coffee, made a face, and then smiled. "If they'd only known what they were letting us see! Ol' Victor Charlie, man. He showed us it could work. We can do it here, too."

"If," Walker said, "we are as dedicated as the VC are."

Williams nodded as Walker lit a cigarette and sent a

cloud of smoke into the hard light streaming through the window.

"We're as dedicated, Vernon."

"Maybe we can be, but not yet we're not."

Chuck drained the cup and crushed it. He stood up and bounced the remains into the wastebasket next to Walker's desk. A twitch of muscle rippled in his jaw and he said, "I'll give Spider a hand." But he didn't move from where he stood, aware that Walker had more to say.

"If I ask them to put it all on the line, Chuck, to commit everything—will they? Or will we all start thinking of what might happen to us? Will we hesitate? Will you hesitate, Prime Minister? Will I? You know about second thoughts when the shit hits the fan. When it comes to that time are we going to be running in the other direction?"

Williams ran his tongue over full lips and shook his head. "No, Chief. I don't think so. I'm one of your main men. I've been with you from the start. I think I can be straight with you. And I say it won't happen that way."

Dropping his hand from Mao's book, Vernon stared up at his friend and second-in-command, and laughed. Chuck recoiled as if struck in the face. His eyes glowed angrily, but Walker held up his hand and shook his head.

"No, man. Com' on! Cool down! I just want to make you understand what the hell I'm talking about. I want you, above all of them, to see the size of the thing we are into!" He opened Giap's book, *The People's Army*. His left hand smacked down on the white pages. He dropped the volume back to the desk.

"Eat away at their flanks," he said, and his eyes were no longer an almost opaque brown. Now, Walker's look held the uncompromising image of his special vision. "Harass them and destroy confidence in their ability to protect the people. Break lines of communication. Set ambushes and booby traps. Snipe at them, Chuck! Make them crawl. Tease the beast in them until they're striking back at anything that moves! And when they're weak from a thousand little wounds, when they wish for nothing more than a good night's sleep, then go at them with all your power!"

Walker leaned back and caught his breath. He looked at his hand, resting on the open pages of the North Vietnamese general's writings and he observed that his fingertips trembled. He closed the hand into a fist.

"They'll be beat, Vernon!" Williams said. He was bent over, trying to hold Walker's eyes with his own, trying to convince his chief that it was all true already. "I swear to you we can win. They won't have a chance!"

"But who are 'they,' Chuck? Do you know who they are?"

"The police," Williams said without hesitation. "Then the army if we have to. Every pig, in uniform and out, in this two-faced country!"

"Kill the pigs," Walker murmured. "Off the pigs. . . ."

"You sound like you're questioning it all, Vernon. You sound like you don't know, man, like you're undecided."

"You're damned right, I don't know! And I do question! And I am undecided!" Walker's face was suddenly twisted with the agony of trying to express the inexpressible. "This ain't games, Chuck! This is something that could explode into the most important thing in our lives or turn the whole cart upside down and run us into the gutters!"

"We've been in the gutters before." Williams stood straight. He breathed deeply and held his voice very steady. "But I understand, Vernon. I know what you're talking about, and if I didn't believe all the way before, I do now. And I'm not going back to the gutter. Not alive, anyway."

"Just so you understand, PM," Walker said, and turned on a smile that strained his face. Williams nodded and opened the door to the main room. The mimeograph clattered and banged. Chuck turned back one time before shutting the door behind him.

"We can be as dedicated, Chief," he said, nodding

toward the pile of books, and then the door shut his face from view.

Walker listened to the thumping beat of his heart and closed his eyes. As he had talked he'd dragged things out of himself that should never have been said in front of one of his men. It showed poor leadership. And he saw his doubts laid out in heaps like alley trash, like the stained cassock of a failed priest. He was sorry now that it was too late . . . that he'd talked about his fears. He wondered if Chuck, or anyone in the Party, truly understood what was ahead for each of them or knew the stakes involved.

There is only one man, Walker decided, who has a feeling about what I am doing. And that one man is on the other-side part of the "they" he now fought.

Joe Mason.

Walker murmured the vilest curse he could think of. He was suddenly sick to death of his mind's constant tricks, its endless vacillation and indecision. He wanted to rip out all the old weaknesses and memories, burn them away with pure, hot fire. He was tired of trying to find excuses for what he was attempting to do. There were hundreds of reasons why things had to be changed, and thousands of reasons why the police, and Joe Mason with them, had to come first on the target list. He thought of what Mason had said to Little Bit, the message he'd sent the night before, and smiled bitterly. Old Joe's got a feeling all right. Old Sarge knows.

He pulled out a yellow legal pad and ballpoint pen. He wrote quickly, and his scrawled words glared up at him, possessing a life of them own.

IF EITHER OF US—MASON OR ME—DIES IN THIS, THEN IT'S BECAUSE WE HAVE CHOSEN A WAY OF GETTING WHAT WE WANT THAT AVOIDS ALL THE SAFE WAYS, THAT. . . .

He ripped the page out and crushed it, then sat very still for a moment, staring out at all the shit stacked around the alley.

Chapter Three

JOE AND Mona sat at his tiny kitchen table, surrounded by the white domesticity of stove, refrigerator, and sink, and ate breakfast with hardly a word. Joe had showered while Mona cooked, but he still wore his faded green robe and a pair of rubber thongs. Mona looked strangely youthful, like a teenager the morning after a slumber party, wearing only one of Mason's light-blue long-sleeved police shirts. Her short hair was brushed straight back, which emphasized her big eyes and high cheekbones. She looked fresh, young, and healthy.

Mason looked awful. He sipped black coffee and chewed toast, the remains of an enormous eggs-and-bacon breakfast, and grinned at Mona's somber assault on a single fried egg.

"You're very serious, lady."

"Hmmm...."

"Never speak with your mouth full."

"Mmmm." Mona swallowed, and took a gulp of cold milk from a glass tumbler decorated with comic-book characters. "That's right."

"Very polite. Very correct. You look like a virgin."

"You know better than that!" she snapped, but the grin he expected did not accompany her reply.

"What's bothering you?"

She shook her head. "No, Mason. It's something bothering you."

"What that's supposed to mean?"

"Something is hanging you up."

"I'm not hung up," he said, smiling ruefully. "I am just hungover. There's a difference."

"I know the difference, and you're full of crap. It's something more than your hangover."

Mason's smile faded. He stared at her through a cloud of exhaled smoke and lit his fourth cigarette of the morning. Mona thought to herself that right this minute he was trying to look as tough and unconcerned as he could manage. But like a taut wire between them, she felt the tension in Mason. She felt the anger that lay just below his manufactured surface.

"I spent the night with you, Mason, remember?"

"I remember. Com' on, knock it off."

She ignored him. "It's been like that before, but last night was really bad. I could tell. It was real damned bad."

"What is this?" he asked, touching the side of his head with a rigid fingertip. "You want to be my shrink, or something?"

"I'm worried."

"There's no need to worry."

"Vernon Walker," she said calmly, and pulled back at the sudden change in Mason's eyes. "You and Walker worry me. Why don't you just leave it alone, Joe?"

"You can't be that stupid, Mona." he laughed, and the sound of it was harshly bitter. "Jesus! 'Leave it alone'!"

She stood up and gathered the plates. Her lips were tightly pressed together. She started water in the sink and squirted a stream of liquid soap onto the egg stains and streaks of butter. Mason stared away from her, at the far wall. His cigarette smoked between his fingers.

"He's on my beat," he said. "He's stirring up the shit, and the shit is rolling down on my goddamned head."

"Fuck both of you," Mona said, and busied herself washing the dishes. "I sure as hell ain't going to worry about a couple of salt-and-pepper assholes looking to do each other in."

"That's my smart lady," he said, and reached over the small table to grab at the coffeepot and pour into his cup. He stirred in a spoonful of sugar. "That's being smart."

Mona muttered an obscenity that would've shocked Mason if he hadn't known her so well, and scrubbed viciously at the greasy frying pan.

"There ain't no doubt in my mind," she said vehemently, "why your old lady left your ass!" But even as the words slipped past her lips, she turned and stared at him over her shoulder with suddenly fearful eyes.

Mason stared back for a long minute, and then said, "That's enough of that shit. You are not the one to be pointing at anyone else. You understand?"

Mona nodded—four quick jerks of her head—her hands submerged in soapy water, and took a deep shuddering breath before answering.

"I'm just looking out for myself, Mason," she said. "Without you I wouldn't have any insurance left. You keep the heat off, and I appreciate that."

He patted her rump and a hard smile erased his frown.

"This is true," he said cheerfully. "Now you're talking sense. And don't worry—I'm not going to get blown away. This thing with Walker's just something that can't be put off."

And as Mason said the words he knew they were what he'd been searching for—the answer to what had been itching him for weeks. *Something that can't be put off.* That was it. It had been there all the time, but he hadn't wanted to admit that it frightened him so much it made him want to run and hide. "Because, it can't be put off," he murmured, and took a long sip of his coffee. The coffee was still very hot. It burned his lips, but he hardly noticed.

An hour later Mason watched from the living-room windows as Mona crossed the street below the apartment. She moved lightly, making a run through traffic look graceful, then turned on the opposite sidewalk and gave him a choppy wave. He lifted his own hand, though he knew she wouldn't be able to see it, and she walked east as he turned away.

In the bedroom he dressed quickly, buttoning a

blue-plaid shirt and pushing the tails
He buckled on a thick, brown-leather
at his image in the full-length mirror
blue-steel .45 automatic and pulled t̄
check the gleam of brass slipped halfway
chamber. The slide moved forward as he rele
pressure and the sight of the first round was
Safety on, he slid the pistol into his shoulder ho
and struggled into the leather harness. He shrugged
arms through the loops and straightened into
slouching stance.

Mona, he thought, and recalled the tense silence
tween them as she dressed and kissed him good-bye. It
was a leftover from the talk they'd had in the kitchen,
and the kiss had been a seal to everything they both
knew. She was a hooker. He was a cop. But there were
hungers in both of them that made the relationship
comfortable; neither denied the fact that they both
needed each other. Too, each knew enough to let the
other be what he was. Mason had never tried to "save"
Mona from the life she'd chosen, and now she knew
she couldn't try and "rescue" him. They played
straight with each other. They were both on paths that
held them fast.

The weight of the automatic was steel reality under
Mason's left arm. It returned everything to its proper
perspective. He was sure of himself again, and sure also
that life was exactly as he knew it was: a matter of attack and defense and always a simple choice of
whether to charge or retreat.

Striking a pose, he scrutinized himself in the long
mirror. The shoulder holster and the gun pleased him
enormously. He felt Bogart and Edward G. Robinson
pulse within his chest. His lips curled over his long
teeth and he hoisted his jeans with stiff wrists. "Aw
right, you guys. . . ." A laugh burst free at what he saw
in himself—at the small boy playing cops and robbers—and he shook his head. He moved the chest of
drawers and hefted his badge up and pinned it to the
inside of his wallet, and then raised his eyes to the
framed photo hanging above the dressertop.

marines. It had been a bad number

...ers. The original crew. The first squad, ...a Company.

...ow kneeling, back row standing, hands on ...ds thrown back with cocky indifference, hel-...nted to the side, and Buck Rogers M-16 rifles ...speartips stark against the dull evening sky of An ... Province, South Vietnam.

...here had been replacements for most of these after ... photo had been taken. Joe stared at the small ...rks next to the heads of eleven of his initial thirteen men. Six of those first Raiders had been killed in action, and five had been wounded and flown out in helicopters. Those faces, those men, were marked, but two were not: one man white, the other black. The two of them knelt in the front row, side by side, but separated and stiffly aware of each other; narrow, sidelong glances marked boundaries between them. Brown eyes and blue, Walker and Mason.

Why just you and me, Vernon?

Joe ground the heels of his hands into aching eyesockets. He stared at the picture and thought that it would be a good idea to take it down, to do what the cowardly part of his mind suggested and wait for things to cool down between him and Walker. Just go to work and forget that Walker's outfit even existed. Avoid any confrontation. Collect your pay and stay out of trouble, maybe transfer to another district.

But Mason knew he could not ignore the threat to his beat, just as he knew he would never remove that photograph. He pushed lanky hair from his forehead and leaned close to the picture. He examined the face of the man he had been then, but instead of holding to his own features his eyes were drawn to the black face next to his.

"Damn you to hell, Vernon," he whispered. "Why'd you have to pick my streets to start your little revolution?"

Something that can't be put off.

And Mason felt Walker tied to his neck and, like

the mariner's albatross, weighing him down with frustration and anger.

There were scenes he could never erase from his memory and Walker was part of most of them. There were times he had willed himself to forget, but he could not. And Vernon Walker was the only part of those times close enough for him to communi[cate] with, as much a souvenir of it all as the photo of t[hir]teen marines. Six doomed to die, five ripped apart [by] flying steel, and two destined to—what? To [do] penance for all the times recalled in weeping a[nd] screaming?

Mason shivered, remembering a phrase from church Latin. *Mea Culpa. Mea Culpa. Mea Maxima Culpa.* Through my fault. Through my fault. Through my most grievous fault.

He threw on his jacket and hurried out of the apartment. The drunk night before, Mona that morning, the flood of old memories—all of it had come together to bring the truth to the top of his consciousness. He pounded down the stairs two at a time and lunged into the cold morning. Dodging traffic, he crossed the street and jumped into the old Chevy. He felt suddenly alive and strangely anxious. The hangover was gone. The doubt, too, was gone. He was charging now, and no hesitation or turning back would be allowed. His stomach clenched as he turned the key and started the car.

We'll either make a truce that'll work, he told himself, or that black bastard and me will fight it down to the line and end it. And Mason saw the nightmare, even as his mind echoed with brave resolutions. He felt himself, once again, holding on to Vernon Walker's sweating neck, the pain charging through his legs, and he tasted a razor-sharp flavor of remorse. But to hell with that, he thought, and said out loud, as he turned the Chevy east, "To hell with that, Walker!"

Chapter Four

CHUCK WILLIAMS stood at the sandbagged wall that enclosed the front section of Party headquarters. He stared through the firing slits at Delmar Avenue. All of what Vernon had said ran through his thinking like an old newsreel, spotty and dark-colored with urgency and danger. He watched a group of white hippies gathered on the corner and wondered if they would be with the Party when the fighting started. He hoped they wouldn't be. He would rather go under than have bloods fighting alongside punk-ass whites.

But then he thought of Eileen. White. White as snow, baby, but not cold like snow. Eileen was pure and deep and fresh, but once plunged into—burning hot. Where would she fit in when the fighting turned these streets into a snipe-and-run, urban battlefield?

And there would be fighting. Of that he was sure. For the first time since he'd helped Vernon build the Party to what it was, Chuck Williams was positive the guerrilla war they had once envisioned would happen. This knowledge excited and sobered him at once. It rippled over his volatile spirit and he felt much older than his twenty-four years, and much more the spearhead of deadly purpose. He felt that he had enough violence stored within him to destroy an entire city if he should ever blow loose. He felt that everyone but those in his group, and perhaps a few knowledgeable cops, was living in a dream world. He, his friends, and his enemies knew the truth. They were the haunted possessors of the key. When it comes, Chuck reminded himself, it'll come because we unlock what everyone else is just too damned afraid to look into. That moment was what he lived for, and he had nurtured his desire for violent glory since he was a small boy, perfecting it through a thousand movies, a million comic books, and the TV set that almost every dingy apartment in the city boasted, no matter how poor it happened to be.

The time would arrive, he knew, when Chu(ck) Williams would be known as Vernon Walker's Pr(ime) Minister. He would not be a faceless black man, h(us)tling and running from the system. He would ba(ttle) and possibly destroy that system.

The sound of the mimeograph maching pushed hi(m) from his thoughts. Chuck stared at Spider Washington's hunched figure, hovering demonlike over the rattling printing press. Spider was short, but broad in the chest with a skin color closer to purple than to the black of his shaggy beard, mustache, and bushy hair. Youthful acne had scarred his flat, mongol face with a scattering of dots and dashes that moved into more serious knife scars and ran along his dark cheeks to the sides of a widespread nose. Spider's personality was as wild as his ebony eyes. Depression constantly battled for a surpreme place in his soul, but not against joy. For Spider was always down to brood or up to hate.

Glancing up and meeting Williams's calm stare, Spider jerked his hand off the machine's crank and let it spin for a moment before he stopped it with a clenched fist. He stood very still, but his breath came and went like a bellows. Williams blinked at him and smiled with wry amusement. "I told Vernon you was kicking that mimeograph's ass, Spider. Not the other way around."

"This bullshit!" Washington turned and stalked over to the end of the wood plank propped on the carpenter's horses. He pointed at a stack of finished handbills. "This ain't what I joined you for!"

Chuck's smile vanished.

"If you want out, go back there and tell it to Vernon."

"I didn't say I wanted out!"

"You might not have said it, man, but you made

clear what you feel about this." Chuck held up a single handbill, a square of white paper with the Party's insignia stamped across the top and thick print beneath. Spider reached out and snatched it from Chuck's hand. He read it aloud, his gravelly voice quickly going hoarse with suppressed fury.

"Brothers and sisters, resist oppression! Resist police ...der and political arrest! Fight for the release ... shit!" He flung the handbill to the floor. "Words! ...ords, man! Words and more fucking words!"

Williams folded his arms across his chest and said, "You're an orator, Spiderman. You know that? Bet you didn't know that, did you? You have a hidden talent. You're a motherfucking orator!"

"I come into this outfit," Spider growled, "to fucking fight!"

"You are just going to have to do your fighting with these funky words, man, until you are told to fight with something more dangerous." Chuck sat on the edge of the makeshift table. "You can always go back to that cycle gang if you don't like what we're doing, Washington. You can always go back and frighten little girls with your bad-ass motorcycles and chains."

"The Warlords weren't what I wanted," Spider said, and had to swallow quickly. His eyes snapped out anger as Chuck continued to stare at him as though he were an interesting, amusing specimen. "They weren't what I wanted," Spider repeated. "I thought you dudes were what I wanted."

"That's good," Williams intoned. "'Cause around here we don't go for that kind of punk-ass Warlord shit. You know, my man, you and Terry T. ought to start going steady. You two are more than just skin brothers. You're stupid brothers, too."

"Why am I here, then?" A thick vein pulsed in Spider's neck. "Why are you trying so hard to spring Terry T. if he's so stupid?"

Williams replied in the same even tone of voice, his expression unchanged. "Because if Vernon told you two to puke gold nuggets, you'd both give it a try, that is why, bad man."

Leaning heavily on the table, Spider stood very close to Williams and said, "The run Little Bit and Walleye are on—"

"What about it?"

"It's for guns, ain't it? It's for pieces."

"Ask Vernon." Williams let his eyelids droop over the anger he knew was beginning to light his eyes. "Ask the chief; don't be asking me that shit."

"Are we finally getting off our asses, PM? That's what I'm asking you!"

"Like I said, Spider, you ask Vernon."

"You tell me! I'm asking you!" Spider grabbed Chuck's arm, but the Prime Minister neither drew back nor appeared frightened. He merely glanced down at something that seemed to interest him greatly, unaffected by the big hand gripping his bicep.

For a moment Spider was confused by Chuck's calm, then his eyes followed the other man's stare and he saw the knife blade touching the front of his sleeveless denim jacket. He dropped his hand and stood back. Chuck grinned broadly.

"You have to have a brain to be really bad-ass, cycleman," he said. "Or didn't you know that? I've always known it, and that's why I could've spilled your nigger guts before you even messed up my shirt." Williams held the knife out for a moment, then drew it back, chuckling to himself. He kept glancing at Spider's heaving chest, then at the six inches of shiny steel. "And you wanted to get out there and fight!"

Spider nodded slowly. "I still do," he began, but turned as Williams did and saw Walker standing in the open doorway to his small office-bedroom.

"What's going down out here?"

Chuck folded the blade back into its handle. He slipped the knife into his back pocket. "Me and the Spiderman was just talking, Vernon."

"We're just having a little talk," Spider mumbled. "Wasn't nothing to it."

"Is the Spider upset about something?" Vernon's voice was like spun silk. Washington turned away and moved back to the mimeograph machine and placed a new stack of unprinted paper in the carriage. He glared over his shoulder at Williams.

"I just asked the PM a question, President Walker." Spider pronounced ask as "ax," and Vernon imitated the pronunciation when he spoke again.

"What did you ax the PM that made things so hot in this cold-ass room, Spiderman?"

"When, I wanted to know, are we going to start doing what these little pieces of paper preach? When are we going to start downing pigs?"

A sharp squeal of tires in the back alley interrupted Vernon's answer. He spun around and stepped back into his office. He stared out the window. The green pickup slammed to a stop and rocked on its springs. The doors flew open and Little Bit and Walleye leaped down. They ran to the rear of the truck, which had backed up to the steel door, and out of Vernon's field of vision. Instantly, the sound of a banging fist on the rear door echoed through the high-ceilinged hallway.

"Trouble," Vernon said, and jumped over his cluttered desk. He dragged open a lower drawer and yanked out two .38 revolvers.

As Chuck and Washington ran to him, Vernon shoved the pistols into their reaching hands.

"Maybe you'll get your chance now, Spider!" he said, and led them to the hall door. He knew something had gone wrong or was about to go wrong. Little Bit wouldn't be beating on the back door like a madman if everything was still cool.

The door was swung open by Williams and the three men were met with a blast of cold air and Stanton's panting voice. Chuck and Spider pushed past Vernon to help Walleye, who was struggling with a long case, trying desperately to drag it from the truckbed of the battered Ford.

"Mason!" Little Bit said, spitting to the side and coughing with exertion. "He passed us on Delmar and eyeballed the back of the truck. The motherfucker made a U-turn and we split down the alley. Don't know if he came after us or not!"

For a second Walker's brain refused to function. The sudden appearance of the truck and his two men, who were not expected back until later that afternoon, and the materialization of Joe Mason somewhere close (front or back?) momentarily unnerved him. Does thinking about that bastard make him show up? He clutched Little Bit's trembling shoulder. The obvious fear in the other man steadied Vernon's voice.

"Give the PM and Spider a hand! Hold your piss, Little Bit! Just stay cool. You got anything in the cab?"

"Just one," Stanton stuttered. His head snapped up and down and cold sweat seeped down from beneath the leather band of his scruffy beret. Vernon smiled.

"Okay, I'll get it. Go on and give them a hand!"

Little Bit whirled to help the others. His high-pitched voice spit out a steady stream of obscenities, as Walker ran to where he could look down the alley. For a second he thought that Mason might have gone to the front, or not bothered to check the truck out at all, but then he saw the Chevy turn into the alleyway from the Star Theater's parking lot.

"He's headed this way," he said, speaking as calmly as possible. "Let's move it, people. Move it. Move it."

The others stared at him, frozen into attitudes of flight, the long wooden case between them. Vernon waved them on and they moved again, but Walker himself suddenly felt icy sweat gather in his armpits and his stomach congeal into a lump of leaden heaviness. Move! he told himself, and opened the door to the truck's cab. He jumped in and dug under the seat until he located a tubular package, about a meter long, wrapped in brown paper. He clambered out of the truck with it as Mason's car pulled up in front of the parked pickup. A quick glance showed Vernon that Chuck had managed to get everything inside and close the door. They all made it, he thought, but was immediately aware of the heavy package in his arms. He shuffled his boots on the alley's cobblestones as Mason parked the Chevy and climbed out.

(Here you are again, Mason. I can barely keep my

53

eyes open and I'm hurt in the chest where you first punched me, and I'm wondering why the fuck do you keep crawling to your feet and swinging back at me when you should be fucking out? Damn you, Sarge, you bigoted motherfucker, here you are again, swinging like a wild man but not hitting with each one, hitting just enough to hurt me before I put you down again. And the whole damned platoon watching Vernon and Joe go at it, with someone always making the inevitable comments, "Won't those two fools ever get tired of fighting each other?")

"Vernon," Mason said, warningly, and walked toward him. Walker nodded and was painfully aware of the wrapped rifle in the crook of his arm.

"Joe. What's happening?"

Mason grinned and kept his hands jammed into his jacket's pockets. His nose and cheeks were red from the cold wind.

"Nothing much, Vernon. Thought I'd just drop by and pass the time of day. You know, say hello."

They were both grinning now, Mason shifting from one foot to the other, and Walker beginning to shiver, being coatless. Vernon held the package like something not important enough to notice, except that Mason did notice. Vernon could see it in his eyes, those damned blue eyes that always reminded him of chipped ice, and which had the uncanny ability to change with Mason's moods: dark blue, gray, and even a freezing green. They flickered over the long bundle, then lifted to meet Vernon's own carefully controlled stare. Vernon knew also that Mason was aware of the men covering their chief from the back window of Party headquarters.

"What can we do for you, Joe?"

"How about a cup of coffee for openers? It's cold as a witch's tit out here."

"We've got some coffee inside," Vernon said, but there was no invitation in the statement. His hands clutched the brown paper and pressed down on the hard outlines of what was concealed beneath.

"I wanted to talk," Mason said.

"We're busy."

"We at least used to be able to talk, Walker!"

"Between the times when we weren't trying to punch each other's teeth out, do you mean? And the 'talk' we did was more like, 'argue,' wasn't it?"

"We have our differences."

"And they're as clear as black and white. I'm black and you're white."

Mason seemed to ignore that, but Vernon saw at once that the words had struck home. He saw the change in Mason's eyes and the flush of color, that had nothing to do with the cold, rise up into the other man's cheeks.

Mason said, "All right. If that's the way you're playing it. Yes, the differences were, and are, as clear as black and white."

Vernon nodded. "Anyway, in Nam, was when we were supposed to be on the same side. But now is now, Joe. Things are strictly nigger and honky." Walker took up a more relaxed stance, though inside he was tensing for Mason to make his move.

"The hard guy," Mason said. "Always got to be the big, bad militant. And here I thought that maybe—just maybe—I could get through this day without being impressed by some cheap imitation of Eldridge Cleaver. But I'm impressed, Vernon. I have to admit I'm impressed."

"What the fuck do you want?" Walker was suddenly confused. Mason wasn't acting according to his nature. "How can you and me talk? What do we have to say to each other that hasn't been said before?"

"We could throw a few words around about these streets we both love so dearly."

"You and me?" Walker was incredulous.

"It's easy," Mason said, and unsnapped his jacket. He spread it away from his side, showing Walker an empty holster. "I left my heat in the car," he said. "I didn't figure on needing it with you, so why are you trying to prove something to me?" His eyes settled on the package and Walker knew that Mason was perfectly aware of what was inside. The bastard knows,

Vernon thought, and he's using it to bargain with. He's not going to do anything about it—at least not yet. So, okay. Now, he's more like the old sarge again. He playing deals. He's got deals in his head and he's horse trading. So, okay.

The two men stared at each other, and finally Vernon nodded, breaking the silence at the same time.

"Wait here." He turned away. He forced himself to walk slowly to the door, which swung open as soon as he reached it. Chuck stared at him anxiously, but he pushed past the PM and stood in the hallway getting his breath. Spider, pistol in hand, and Little Bit, also armed now, stared at him from the bedroom office doorway. Walleye must still be covering Mason, he decided, and handed the paper-wrapped rifle to Chuck.

"Get them all out of their cases. Contact as many of the other members as you can get hold of. Clean these pieces up. I'll be back."

"You're not going with that pig, Vernon?"

"He says he just wants to talk." He smiled at his Prime Minister's look of intense suspicion. "No sweat. Mason doesn't double cross. It isn't his style."

"Did he—?" Chuck hefted the package. "Do you figure he knew what was in here?"

"I don't think he thought it was long-stemmed roses, no. He knew. He could've busted me, but he didn't."

"He could've tried," Spider said.

"What's that dude up to, Chief?" Little Bit wanted to know. "What's his hustle? He's got to have a game."

"That's what I'm going to find out."

"He knew we had you covered." Spider held his .38 as if for inspection, straight alongside his neck and pointing at the ceiling. Walker glanced at the new man and nodded.

"That could be part of it," he said. "But Mason has nerve. He doesn't scare. He wouldn't have let me slide unless he's got a reason. I think he's using this to make me trust him."

"Then he's got to be out of his fucking mind," said

Spider, "if he thinks Vernon Walker's gonna trust a pig!"

"Get the president his jacket, cycleman," Chuck said, but Washington didn't move. He stood crouched and tight in the doorway, glaring around the corner of the doorframe and into the office-bedroom.

"Just give the word, Chief," he whispered, "and that is not only a crazy pig, but a dead one, too."

Walker knew Spider was looking over Walleye's bent back, out the window, and dead center at Mason's chest. He also knew that all he had to do was speak one word and Joe Mason would die—hard and fast. But double crosses weren't his style either.

"Negative," he said, and felt the power of control turn his back and neck muscles rigid. "I said, negative, Spider. Now, all of you—put up your fucking heat. It is only one damned white man out there!"

Chapter Five

MASON STOOD in the cold alley, waiting for Vernon Walker to reappear. His eyes watered from the icy wind, and his arms and legs trembled with an almost spastic shiver that was close to real pain, but he had decided not to move from the spot where he was standing.

I won't even wipe my goddamned eyes, he thought.

Let them see me hard and bad-ass: cool, don't-give-a-damn Mason. I know they have guns on me. You could sink a ship with the guns they've collected in that little fort of theirs. If they opened up now, right this minute, I might have one chance in a hundred of getting down and reaching my car. Maybe.

He stared at the reflecting window and steel door, but saw a sudden flickering of technicolor film, instead of the rear of an old building.

(Young calvary officer, and buckskinned scout ride slowly into the midst of hostile Sioux. The scout hisses at the frightened officer: "Don't let the critters know you're scart, Lootenant, or they'll have our hair for damned sure!")

Mason grinned at his vision, then indulged himself in a chilled and almost childish giggle.

"Shoot, ya dirty redskins," he whispered, and felt his body respond like one unified nerve. All of me, he thought, is suddenly sensitive to everything. And he stood in the biting cold and let the tears well up in his eyes as the hard wind buffeted his face. He thought about all the things he *knew* would be now, and waited for Vernon to come back out through his steel door.

The telephone poles that lined the alley threw dusty shadows across Mason's stooped figure. He stared at their elongated shapes criss-crossing the cracked concrete and cobblestones, and still he did not move. He felt frozen to the alley. He felt numb clear through and into his heart, and he remembered what Mona had said earlier that morning: "There ain't no doubt in my mind why your old lady left your ass!" And he saw the marriage, the honeymoon, the boy she'd given him, the arguments, the tears, the divorce-court judge's dim eyes behind shiny glasses.

Everything that had once been, and what was his reality now, filled him with a sadness so pervading that he no longer felt the cold.

"Shit," he said, then saw Walker emerge from the doorway, a single figure in the shadows.

"Ready when you are, Sarge," Walker said, and stopped in front of Mason's two-inch-shorter form. Vernon was all black: trousers, boots, shirt, jacket, and beret.

"You can cease the Sarge shit. That's all over now."

"Is it?"

"That's what they tell me. They tell me I'm back home. Returned to the warm bosom of my peaceful country."

"To bosoms, maybe, but that's all, Sarge."

"Okay, so keep the Sarge, Vernon. If it makes you feel good, keep it. I wouldn't deny you a simple pleasure."

Walker slipped on a pair of violet sunglasses.

"Thank you, Joe."

And once again the slow smile tugged at both their mouths, but this time it refused to grow any further. They stood next to Mason's Chevy in a bright band of sunlight that lanced from between dark buildings.

"I'll leave my ride here," Mason said. "Unless you have another shipment coming in today."

Walker's eyes were invisible behind the sunglasses and Mason couldn't tell if he'd blinked or not. But he thought that maybe a flicker had moved across Vernon's set face.

"You mind?" he asked, and Walker shook his head.
"Nothing to me. We'll foot it."
"It's only around the corner."
"No sweat. Leave your ride here."
"I'll have to take my heat with me."
"Never doubted it for a minute."

Mason opened the Chevy's door and reached under the front seat, pulling out the automatic. Walker peered over his shoulder as he slipped the big .45 out of sight under his jacket.

"What a mean old cannon," Walker murmured.

"It makes a nice hole," Mason said, slamming the car door and striding off down the alley. Walker caught up to him and got in step. They threaded their way past spilled trash cans and smoking brick pits used to burn garbage. The alley spawned filthy cats and hopeless dogs who fled at the first sight of the two men. A smell hung in the air that was so pungent Mason began to think he could taste it.

"I had a dream last night," he said, staring ahead and now slowing his pace. "It was the mother of bad dreams."

Walker glanced at the man walking next to him. His eyes widened behind their violet shields, then he turned away.

"Don't feel like the Lone Ranger. Bad dreams seem to be getting kind of common nowadays. People even have bad dreams about us niggers becoming the majority instead of the minority."

"Maybe everyone's going Section Eight."
"Could be. It's very possible."
"What's possible?"

"Anything, man," Walker said, and smiled. Mason was not watching and his own face stayed as grim as before. "Yeah," he mumbled, and they walked on in silence through the Star Theater's parking lot and out to the sidewalk on the south side of Delmar. Their breath puffed out white and steaming in front of them, but was quickly whipped away by the gusting wind. A police car crawled slowly past, moving east.

Mason couldn't see who was driving, but the shotgun man glared back at them over his headrest and Joe recognized him immediately. Sam Oakland. Oakland was on Mason's crew and a broadcaster of the latest dirt. Mason felt a flush of embarrassment wash hotly over his cold face. He thrust his hands into his jacket pockets.

"Your buddy don't believe his eyes," Walker said. "Could that be Joe Mason, strollin' along with Vernon Walker? Outrageous!"

"Jealous," Mason said, but the quip rang hollow, and he had to lengthen his stride to match Walker's sudden burst of speed.

The prowl car made a lazy U-turn and came back past them. Mason stopped walking and faced the two white faces that stared out at him. The driver was a rookie, fresh out of the academy. Lablonski, Lacowski—something like that—and he wore a friendly grin. Oakland, however, looked as if he'd just discovered Mason screwing his baby sister. That look of indignant anger triggered Mason's shout.

"You got nothing better to do, Oakland?"

"What are you doing, Joe? Fraternizing with the enemy?"

"I live in this beat!" Mason yelled back, and lifted an obscene finger as the car passed by.

Walker said, "If you were black, if you weren't a cop, that finger'd be broke off and jammed up your ass."

"That's right," Mason said, and stared at the retreating police vehicle: POLICE 344, dark-green Plymouth Fury, twin red lights and centered electronic siren-loudspeaker on the roof. POLICE 344. "And so what, Vernon? What the hell does that prove? That there are advantages to being white, to being a cop? Shit! There are advantages to being black and a well-known militant, too!"

Walker shook his head and stepped through the steamed glass door of "OPEN 24 HRS! PHELPS HOUSE COFFEE SHOPPE!" Pink walls rolled by them to the clink of glasses and spoons, and the sizzling, smells of grease, onion and disinfectant.

The two men settled into an orange leatherette booth at the back of the narrow room and Mason signaled to the redheaded girl behind the counter. She came down and out into the aisle, sniffing at Walker but giving Mason a rotten-toothed smile.

"Hi, Joe."

"Two black and sweets, Ida."

"Anything to eat, Joe?"

"No, just the coffee."

The waitress nodded.

"You off or something today, Joe?"

"Yeah. My day off. Get those coffees, will you?"

"Cold enough for you?" she asked.

"Freezing, Ida. That's why we'd like those coffees!"

The girl compressed her lips and hurried back behind the counter. Walker chuckled and Mason slumped back in the booth, loosening his jacket. He felt the heated interior of the café slowly warming him, sniffed at the dark scents of people and food, then looked up and faced Walker.

Vernon's face was all black, the violet sunglasses startling against the dark skin. The eyes were hidden behind the violet. The beret was still arrogantly cocked to the left and all Mason could think of, with Walker so close to him, so near he could have lifted a hand and touched the man's face, was: black.

"I am jealous, now." Vernon rubbed his hands together.

"Why's that?"

"Ida likes you better'n me."

But Mason wasn't smiling. He didn't think he could smile. Not at that moment and not if his life had suddenly depended on it. What he knew was fact, but had no proof for, was rising in front of him.

"You're serious as a judge with noble intentions, Joe. What's bugging you?"

Mason said it, without beating around the bush, "You're thinking of being a Viet Cong, an American Viet Cong aren't you, Vernon?"

Walker lost none of his composure. He sighed, however, and removed the sunglasses. He set them aside carefully, next to his right hand, and rubbed his forehead.

"You tell me, Joe. You're a member in good standing with the white-hatted, white-skinned, good guys. Don't the forces of light know what the forces of darkness are doing?"

Ida chose that moment to return with the coffee. She set the cups and saucers down and glanced nervously at the men who sat staring so intensely at each other. There was something in their attitudes that signaled an approaching explosion and the waitress retreated behind her counter without saying a single word.

Mason sipped his coffee, found it tasteless and too hot, and set it down slowly on its saucer.

"Okay," he said. "I think you're getting ready for something. I think you're going to start a war, Vernon. I think you're going to try and make the cops come down hard on everybody, the way the VC made us come down hard on the Vietnamese. I think you're going to start your war here, on my streets, that you picked this district because you think knowing me in Nam will give you some kind of fucking edge."

Walker took a moment to light a cigarette, and collect his thoughts. "So I'm about ready to start a war?"

"That's what I think."

"You're thinking wrong, Joe." Walker's long-fingered hand toyed with the sunglasses. "We'd have to be nuts to go up against the police and everything else they'd throw in the game."

"Don't give me that crap." Mason helped himself to one of Walker's Kools. Both men hissed smoke at each other, and Mason said: "The VC weren't nuts. They put a hell of a lot on the table against Diem and then us, and they almost—no, man—they are getting away with it!"

"You're on the wrong track, Joe." Walker flicked ashes into the puddle of coffee next to his cup. "You're wrong. We may not be a social club, but we're not looking for a war."

"If I'm wrong, then I'll apologize. But I don't think

I am." Mason dropped the tone of his voice to an almost purring insistence. "I've heard you talking to the young bloods who come flocking to your outfit. I've heard a few of your remarks on TV, and I've seen the dudes you've recruited in the past two months." Mason began ticking off the names on his fingers. "Terry T. Logan, Jewel Johnson, Sonny Max, Chino what's-his-name, and that madman from the Warlords, Spider Washington. If you're going to sit on your ass and tell me that guys like those are going to be satisfied with breakfast programs for the kiddies, then you must think I'm just plain stupid. Goddamn, man! Do you really think I'm believing that crap about righting social injustice, Vernon? Man, you are filling your squads with fucking killers. You are getting ready to fight, and that's it!"

Walker butted out his cigarette in his saucer, a hiss in the brown coffee.

"You weren't there when Lee Tillman was shot, were you, Mason?"

"No!" Joe pushed his cup and saucer away, exasperated now that he knew what direction Walker was trying to push the conversation. "No, I wasn't there."

"That's where it started. And I'm not beginning anything that hasn't already begun—all over the country. Whatever goes down now, man—is their fault, not ours!"

"Whose fault, Vernon? The cops? Jesus! It was some poor idiot kid who killed Lee that night! Not cops! Some nutty kid who thought he was Hitler or something!"

"A white kid."

"So? What's that supposed to mean?"

"You're all part of what that kid believed. King, Evers, Tillman, and a whole lot more brothers were killed by whites."

"You think I believe the way that kid did, or Ray?"

"Finish your coffee, Sarge. You're blowing up."

"I just can't see your reasoning behind this, Vernon. Damn it all to fucking hell!"

"Cool down, man."

"Cool down?" Mason's hand clenched into a fist in front of Walker's tight face. "You're going to start a goddamned civil war in the streets, and you got the balls to tell me to cool down! Christ on a stick!"

Walker smiled at Mason's anger.

"Joe, listen. How about shitcanning that badge of yours and coming in with me?"

Mason swallowed hard, pinched an inch of skin from the top of his hand, and said, "You can't run your mouth off, and then tell me you could trust my color."

"Not the color," Walker said, "but the brain in you is something I do trust. Listen, I know you ain't a screaming KKK. You got a feeling for the people on this beat. I know that. You're fair, to a point, so you must see the difference between their treatment and the treatment the whites in the suburbs receive from the system—the police, courts, everything. You know you're on the wrong side, man." Walker was excited now, caught up in what he was saying. "You wouldn't have to be out in the open. Just work with me. Fuck, I know we got very basic differences, but if you really want to help the people, man—I mean, this is going to be different, Joe! This is going to be like Nam!"

Mason's eyes went half-lidded and lazy-looking then, and Walker clamped his mouth shut and sat straight.

"A war," Mason said softly. "Like I said, Vernon. A motherfucking war."

"It doesn't matter that you know it. I knew you'd get on to it, maybe a few others have, too. It doesn't matter that any of you know it."

"I'll stop you."

"Nothing, and no one dude can stop me."

"This city'll stop you, man. The people, Vernon— black and white. They won't let it happen—not the way you want it to happen. You think they're going to rise up behind you like the Russians behind Lenin, or something? You think they're going to throw away their jobs and their cars, and their color TVs they're paying for on time? Shit, things might be bad, but they were worse." Mason shook his head. "No, man.

The black people I know remember those days. They remember, and they don't want it back. They're not going to put their asses on the line for a lot of mumble-jumbo, commie bullshit!"

"Enough of them will," Walker said, his voice hard and his smile gone. "The young ones will come in, and we don't want the Toms anyway!"

Mason still shook his head, and Walker suddenly hated him as he had never hated anything else. Mason was so *close* to it—and he couldn't see anything. Joe knew what it was, but wouldn't accept it, could never accept it. He was steeped in their propaganda, the smooth and simple "way things were."

And the hatred that Vernon felt was absorbed by Mason, too. He had never thought that Walker was stupid, but now stupidity was the only label he could put on the kind of talk he'd just heard.

"This rap ain't getting us anywhere," he said. "Nothing is going to get us anywhere. We don't agree on anything. We're too far apart now, Vernon. I guess we always were."

"Glad you finally realize that."

"But we were good when we weren't trying to beat each other's brains out."

"When we were killing something, then we were good. We got together killing people, didn't we—Sarge?"

Mason ignored the remark. "Listen, Vernon. Tillman...."

"Lee Tillman is dead. He isn't President anymore, and we don't follow his way of doing things."

"You used to."

"Not anymore."

"But he knew how to work through—"

"Don't!" Walker said, his voice rising with anger. "Don't you be giving me any of that shit about working through the system! The motherfucking system is what we are fighting!"

Ida, and the few customers in the café, turned and stared at Mason and Walker, then turned back to their hamburgers and coffee.

"All right," Mason said, and his voice dropped to the barest whisper. "All-fucking-right."

Walker replaced the violet sunglasses—cutting off the sight of his hot, black eyes—and stood up.

"That about does it," he said, and Joe nodded, feeling weak and tired of talking about anything.

"Right."

Chapter Six

"I'M SORRY it has to be like this, Vernon," Mason said, as they stepped back out to the cold, "but in another way, I'm not sorry. You understand?"

"Heart throbs and gut aches," Walker said. "Yeah, man. I can understand that shit."

"At least we know where we stand."

"We do know where we stand."

They walked on in silence to the alley and back to Mason's Chevy. Vernon stood a few feet away, his hands hanging loose at his sides, as Mason got into the car and started the engine, rolling the window down and staring up at the face which still ran with him in nightmares. There was little anger left in his thoughts of Walker. Instead, he was calm and thinking of all he had to do, and of the short time left to get it done. He must plan! He knew the line was drawn and there was only one path to take along its narrow limits. Above all else, Joe Mason was a realist. He had always been a realist.

"So long, Vernon," he said. "I'll be in touch."

"I'm sure you will be, Joe."

"It's a fucking shame."

"What?"

"That it has to be this way."

Walker shook his head. No, man. You don't mean that. You know it isn any kind of fucking shame."

Mason considered this, then nodded.

"Maybe you're right. Maybe the other way would've been worse."

"This way," Walker said, "we at least stay men. We come at each other in the open and there's none of the slimy hypocrisy shit you hate as much as I do."

"That's right. You're right about that."

Walker stepped to the side of the vibrating Chevy and put his hand on the doorframe. He slid his sunglasses off and a muscle in his left jaw twitched once, then froze into black immobility. His face was ebony stone. The car's engine throbbed under Mason and he felt the sunlight that gave off no heat, and the world turning.

For the first time in a very long time, Joe felt how damned good it was to be breathing.

"You were right about one thing, Joe," Walker said. "I guessed your district because I thought I could make it easier on myself. But now, I don't think it was that way at all. I think I wanted it to be as tough as it could possibly be. I remember how you never quit swinging at me until you were out."

"It'll be as tough as I can make it."

"I know that. I want it that way. I'll be playing the same way."

"And I'll stop you, Vernon." Mason released his emergency brake and shifted into reverse. "I'll stop you, you black bastard."

"You will try and stop me, you honky son of a bitch."

Mason grinned and let out the clutch. He backed the Chevy into the alley and shifted into first, then lurched forward. He had not answered Walker's last challenge. He knew there was no need to. Their eyes had said everything each of them already knew. It was all laid out, and ready.

(The squad was leaving the perimeter with Walker's fireteam at point. Mason was three men behind the black corporal, and peering into the gloom, trying to see the way, as his men threaded a slow path through the rolls of barbed wire. It had rained hard all day and Mason's boots dragged in the thick mud. He cursed the rotten, stinking, mud and silently damned all of Vietnam, then a flash of lightning ruptured the night sky.

The flare of blue-white outlined the marines in front of Joe, etched them darkly against a background of far mountains and clustered trees. Walker was turned around, looking back to where Mason stood rooted to the earth, and the corporal's eyes were like twin pools of bright white in his sweat-and-rain-streaked face; and Mason felt that for the first time he was looking through Vernon's flesh and getting a glimpse of the man's soul, ripping skin from the skeleton and leaving Walker bare and ivory white.

The lightning faded. Its rumble of thunder followed, thumping through the earth, and the squad moved on. Joe Mason began to shiver at the image of Vernon's death mask burned into his brain forever.)

Vernon stepped back and watched Mason drive away. He felt, for no apparent reason, that he'd lost something important, yet gained a gift he had no name for, and could place no value on. He knew Mason felt the same.

And maybe that's it, he thought. Perhaps what we both gain is simply the ability to reach each other honestly. Christ, how many people are truly honest with me, even fellow black men?

He knocked on the steel door, and Chuck's muffled voice asked, "Vernon?"

"Yeah."

The door opened and he stepped in. Chuck followed him into the main room. The smell of oil and cleaning solvent filled the stuffy air. The rifles were laid out in rows on the improvised table and the steel desk. Spider, Walleye, Little Bit, and other members of the Party were stripping the weapons down and cleaning the dissected parts.

"How do they look?" Walker asked Washington. "Are you happy now, motorcycle man?"

Spider lifted his head and grinned with each tooth in his black face standing out like a white light. It was the first time Walker had seen him really smile and it sent an unexplainable chill racing along his spine.

"The handbills still get printed though, motorcycle man. We still put up all the camouflage we can manage."

"That's okay, Vernon. As long as I know we will be using these bad-ass pieces."

"We'll be using them," Walker said. "The power of the pen has about run out."

"Mason?" Chuck asked, hovering at his side, and Walker nodded. He stepped over to the table. He looked down at the pried-open crate and the gleam of brass cartridges. He picked up one of the carbines and worked its bolt. The weapon had not yet been cleaned and was still smeared with Cosmoline, a thick grease used during storage. Walker walked to the sandbagged wall. Peering out at the street through one of the slits in the outside boards, he aimed the rifle at a white man in crumpled overcoat and smashed fedora. The man was staggering past the Tip-Top Market, Marcel's Beauty Shop, and Hank's Auto Parts. A bottle in a brown paper bag protruded from his grimy coat pocket. Walker centered the drunk in the M-1 carbine's peep sight and pulled the trigger. The resulting *snap!* was loud in the echoing room, and for a moment the members behind him stopped working and talking to each other.

"Zap," murmured Walker, as Chuck leaned against the sandbags on his left. "One less wino. I always was for a stricter antilitter law."

"What'd Mason want?" Chuck asked.

"A peace treaty," Walker said, still aiming through the grease-coated sight. "He thought he could talk me into some kind of peace treaty, but it came down pretty quick that we couldn't get together on the truce route."

Spider had overheard, and snorted with disgust. He held up the rifle he was cleaning. "This is the only peace that Mason pig's gonna get!"

Walker straightened and set the carbine down alongside the others in the crate. "He knows that. He knows that, now."

Mason drove as fast as he was able through the heavy afternoon traffic. His heart slammed against his rib cage and he found himself laughing for no reason, giggling at the people on the sidewalks, and thinking, You're all going to be turned upside down. You're all walking and driving and living every day in a hurry to get nowhere, and you don't even know there's an earthquake building up under your feet!"

He had never felt so alive, so ready to come up against anything, but below that a dread nagged at him. He mistrusted the elation for the same reason he was so happy. He couldn't afford this excitement. You can't get too cocky, he told himself. You have to be smart. You have to stop, and think like Walker will think, know what he will do, anticipate him. Mistakes aren't allowed in this game. Not now. Because you won't have a chance to do it right the next time. There just won't be no fucking next time, and so you have to lay traps and stay out of the ones Vernon'll be laying for you.

His hands tightened on the steering wheel and a smile spread across his face. His blue eyes turned smoky gray and he hummed through tightly clenched teeth at the honking cars and scurrying pedestrians to either side of him. "You're all going to be turned upside down . . . you're all going to be turned upside down."

Chapter Seven

THE MAIN room at Party headquarters was crowded with members, most of them silent and holding their excitement with a studied, distainful calm, a cool unemotion which was unreal in the heated atmosphere. For just below the surfaces of smooth faces and glasslike eyes, the boiling was already starting as Vernon Walker stood to face their seated ranks.

The metal desk squatted in front of him. He felt the cold steel press against his thighs as he raised his right arm, fist clenched. The ring of black men lurched to their feet and raised an exact imitation of the salute, and a murmur passed along their staggered rows. The growling sound changed to shouted response as Vernon said with vibrant clarity: "Dedication!"

"Dedication!"

"Determination!" he shouted, and their voices took up the chant: "Determination!"

"And death to every foe and traitor!"

"Death to every foe and traitor!"

The clenched fists vibrated in the smoky room until Vernon snapped his own fist down to his side. The others followed suit. The members sat back down, looking fierce, twenty-eight young men who would rather shout than assume defiant silence.

Walker turned and smiled down at Henry Lehr, the only white man in the room. Lehr sat to Walker's left rear, looking as garishly out of place as usual in a blue-and-maroon-checked suit with contrasting purple tie. Henry wiped at his red cheeks with an initialed handkerchief, and nodded back at Walker's grin. Lehr's eyes were wide and barely contained his hound-dog sadness, his unabashed fear.

"I couldn't reach him at his place, Vernon," the attorney said, and Walker glanced once more at the chair where Chuck Williams should have been sitting. The folding chair was empty, and Walker shook off what was in his mind and forced the confident smile back upon his square face. He murmured to Lehr: "He'll be here." Then he threw his dark stare at the gathered men.

"Brothers, tonight I'm going to let you know for sure what most of you have been guessing at. Tonight, I'm going to tell it like it really is going to be."

Grins flashed between the members and hands turned to fists on bent knees. Little Bit moved up to the very front of the half ring and sat on the dusty floor, his legs curled up beneath him. He pulled off his battered beret and gripped it between his thighs. He snapped his head around, gesturing to Walleye to join him in front, but Walleye shook his head and looked more mournful than ever. "Tell 'em, President Walker," he said, and his voice was almost a moan. "Tell em the way it's going to be so we can get it goin', and get it over with!"

"I'm telling, fat man," Walker said, "if you just give me the chance."

Laughter rippled up to him like an offering which he accepted and then set quickly aside. The mood of the chilly room changed with the settling of his face. Once more the men were silent and waiting.

"We are—" he began, but stopped. With the sudden instincts that had saved his life many times in the past, Vernon turned to the white lawyer and suggested politely that he leave the room. "It's about time for you to be down to bail Terry T. out, anyway, isn't it, Counselor? You don't want to have to perjure yourself someday, in some courtroom, because of what you might hear here tonight."

Lehr stood up, and with jerking motions gathered briefcase and overcoat into his arms.

"Chuck will be here, Vernon. I've called all the district stations and he hasn't been picked up."

"Don't worry about the PM," Walker said.

"Vernon—"

"Won't do any good," Walker said softly. "You had your say the other night. I listened, Henry, because you're a good lawyer, but that's the only reason. Now, go and do what we pay you for."

Lehr's dark-brown eyes examined Vernon's impassive face, then stared at the assembled members. "Fine," he said, and hurried from the room.

Walker waited until Lehr had vanished down the hallway before turning back to his briefing. I am going to have to ease up on that dude, he thought. I am going to have to cool it with that blob of jelly before he starts talking to the wrong people.

"Whitey's gone," he said, and once again felt the wave of excitement radiate out from the faces and eyes and open mouths. Everyone began to talk at once, and he signaled for silence. "Okay! That's all, brothers. This is serious shit. I am talking very serious shit. So you better get your heads on real tight, because this is rough and you may be feeling scary in the next few minutes!"

Their eyes flashed indignation—except for the fat man's. He nodded mournful agreement.

"You think maybe I'm putting a bad name on you?" Vernon asked. "You think I'm saying you don't have heart? Well, you wouldn't be sitting here, hearing this if I thought that was true! You all got more heart than you know what to do with, or you wouldn't be members, but I want you to understand that this ain't playtime anymore. We are going to do from now on, instead of talk! And I want you all to think about that for a minute. That's why this meeting isn't open to the public or to recruits who aren't full-fledged members." Vernon looked pointedly at Spider Washington, who had only yesterday taken the oath and entered the inner circle of Party members. Spider let his chest puff up and set his bearded face into a scowl of dedicated fervor. Walker smiled slightly and let his last words sink into the thick air. I am getting to them good, he decided. I have to find them where they live; fire them; shame some of them; threaten others. But in the end they'll all be with me. He gestured to the cases stacked on either side of the room.

"You've all got a good idea about them, don't you?"

This time there was no shouting, but only a slow nod from each man, as if Walker were addressing him and him alone.

"Heat!" Little Bit shouted, and Vernon motioned to him. "Stay cool, man!"

Stanton swallowed. His eyes were bright. He bobbed his head and said, "Okay, Chief . . . okay."

"There is going to be blood—for bloods and by bloods." Walker spoke carefully. "There is going to be sniping, and booby traps in the alleys and dead cops and cops who'll try and shoot back, but won't be able to see us. And there'll be cops who'll shoot at anything black before we're finished, and they"—he stopped and felt them hanging by his taut words—"they will do our job for us, brothers! *They* will turn this entire, motherfucking district against them. And then, brothers, we will start to get it on really heavy!"

"Goddamn! Goddamn!" Stanton screeched. "We are with you, Chief!"

Vernon held up both hands and felt the sweat crawl down his chest and sides. His face streamed and his muscles ached.

"Many black people in this city, in every stinking hole of a city in this country, think that to go along with the program is the only way to make it. We are going to show them how wrong they are! We are going to show them that Whitey and Officer Pig can bleed and suffer and be just as afraid as they are now. We are going to be the point of the spear! We will show the way, and we will force the undecided to decide, or to die under a police state made to defend the system against us! And we will make them have to win to survive. Because the cops, and even the army, 'll be grabbing any nigger they can get their hands on!" He swallowed and coughed to the side. He slammed his open hand down on the metal desk. It boomed like a drum, and he saw his men jerk to the sound. "And what about the fucking army? The marines? How many brothers are in the army and marines—in all the armed forces? Are they going to turn their guns on us or on their white masters?

"No, brothers! I don't think we have too damned much to sweat from the armed forces of the United States of America. Why, more than half the infantry units in this country are black! We will make Whitey wish to God they'd never put their boots on our necks!"

Walker straightened his arm and his fist punched upward once more.

Twenty-eight fists rose and answered his, and twenty-eight black men jumped to their feet and answered him. And the moment would have been his complete, but for the duel that morning with Mason and the empty chair behind him.

The members shouted, rolled their eyes, slapped hands, laughed, chattered. Vernon let them blow off their accumulated steam. He lit a cigarette and stared at its glowing tip.

Mason, and the Vietnam memories, had stalked him all that day. His and Joe's acceptance of the simple fact that they would each try to destroy the other had opened a chink in Vernon's personal armor. He knew now that he had always respected Mason, even more than he had hated his possible racism.

It shook him to his roots, this discovery. In the man he was planning to wage war against was something strong, something admirable, something he could damn near love! Still, he wouldn't let it turn him from what he knew he had to do.

"Spider," he called, and Washington separated himself from the milling group of young men and stepped around the desk to Vernon's side. The biker said nothing, but he didn't have to. His happiness, the pure, savage joy of it, gleamed from dilated eyeballs that seemed to simmer in the hot oil of their shadowed sockets.

"I want to get these guns checked out to our people."

"Yes, Chief."

"I want you to see to it." Walker sat down. "I want them to know their weapons inside and out. Help the ones who've never broke a piece down, and get the pieces cleaned up that we didn't have time for this afternoon. Spend as much time as you need on it, then get all the weapons down into the basement where the furnace is built into the wall. Take Little Bit with you. He knows where they're supposed to go. Brown, too—let him help you. He was in Nam."

"Isn't this all the PM's job, Chief?"

"You just do what I told you and don't worry about the PM."

"Where is he tonight?"

Vernon brought his eyes into focus and glared at Washington's answering grin. "You want to say something, then say it, Spider."

"Chino seen the PM tonight." Spider's grin slipped off his darkly shining face at Vernon's sudden change of expression. "He seen him, honest to God!"

"Where?" Walker demanded, then held up his hand. "Wait a minute. Chino!"

The tall, yellowish-skinned youth sidled to the desk. "Yeah, Chief?"

"Spider says you saw the PM."

Chino glanced at Washington, who shrugged, and he said, "I'm not bullshitting you, Vernon."

Walker stared at Chino.

"Where?"

"Walking down Skinker from the college. About two hours ago. On my way here."

"Who was he with, man?" Spider asked, and moved closer to Walker while he answered his own question. "He was with some white trim, Vernon. That's what I was going to tell you. That's what Chino ran down to me before the meeting."

Walker shook his head. He allowed himself a tight smile, and without lifting his head to look at the new member, he said, "You are hungry, aren't you, Spider? You are starving to death."

"I just want what you want, President Walker."

"You're just hungry for the power and the killing. You don't want what I want, man."

"I want to fight them. I'm loyal."

"Do what you're told then," Walker said, and waved at Little Bit. "Give the Spider a hand, little soldier."

Chino had watched the exchange without a word. He still stood in front of the desk and waited as Washington spun around and stalked off with Little Bit Stanton. The members began breaking open the closed crates and Chino's serious black eyes squinted around grinning folds of skin. "She's a hunk of good-looking trim, Boss, even if she is white. I don't think the PM's really strung out on her or nothing."

"How long's he been seeing this good-looking piece of white trim?"

"I don't know. A month, maybe. Maybe longer."

"Why the secret shit?"

Chino lifted his shoulders expressively.

"Don't know, Boss. The PM's always been tight about his private life. Maybe he don't want no one ace'n him out."

"Okay." Vernon lit a cigarette and set the problem aside. He looked at Chino, still standing very still and watchful. "You know the cop, Mason, Chi, man?"

"Sure. Seen the dude on the block enough."

"Good. I want you to give the street a good eyeball, then take a walk over to the Fireball, and eyeball some more. You see Mason, give me a call, then bird-dog him. Let me know what he's doing."

"Like the FBI," Chino said, and smiled. Walker stared into the man's flat-black eyes.

"Yeah, Chi, man. Just like the FBI."

"You want me to introduce myself, Boss, if he spots me?"

"No. Just turn around and come back here. Just watch him. I want to know what that dude is doing."

But Chino Poole would not see Mason that night.

Joe was pulling his Chevy to the curb on Finney Street in Clayton, a suburb of St. Louis's bright-lit Inner City, a place of tree-lined streets, old homes, and good apartments, boasting a brightly shining business district patrolled by well-paid police officers who could easily expect to work twenty years without seeing a homicide victim. The Chevy's right wheel bumped up and over the concrete curb line and bounced heavily in the gutter as Joe switched off the rumbling engine. The car rocked on its shocks and settled into a crackling stillness. Mason lifted the bottle riding next to him on the front seat and unscrewed the top. He took a long pull, gasping as the Scotch burned over his lips and down his throat. Resealing the cap, he searched his pockets and found a pack of gum. He unwrapped a stick and jammed it into his mouth. He chewed slowly, opening the car door and standing for a moment in weaving indecision as he stared up at the apartment he'd parked in front of.

"To hell with it."

He climbed the steps to the right-side door, took a ring of keys from his pocket, and fitted one into the lock. The door swung inward and Mason climbed the short flight of wooden stairs. In the living room he paused and regained his steady rate of breathing.

The smells are all the same. You remember the smells first and last: wood smoke from the fireplace, the incense she liked to burn with the old logs, and the faint odor of her too-heavy perfume. Even little Mark's smell: that sweet-sour smell of baby boy, that talcumy fragrance of infancy.

You carried all this furniture up here, Mason. You made love to her on that couch. Christ, you bought the damned couch and the rugs and chairs and paintings. You started the first fire in the fireplace and forgot to open the damper. Smoke all over the place and Ellen running out to the balcony with Mark in her arms, giggling at you.

Mason moved quietly through the living and dining rooms to the short hall which separated the two bedrooms, the kitchen, and bathroom. The bathroom light was on, but the door was shut to a bare crack, emitting only the slightest illumination.

He knew they were both asleep, his son and ex-wife, deep in sleep, and he could feel them—one to each bedroom. They had no idea he was here, half-drunk and wondering why he'd come in the first place. The marriage, his mind told him indignantly, is dead. But I want, Mason answered himself, to see Mark.

Open his door, then. See him curled in the baby bed, fists to either side of his damp head, mouth slightly open, and eyes closed under heavy lids.

You made him come to life, Joe. He exists because of you. Mason bent slowly over the wooden bars on the bed to brush his big hand across his son's rounded forehead. Little Mark. The trooper.

How you been, Trooper?

The boy stirred in his sleep and rolled onto his side. The bed was littered with stuffed animals and plastic cars. Mark was always a nut about cars, Mason thought, and look how damned big he's getting. This darn kid'll be twice my size someday. Old trooper.

And you don't want to wake him, but at the same time you wish for him to open his huge glowing eyes and look up at you and speak his strange, lisping, child language.

Move out, Mason. Retreat before it gets to you too bad and you're bawling like a broad.

He backed to the half-open door, glancing right and left at the stacks of toys (red-plastic truck, yellow bulldozer, wood Fort Ticonderoga) under the bed and in the far corner, and at the silly kid things Ellen had hung from the walls and ceilings: clown faces, a toy soldier, cut-out fish with brightly painted human smiles swinging from dangling strings.

Close the door on all of it; grin and bear it, man.

He crossed the hall and opened Ellen's door. He saw his ex-wife just as soundly asleep as his ex-son, in his ex-apartment, amid all his ex-furniture.

Sitting as gently as he could upon the edge of her bed, Joe stared down at Ellen's sleep-composed face. He was amazed, as always, at his son's resemblance to this woman who had laughed so gaily on their wedding day, fed him white cake, white body, and whispered to him, "We will never end, Joe."

Mason spoke the words aloud and Ellen's eyes snapped open at the first sound of his voice. Her breath hissed in and she shoved back against the headboard, rising up from the mattress, her long brown hair hanging over naked shoulders. She clutched the blankets to her breasts.

"You look like some silent movie star, just waking up and seeing the bad guy," Mason said.

"Joe! Jesus, how—what are you doing here?"

"I'm checking the house for leaks. I was driving past and I thought I smelled love leaking out of this house, so I grabbed my love meter and came inside to check."

"How'd you get in for God's sake—and why?"

"I still have a key," he said softly. "And it's true, Ellen. I'm checking on love leaks."

"Oh, Joe! Get out of here!" Her voice rose with each word and Mason raised his hand. She flinched back against the crushed pillow. He pulled the hand back as if he'd been burnt.

"Just be a little quiet, Ellen. You'll wake Mark."

"Joe," she said carefully, holding a trembling hand to her forehead, "I want you out of here, please. This isn't accomplishing anything. You are frightening me, Joe. I'm really afraid."

"Afraid? Ellen, dammit to hell, how could you be afraid of me? Have I ever hit you? I couldn't—"

"You've been drinking."

"That's right," he said, and grinned. "You're right. I have been drinking."

Ellen swiped at tears trying to spill from her wide eyes and drew in a deep breath. She glanced at the alarm clock on the nightstand next to the bed.

"What do you want, Joe?"

"I want to see Mark and I wanted to see you."

"It's two o'clock in the morning."

"If you hadn't waked up, I wouldn't be sitting here talking to you. I wouldn't've waked you up. I was leaving in a minute."

"You can leave now," she murmured. "And give me the key you still have."

"How's Mark?" he asked, ignoring both her requests. "How's the trooper been, Ellen?"

"Mark," she said, "is always fine. Can I have that key?"

He stood up and tried to straighten his back, but felt wired into a perpetual slouch. He rubbed at the back of his neck and felt his eyes clear themselves of the dizziness that had accompanied his rising. His hand searched through the change in his pocket and he drew out the key. He held it for a moment, then laid it down next to the alarm clock.

Ellen still held the sheets up to her nakedness and Mason felt a flash of the old feelings assault his groin. This bedroom held more than its share of sexual memories.

"It's really over," he said.

Ellen nodded and spoke in a flat voice. "There's a paper saying it is."

"To flaming hell with a bunch of fucking papers!"

"Joe—"

"All right," he whispered harshly, and turned and centered himself in the doorway, his back to her breathing. He stared at his son's closed doorway and felt Ellen's presence. He wished to reach out and touch her—she still lived so strongly inside of him—but he would not give her that much victory. Instead, he drew a sudden picture for his mind to contemplate: Mona, the Fireball, Frank Brown, Vernon Walker, his beat, the black faces growling, smiling, noncommittal. His beat.

"You know I have to do the kind of work—" he began, but her voice cut him off.

"No, Joe. Let's don't go through all of that all over again. Please. It's so late."

"Yeah," he said, "I suppose it is."

"You can come and see Mark." Ellen's words were like ghosts floating through the darkness. "You know you can come and see him whenever you want."

"I'd rather not see him at all, than just part-time.

You know how I feel about that." He twisted sideways in the doorway and stared at her. "Dammit, you know how I feel about everything!"

She lowered her dark eyes and nodded.

"The words sound so clinched, Joe," she said. "And I've said them all a thousand times ... I don't want to be a policeman's wife. I don't want any part of it. My friends, the people I care about, and the people I've always associated with, aren't part of that world. I can't be part of it, either. I don't understand it. I hate it."

"You've just explained the whole thing to yourself," he said, "and you don't even know it."

"What do you mean?"

"You don't understand something, so you hate it."

"That's not fair, Joe. I never hated you. I don't hate you now."

"So what the fuck is 'fair' anyway, huh?" He lifted his hand, saw it trembling, dropped it, and said: "See you, baby."

Then will your legs to move, Mason. Turn through the short hall, the dining room, living room, and down the creaking wooden stairs. Step out into the cold night and climb into the Chevy. Stare up at pinpoint stars, and then down at the slowly dwindling bottle of Scotch, clutched in a shaking hand.

Strangely enough, you're not thinking of Ellen and Mark. It's your dad you're seeing now. Dead Dad. Killed-in-stupid-car-wreck Dad. And you remember something he always used to say.

"If a man's got enemies, then he's probably a good man. You can judge a man by the quality of his enemies."

"That's nuts!" You're seventeen. Everything anyone over twenty says is nuts. "You don't have any enemies, and you're a good man, Pop."

"I'm just an easy man to get along with, Joe. I make friends easy. I don't want people to dislike me. I want to be everybody's buddy."

"What's wrong with that?"

"Oh, nothing, I suppose, except that men like me are never really doing what they want to do. We're

84

never really independent. We don't go our own way or stand by a set of hard principles." His father rubbed a gnarled hand over his clean-shaven face. The pale-blue eyes stared at young Joe Mason, and the thin lips curled into a grimace of disgust. "We're flexible."

And a few months later Joe cried on his father's grave. But only after everyone else had left. And it started to snow as he wept, as he choked and laughed, kneeling and shouting at the freshly turned earth:

"Dad! Aw, goddammit, Dad!"

Because his father had always opened himself to the world, and to his son; because George R. Mason, insurance salesman and good buddy to all mankind, had never known the pleasure of telling someone to go to hell.

But you have an enemy, Mason. You have Vernon Walker and he has you. You're both wealthy.

He drained the Scotch remaining in the bottle and shuddered. He took a final look at the place where his past lay sleeping. He remembered everything for the last time—his father, his mother who sat each day in an empty house with six cats and did needlepoint and talked to herself, his sister who had moved to Saginaw, Michigan, with her appliance-salesman husband, and the boy he'd once been. The boy who wept in the snow.

"Now," he mumbled, starting the car's cold engine, "I'm just like Cortez. Burn all the fucking ships, so there's no way to retreat. Nothing to come back to but a good old reliable—enemy!"

He drove from the middle-class serenity of Finney Street in Clayton and headed for the slum lights and burnt, wet smell of his adopted neighborhood. He would call Mona first to make sure she wasn't with a "friend" before he went to her brown arms, small bobbing breasts, and leg-clasping love. Then, tomorrow afternoon, work again. Vernon Walker, and work.

The city dragged its ass through another night. The streets were mostly deserted, except for the small havens provided by barfronts, recessed doorways in crumbling brownstones, and enclosed aluminum bus stops where winos and wanderers from the hippie underground huddled out of the November wind.

The city, built on the refuse of almost two hundred years as a major riverport, ate the garbage of yesterday and swallowed the garbage of the day before and digested the sludge of a week ago. And it grew; brick cell upon steel girders upon mud upon concrete. Ever more monstrous, hideously pockmarked, it grew.

And down a street, deserted and ice-slick, drove a dark blue '57 Chevy, carrying Joe Mason to that place within the city's bowels which would be his resting place this night.

Walker woke suddenly, startled. It was morning, and he was surprised at how fast the darkness had passed. He got off the bunk, washed, and dressed. No one was in the headquarters, but that didn't bother him. He was glad that on this particular day he was alone for a while with his own thoughts.

No dreams last night, he realized: a sleep that was deep and untroubled, the first such heavy sleep in a long time. Me, he thought, with enough problems to fill Busch Stadium and I sleep like a kid. Why? Is it because I don't feel worried? Christ, I should be worried. . . .

He was moving slow, with the easy grace of a man with some time on his hands, when Chuck Williams opened the door.

The Prime Minister held a white paper bag covered with grease spots.

"Couple White Castles, and coffee, Chief. Peace offering from the prodigal son."

"Okay," Vernon said. "Sit down."

Williams sat on the cot and smiled uneasily.

"How'd it go last night?" he asked.

"You'd like to know?" Walker pried open a styrofoam cup and sucked at the strong hot coffee. He decided he hated styrofoam cups more than anything else in the world. "You'd really like to know how it went? You're interested?"

"Listen, I'm sorry, Vernon."

"The white chick. Is she sorry, Chuck?"

"I am sorry, man!"

"'I am sorry, man,'" Vernon mimicked. "Sorry don't cut it, Chuck. This isn't games, now. I thought we got that straight with each other. I thought we sat here and talked about dedication, and how we were as good as the VC. No, man. Sorry don't mean shit, PM."

"It won't happen again, Vernon."

"You're goddamned right, it won't happen again!"

Walker lowered himself into the chair behind the small desk. The peaceful beginnings of this morning were dissolving fast. "You are the PM, Chuck! You have to be here, man. You can't be out trimming white trash every time you get a hard on!"

Walker studied Chuck's angry face, the light brown skin darkening, the fine-fingered, piano-player hands linked together, knuckles straining.

"You're the PM, and your world don't revolve around the head of your penis anymore, Chuck."

"It's not like that, Vernon." Williams pulled off his black beret. "She's not like—she's not a piece of white trash."

Walker swallowed another mouthful of coffee. It tasted like raw acid in his throat as it mixed with the anger that pulsed there. He reached into the bag and unwrapped a hamburger, White Castle's contribution to ghetto indigestion, and bit into the greasy mess.

"Eat a hamburger, PM. Drink your stinking coffee."

Williams ignored him. His eyes were still wide with rage.

"You can't tell me how to live my personal life!"

"If it affects the Party, then I sure the fuck can tell you—and I will!"

Silence thudded between them, and held them for an agonized moment, then slipped away into the cold light sifting through the dusty window. Williams shifted his boots and lowered his gaze.

"I told you I was sorry, Vernon."

"And I told you," Walker said between clenched teeth, "that sorry don't mean shit! Things are going to start hitting the fan around here, Chuck. Where are you going to be when that happens, when I need you, man? Are you going to be shacked up? She's stealing your balls! Whitey's eating your goddamned pride if you rate her above your brothers!"

"My life!" Williams shouted. "It's my life, Vernon. Like my woman's mine. And what I do away from here is up to me!" Chuck looked at Walker, his eyes pleading for understanding. "Don't be coming down on me this way, man! We've been through too much shit for you to come down on me about a girl!"

"It's not just a girl." Walker threw the remains of the hamburger at the overflowing wastebasket. "It's her color. Wasn't it you, Chuck, who stood here and came down on Lehr for not being black, for not understanding blacks? Wasn't it you who talked about what our members would think if we didn't spring Terry T.? Shit! What do you think the members are going to think when they see you with Whitey? You do not have a personal life anymore, Prime Minister. You have to be in this all the way—or out! Now, make up your mind, Chuck. You decide whether you want to be a man, or go back to being a nigger!"

Chuck lunged off the cot and stood trembling on the far side of the room, his back to Vernon, who passed a hand over his face and took a deep breath. Christ, he thought. My main man is falling over the edge—slipping away from me. The one dude I thought for sure I could depend on.

"I am a man," Williams said, his voice low and full of what was in him now, what was spreading through the room like fresh air. "I'll never be a nigger again, Vernon."

"Then you get rid of that white chick," Walker said, knowing that even as the words passed his lips he pushed his friend too hard.

"I'll think about it, Vernon. I don't want to go against—"

It enraged him. Chuck acting like a spoiled child blew his cool completely. There was so much at stake,

88

and all his Prime Minister, his main man, could offer was, "I'll think about it—"

"You'll do what I tell you," Walker said. "You'll do what's best for the group, *all the time*, or you will get the fuck out!"

Chuck growled something unintelligible and spun around. He lurched against the cot and kicked over his cup of coffee sitting on the floor. The coffee rolled out into a puddle and Williams stood for a moment staring from Walker's uncompromising eyes to the spilled coffee, and then back to Walker before stumbling out of the room. His answer floated back as he stomped through the main office and out the front door: "I'm still the goddamned PM!"

Spider Washington appeared, as if by magic, and leaned into the doorjamb. He grinned at Walker's slumped figure.

"You two really hassling."

"Where the fuck did you come from?"

"I was in the basement."

"What do you want."

"I got Little Bit down there. We're finishing up on the guns."

"Then finish and stop trying to use your pea-sized brain, motocycle man."

"Sounded like our PM's not as dedicated as—"

"Get your black ass out of my office!" Walker stood up and took one step forward.

Spider's eyes lingered on Walker in a calculating appraisal, then shifted away.

"Right, Chief."

Chapter Eight

JOE MASON was back at work and suffering from another monumental hangover. He was also more enraged than he could ever remember as each word drawled from the corner of Captain Roy Slater's mouth.

"Black Panthers crawling out of the woodwork, yeah ... uh, everybody's seeing militants in their sleep, there, Mason. What was it, now? Yeah, guns. All kinds of deadly armament and plans to take over the world; these panthers are going to do that, huh? These black nationalists?"

Joe nodded, feeling stiff in his starched blue uniform shirt, black clip-on tie, and pressed dark-blue trousers. He tried to speak, but couldn't. Instead, he concentrated on locating the precise source of the nausea that churned his stomach. He squirmed on the chair, facing the chief of detectives, Thirteenth District, and dreamed of the immediate relief just one shot of neat Scotch would accomplish within the frayed conduits of his quivering nervous system.

"The black menace, Joe. Like the red menace when McCarthy held them hearings, you know? That's what it is. A hell of a scare, and—"

Slater, a short but muscular man possessed of a personal stockpile of energy that made each gesture an attack, seemed to bounce up and down with his own need to explain away the obvious. He ran his hands through thinning, white blond hair, rubbed a freckled nose, and fingered the pale scar that ran down the bulge of his left cheekbone. The scar was very white against the flush of his ruddy complexion. It was the source of Roy Slater's claim to fame. He'd received the knife cut while disarming a psycho who'd attacked a group of worshippers at a synagogue, and managed to kill a rabbi and seriously wound six of his congregation before Slater arrived to find the man holding a young girl in front of him, threatening to open her windpipe. The young then-uniformed Roy Slater managed to convince the suspect that the police surrounding him were Gestapo, and that he, Slater, was Adolph Hitler. It had worked—to a point—but the blade had caught Slater's face as the rookie cop grabbed the man's arm, dragging him away from the screaming girl.

That incident was in the dim past and much had happened to cool Slater's fervor since then, not the least of which was promotion to captain. And today, with Joe Mason arguing before him, the chief of detectives was more agitated than usual. This was beginning to have a similar effect on Mason himself. Joe felt that he was starting to imitate each of Captain Slater's gestures—with jerks, jumps, and twitches of his own. It made the anger in him boil into his chest like a bad case of heartburn. He tasted bile in his throat as he forced himself to listen to Slater's lame argument, as the captain informed him that there was "nothing to" what Walker had let slip the day before.

"Listen, Joe. ..." A cough. Straightening of tie. "A lot of bullshit is what it is." Another cough, and Mason felt his throat tickling. He coughed in response as Slater talked on.

"There's nothing to it, Joe. I'll lay odds. They're selling a bunch of phony tickets on themselves. They want us to get hopped up on the idea they got guns in there, that they're going to start using them, popping at the cops. You see? They'd love us to go charging in there and—all over the fucking papers, see? They'd just love that kind of stuff. Do 'em a lot of good."

"I saw Walker bring in a weapon, Captain."

"You saw a package, Joe!" Slater rubbed at his creased neck. He adjusted the lapels of his checked sport coat. "Could you swear in court it was a rifle? You know about probable cause, search warrants—how can you see me trying to get a warrant on just your say-so? Can you see the judge? *I* can see the fucking judge. On that kind of a bullshit tip! To a judge all you saw was a package. Christ. If we went in on that, all hell to pay with the newspapers—if we went in on Walker's little group—with that kind of evidence."

"It was a rifle," Mason said. "I've seen too goddamned many guns not to know a rifle, even if it is wrapped up. I'm telling you, Captain, something's coming. They're going to hit us. I know Walker, and he's ready to ... pull something!"

He stumbled over the last two words, looking for the right way to explain it, so Slater could understand. But Joe knew it was no use, even as he talked. He could feel Slater's interest die, could feel him slip away, sorting the papers on his littered desk, barking something over his shoulder to Cassiday and Reynolds, who were printing a tall, black prisoner and photographing another black man with a red streak dyed into his Afro.

"Captain," Mason said, leaning forward and trying to catch Slater's roaming eyes, "I tell you, I know Vernon Walker. I spent some time with him overseas. We learned all about this crap over there. He knows how to do it and he's going to try, Captain. I know him like myself. He'll try!"

"We can't—" Slater began, but then looked up as Cassiday waved at him through the door of the back room. "What is it, Cass?"

"This bird wants a lawyer. Right this minute, if not sooner, skipper."

"You got the show-up ready?"

"Everything's set. Two guys from the fire department, and one from the day-shift platoon. They're suiting up in overalls. The witness is waiting outside at booking, shitting in his pants."

"Okay," Slater said, and picked up one of his two phones. He punched an outside line and dialed quickly, eager for an excuse to ignore Mason.

Joe stood up, taking the hint, and straightened his dark-blue nylon jacket. Cassiday, a tall rawboned Irishman with a dapper mustache and a taste for flashy suits, winked at him.

"How's everything in the harness bulls, Joey?"

"Still bringing in busts you fuckers take credit for." Mason stared down at Slater on his phone. The detective captain asked for the prosecuting attorney's office, then cupped his hand over the phone's receiver.

"Listen, Mason. I know you've got good intentions, but maybe you're too close to the problem. Maybe you see it in the wrong light. Since they're on your beat, and all."

"Who?" Cassiday asked, lighting a cigar and blowing out a billow of rank smoke. "Who's on his beat?"

"Shitbum Walker and his group on Delmar," Slater said. "What does Intelligence have on them?"

Cassiday studied the glowing tip of his cigar.

"Well, all I know is they ain't been able to infiltrate the punks. But they're nothing. Militant punks is all. Lot of mouth and nothing to back it up with. People in his oufit, though—like that Washington. Now, there are some people in his group with mean records, and all."

"Joe, here, thinks they're bringing guns in," Slater explained. "Says he saw them bring in a bunch yesterday. Isn't that right, Joe?"

"That's right!"

"Nope," said Cassiday. "Don't think so. No offense, Joey, but our information is that they're not going that route. Course, I could be wrong. And sure as hell, that bunch in Intelligence has been fucking wrong before. By the way, Joey. What the hell were you doing down there on your day off?"

Mason ignored the question and turned to speak to Slater, but the detective captain was talking into the phone.

"Yeah, Bob. Slater at the thirteenth. Sure, fine. We got a rape suspect wants a public defender before he'll agree to a show-up. Right. Is he what? Hell, I don't know, but we got a witness. Some guy who was in the park walking his dog. Listen, Bob, we bring the bastards in on a witness."

Mason turned, suddenly disgusted with everything, and started for the door. Roy Slater cupped the phone again.

"Get me something I can use for a warrant Joe, and we'll back you all the way. But we got to have something concrete—something solid." He smiled generously.

"Sure."

Cassiday touched Mason's sleeve.

"Joey, boy. You never told me, kid. What you doing down in that neighborhood on your day off? You got something you're fucking down there, Joey?"

"I live down there, garbage-brain."

"A foul-tongued lad, aren't you?"

"Fuck all of you Peter Gunn's."

"And God bless you, too, Joey."

Mason stepped rapidly down the hall to the assembly room. He pushed open the old wooden door and sank down into an empty desk next to his riding partner, Allen Jones. Jones, a young black officer who resembled Harry Bellafonte so much that girls were always doing double-takes on him, was just out of the academy and eager as hell. Before Joe's session with Slater, Allen had pumped all he could get out of him about Walker. Now, Jones leaned close to Mason and whispered, "Well, what happened, man? You look like you could eat a box of nails!"

"Nothing," Mason said, snorting. "Nothing happened. We got to get 'evidence' before Roy Rogers'll make move number one."

"You're kidding?" Jones's handsome face puckered with concern.

"Sure, I'm fucking kidding," Mason said. "Jesus Ralph Christ! I wish I was kidding!"

"Damn!"

Sergeant Oscar Baker, one of Mason's three platoon sergeants, glared at the two officers from behind his desk at the front of the room.

"Are you two playboys going to listen to these hotsheet corrections, or not? Mason, you've already missed half of the assembly. You had a chance for plainclothes and turned it down. How about making up your mind. You want us, or the dicks?"

This last line brought a scattered chorus of laughter from the men around him, and Mason grimaced at their turned and smiling faces. He lit a cigarette as Allen Jones tried to slide down behind the patrolman in front of him.

I want you, Sergeant Baker," Mason said. "The dicks are stupid, but I decided that you need my help even more than they do."

Another spatter of laughter—partly restrained and frightened—from the platoon members and a dark scowl of anger from Baker.

To hell with all of you, Mason thought, and winked at Jones. You don't have the slightest idea what you're in for. None of you.

And he settled himself into the small school desk and opened his notebook.

Vernon Walker hesitated at the door of the apartment.

Will Chuck be here? he wondered. And he felt hesitation turn to acute nervousness. He was not used to being nervous and it made him angry. He experienced a shaming sense of disloyalty, but wiped that away. It was a necessary thing and he wanted it.

Forget everything, he told himself. She's a piece of white meat. She's white—and wrong. And Chuck's falling for her. She'll take his heart away when I need him. She'll castrate my main man. She'll make him want safety, and I need doomed men for what's about to happen. I need men who have no reason for wanting a safe, peaceful, loving, fucking life. I need men like we were in Nam. Men who know that only blind fighting can save them.

He knocked hard and the door opened almost at once as if she'd been waiting.

The white girl stared up at him, her blue eyes penetrating the thin veil of his sunglasses. Sand-colored hair falling past her shoulders, upturned nose, slightly bucked teeth, freckles, a good figure under a man's shirt and jeans. The All-American Coke Girl. The All-American Liberal. Some of her best friends, he'd be willing to bet, were Negroes.

"Aren't you going to give me the Black Power sign?" he suggested. "Or at least the V for peace?"

"What?" she asked, smiling and Walker knew why Chuck was strung out on her. "What'd you say?"

They have formed our tastes, our desires, to match theirs.

"I'm Vernon Walker," he answered. "Chuck's my man. I want to talk to you about him."

They have given us their Marilyn Monroes, their Ava Gardners, their Ali MacGraws, and told us this is what you will never be allowed to have, but this is what you should look for in women. This is beauty. This is sex appeal. Your own women are fizzy-haired and ugly.

An awful lot of everything that was wrong, Vernon knew, was based on these kind of lies. But here he was looking at this white woman and feeling that familiar stirring of lust. Who's lying to whom? he wondered.

"Come on in," she said. "Chuck's not here, but I know who you are. I've seen you before, man. Once, on TV news. You were beautiful. You'd just been busted. I'm Eileen. Come on in."

Vernon stepped into her living room as she closed the door behind him. She's younger than I figured, he thought, and stared at her flushing features as Eileen gestured at a badly frayed green sofa.

"Sit down. The place looks like hell, I know, but I've never been the house-cleaning type. Gee, this is really sort of weird. It's really kind of strange, you know? Chuck talks so much about you, Vernon. May I call you that? Would you like a beer?"

"Yes, to both questions," he said, and took off his leather jacket. He lowered himself to the sofa.

"Fine," she said. "Gee, this is really strange."

She bustled off to the kitchen. Gee.

Younger than I thought, he repeated to himself, and inspected the room while he lit a cigarette. Her place is exactly like I knew it'd be. Right on the motherfuckin' button.

Posters on the walls. All the really chic posters. And, of course, black and white couples together. Chuck, my love, it's you and me against the world. And stuffed animals. Why are chicks so nuts about stuffed animals? A horse, rabbit, teddy bear—two teddy bears—and a tiger. Christ, a whole zoo of stuffed animals. Teddy bears and Malcolm X. A huge poster of Rap Brown and Bobby Seale. Gee whiz, you're Vernon Walker. Gee whiz, another black militant! Gee. Super. Cool. Wow!

"It's not too cold." The voice next to him spoke, and Vernon turned to stare at the Budweiser can being held out to him. He took off the sunglasses and accepted the beer. He thanked her as he knew she would truly dig.

"Right on, Eileen, baby. You're a real righteous girl. Very righteous, indeed. A true sister."

"Oh, thanks," she said. "I just got back from the store. That's why the beer's not real cold. Chuck loves his really cold. But, like a dummy, I never keep enough in the place."

"It's fine."

"I hate it warm myself." She started for a chair across the room from him.

"Sit here, Eileen. I want to lay some stuff on you and I want you where I can see you close up. You are as good to look at as I expected."

"Gee, Vernon, why the super-heavy stuff?" She took a hesitant step toward him. "Is anything wrong about Chuck and me?"

"No, baby." He dropped his voice low and almost whispered, sipping the beer and staring up at her over the can's rim. He set the beer down on a coffee table made from oh-so-too-cool orange crates. "Nothing is wrong about you and Chuck, but what I want to tell you *is* super-heavy, Eileen. I'm feeling super-heavy ever since I saw you at the door."

"You are unreal," she whispered back, and her eyes glowed at him like twin candles in the dark. She sat down on the couch, holding herself very still.

"Do you mind if I smoke some grass, Vernon? I didn't want anything before, but now..."

"I don't mind a bit," he said. "Don't mind at all."

Joe Mason and Allen Jones settled into the front seat of Department Car 642, a 1971 Plymouth Fury. Mason behind the wheel. Jones at shotgun.

The two men checked the car out like pilots checking out a bomber before takeoff. Mason reached to where the shotgun was bracketed on the lock-up cage separating the front and back seats, and unlocked the twelve-gauge, sawed-off, pump-action Remington. You weren't supposed to unlock the weapon unless it was about to be used, but Joe believed in always being prepared. Jones busied himself changing hot sheets in the illuminated plastic screen, and dropped the small metal writing desk and mike holder which stood on a metal post between his and Mason's bent knees.

Mason was filling out the trip-ticket, writing down the car's number, the date and time, amount of time the vehicle would be used, and beginning mileage. At the end of their tour he would set down the end mileage and off to the side add up the number of miles patroled during their eight-hour shift.

The front seat of the Plymouth was jammed with the two officers' gear. Mason moved around irritably, trying to get everything set up comfortably: moving clipboards to one side, ramming the two nightsticks into the seat so that they stood out like cannons aiming at the car's dash, arranging their briefcases and sheaves of report forms.

"We barely got room for us in this bastard."

"Slater really gave you the runaround, Joe?"

"Don't talk to me yet, Rookie. I'm busy being pissed."

"Pardon me, Bwana Mason."

"Right. Now you got it. That's me. Bwana Mason."

Around them, on the parking lot of the thirteenth district station, to the rear of the station house, the cars that had just finished the day shift were rolling in and parking. Their crews climbed out and left the vehicles to Mason's platoon members. For a few moments there was much organized confusion. Engines revved and sputtered in the cold air; sirens and red lights whooped and flashed as they were tested. Cops got out and got in the many-colored patrol cars. The red lights spun like crimson splashes on the rear wall and windows of the district station and on Sergeant Baker's face as he trotted to the side of Mason's car.

"Couple of warrants," Baker shouted, bellowing over the noise on either side. "And some police demand orders for plates and drivers' licenses!"

"Right!" Mason took the papers and handed them to Jones. "I know what they are!"

"Try real hard to get 'em taken care of before shift change," Baker said, speaking through Mason's open window. "Huh, Mason. Will ya' do that, please?"

"They go on the tail end of everything else, Sarge. If we got crime, we fight crime first. Then, if we get the time, we'll take care of the petty stuff. And I ain't ever seen this district without crime—especially on the afternoon watch!"

"You better stop that cocky shit of yours, Mason. You're going to get your tit in the wringer, you keep on with that cocky shit!"

Fat Baker had attained little besides bland middle age. Fussy, unimaginative, he couldn't understand Mason's attitude toward his job.

"It's my tit, Sarge. Ain't that right?"

"Okay, youngster. Just listen—"

"Okay, what? Are you trying to impress me with your age? All right, I'm impressed. Now what?"

"Just mark my words, Mason," Baker said, a spot of red glowing on each full cheek. "You'll hang yourself someday and I'll be there to pick up the pieces. You think being gung-ho is all it takes to be a cop—you're wrong!"

"Well, you don't have to worry about that, do you, Baker?" Mason laughed as he rolled up the window so that the sergeant had to remove his hands from the doorframe. "So long, glorious leader."

Baker stepped back. His face was solid red now.

Mason dropped his car into gear and squealed rubber across the lot's concrete surface, Jones laughing by his side.

"That Baker dude kills me, man."

"He might someday," Mason said, "when he gives you a more than usually stupid order. Shit. Get us in service, Al. Put us in, man. We've got work to do."

"Right," Jones said, and jerked the hand mike loose from its bracket on the metal desk.

The Plymouth roared into the afternoon's dimness, its headlights on at three-thirty in the afternoon because of lowering clouds. The buildings engulfed them rising up on either side and hiding most of the sky, sending black shadows across the narrow streets.

Mason drove as fast as he could through the developing traffic jams and swerved left, tires squealing onto Boyd. The people on the streets, most of them blacks or hippies, watched the police car go by with a mixture of curiosity, worry, and hatred. Jones waved at them all, remembering his People to People classes at the academy. The rookie had his hat off and was patting the top of a carefully styled, short Afro. His light-brown skin was red-tinged around the cheekbones and nose from the wind racing into his partly open window.

He looks too young, Mason thought, but then remembered his squad in Vietnam, remembered the ones who turned so quickly to being much older than their years, remembering at the same time how his own face had changed. Choir boys into killers. But he buried those thoughts. Get off that shit, he told himself. And forget Slater and Cassiday. You know you're on the right track. You know what has to go down.

He maneuvered the Plymouth into a No Parking Zone and threw the gearshift into park. Jones looked out his window at the sleazy front of Mac's Chicken Palace and groaned horribly.

"Motherfucker. Not chicken again, Joe! Tell me we're not having that goddamned, motherfuckin' chicken again!"

"Did you know you looked too young to be a cop?"

"I'm going to turn into a goddamned chicken."

"Altar boys. That's what they're giving us from the academy, nowadays. Children."

"All this goddamned chicken we've been eating on this shift, man. I'm beginning to cluck!"

"Sounds like a personal problem, kid. Look, it'd be different if we had to pay, but we don't. What more do you want?"

"Steak!"

"It's bad enough we're extorting chicken from the poor black folk, much less motherfuckin' steak!"

"Let the bastards eat cake!"

"Jesus. It's an educated nigger I got." Mason opened the car door, smiling crookedly. "Let 'em eat cake, huh? Jesus."

"Honky motherfucker!" Jones grinned also.

Mason said, "Senior man in the car gives the orders, Rookie. I say it's a fast box of chicken now, and hope for better later." He jumped from the car, crossing in front, and grinning through the front window at Jones. The rookie slumped back on the seat and made a gesture that was totally obscene. Mason threw back his head and laughed, springing up to the sidewalk. "Grin and bear it, kid!" he hollered, and Jones doubled the gesture, using both hands.

Fat Mac, the owner of the Chicken Palace, looked up as Joe pushed open the door. His rotund black face gleamed with sweat under the harsh lights. Behind Mac's bulk and through a slot-cut opening in the wall, Mason glimpsed three young black girls powdering chicken with flour and shifting wire baskets into huge caldrons of boiling grease.

"Be with ya' in a minute, Joe!"

"No hurry, Maxwell."

A long-haired white boy and girl, dressed smartly in shabby work clothes and army field jackets, waited at the far end of the counter. The boy nodded at Mason, but the girl kept her head turned. Joe leaned on the counter and when Mac had finished adding figures down a length of adding-machine paper, he said, "Two boxes, Maxwell. And two coffees to go."

"You hear that, girls?" The black neck swiveled, turning into rolls and creases oiled with sweat. "Two boxes for the Man!" The moon face swung back to Mason, who was unsnapping his jacket and watching the white boy and girl. She isn't more than fourteen, he thought, but Mac's voice moved in on his thinking.

"Sorry, Mac." Joe faced the Palace's owner. "What'd you say, man?"

"I said"—the small brown eyes fluttered mournfully at Mason's lack of attention—"I said, Joe, that those beret-sportin' niggers of Walker's been on me about giving them some of my hard-earned cash. That is what I fucking said, man."

Soul music blared from a hidden radio and one of the girls in the back danced up to the opening in the wall behind Mac and set two boxes on the wooden shelf. Her hand, snapping time to the beat, rang a hotel bell on the shelf. Mac took a chin-quivering breath and turned like a huge black mountain. He grabbed the boxes and handed them over his counter to the long-haired boy. The youth paid him and made as if to leave, but Mason held out his hand.

"Hold on. I'd like to speak to you. Would you wait for just a moment?" Before the boy could answer, Mason asked Fat Mac, "Donations? Is that what you're talking about?"

"Donations shit, Joe! Them niggers are trying to shake ol' Mac down, man! Now I am fat, and I may be old, but I am also a bad dude when angered. And Joe, them punk-ass motherfuckers are angering me!"

Mac glanced back at the kitchen girl, who'd handed him the chicken. He grinned at her, but she affected a look of stylish boredom and turned away. Mac muttered a curse and said to Mason, "I used to be a boxer, Joe. I tell you that, man? Sure! A heavyweight contender. I sparred with Sugar Ray once. Shit! If them dudes...."

"You told me about the boxing, Mac." Mason saw the boy and girl moving toward the door. "You both stay still, kids. I just want to talk. This is no bust. Just stay put."

"Do what the Man says!" Mac roared, and his voice boomed in the small room like a cannon shot. Mason had to grin at the way the two youngsters froze in their tracks. He was going to ask for the boy's ID then, but three black studs dipped through the doorway. They all wore black-leather coats, black berets, and were very, very cool. They eyed Mason's uniform, met his stare, and scowled fiercely. Joe hung on to the smile that Mac's voice had started. He knew the tall stud and just barely inclined his head in greeting.

"What's happening, Terry T.?"

"Nothin' happening, po-lice." The hard eyes regarded Mason's easy slump against the counter, then moved to include Mac in their hate-filled stare. "You what's happening, po-liceman Mason."

"That's what my mama always told me."

The two friends of Terry T.'s stood behind him and to the side and added their own glares to the taller man's play, but Mason turned away from them as the bell rang again.

Mac slung two more boxes into a white bag and filled two cups with coffee. He handed the bags to Mason and nodded his head, his brown eyes speaking volumes. Joe smiled.

"You three know what you want?" Mac's stubby fingers toyed with his soiled tee shirt. "This ain't no lounge."

"We thinking, man." The three smiled at each other. "It strains our poor nigger brains, but we is thinking." His partners cracked up on that line. They slapped hands all around.

Mason set the bag of chicken and coffee on the counter and stepped over to the hippie couple who were still standing, more frightened now, by the steam-streaked window. Terry T. was moving with the loud music, being ultra-cool, and checking Mason's movements at the same time. Joe stood very close to the boy and girl and held on to his smile. His face felt like carved wood. He could taste action coming, and it pulled and tugged at his stomach.

He said to the white boy, his voice hissing,

"Go out to the police car at the curb. Tell the officer in it to come in here, on the double. I know the girl's on our runaway board back at the station, but this is no bust. I recognize her, but I'm not going to take you in. After you tell my partner to come in here, you can split." At the look of resistance on the boy's thin face, he pressed further. "Now, you go on out there. I'm doing you this favor and you can do one for me. If you want to come to the station later and rap about it, okay. No bust. Just tell my partner out there to get his butt in here."

"Do it," the girl whispered.

Resigned, the boy shrugged. "Okay." And they pushed through the door. Mason could just make out their figures as they moved to the side of the car and bent over. He sighed. He hadn't been sure they would follow his instructions, but now he grinned wider and felt confident again. His blood ran like heat, activating his hands and legs. He stepped up to Terry T., forcing the tall youth to stop his dancing and stand with his back against the edge of Mac's counter. Terry's partners shivered. Their faces were belligerent.

"How'd you get sprung so fast?" Mason asked. "You were in on a bad rap, Terry."

"What you getting up in my face for, po-lice? I don't like cops so damned close to my face, man!"

"Tough shit. What's the matter? You prejudiced?"

"Your fucking-A-right, I'm prejudiced!"

"Well, that's tough shit, too, buddy, 'cause you are going to be swamped by the stink of police for a very long time, punk."

"What's with you, Mason? What is this shit?"

"This is a bust, Terry T. Logan."

"What?" The black eyes, the black face, were disbelieving.

Terry's partners started into streams of obscenities at this, but stopped and swung around as Jones came through the door, nightstick in hand.

Mason laughed. He gripped the leather blackjack protruding from his back pocket. He reached and grabbed Terry T.'s right wrist where it vanished into the man's jacket pocket.

"The cavalry's here, punk!"

"You motherfucker!" Logan exploded, bringing his knee up and trying to swing with his left hand. But Mason had the stick out now and brought it down hard on the struggling man's shoulder. He dragged Terry's right arm around and twisted it up behind his back. Logan lost his footing and fell forward, thrashing, face down on the counter, but still managed to keep up a gasping flow of curses. Fat Mac was flattened against the far wall.

During the short scuffle, Jones stood spread-legged and glared down the two friends. They stood still, but cursed with Terry T. Their voices, though, were as beaten as the limp wrists Mason was clicking handcuffs onto.

"One little move," Jones said to his charges, "and I bust heads."

They stood quietly, full of hate, but not moving.

Vernon Walker buried his face in the spreading hair and breathed in the smell of the woman who rocked beneath him. He raised himself to look, breathing hard, at the black length of his body against her whiteness, her white hips, rising and falling white breasts. He saw his blackness penetrating her, prying her open, spearing her, and felt himself wrapped in power. He felt the power guiding her as it guided Willy, Spider, Little Bit, and all the others. He lunged and laughed at once.

Eileen's eyes rolled up. She murmured something. Her nails raked his sides. A spasm arched her slim back off the bed. His name came, strangled and distorted. He covered her mouth with his hand, but the words kept coming. "Vernon! Vernon! Vernon!"

He lifted his head higher. He saw Chuck's face and Joe Mason. He saw his father's seamed visage and milky hopeless stare. He saw his mother sitting in the kitchen after an eight-hour day in the suburbs, cleaning house for whites, her chin held in a wrinkled hand, her children on either side of her, and the bleak city just outside the window. And Vernon felt not the woman's movement, but the dead legs of the first guy he'd ever killed. Just a punk he'd been. And he'd wasted a dude for jumping his kid brother, William. The dude's name was Melvin Jackson and he was cold meat in an alley, where little Vernon Walker stalked him and charged at him from behind with an ice pick in one hand, and a brick in the other. Stabbing and bashing, and the dying Melvin Jackson twitching out his life while Vernon dragged him behind a pile of old garbage cans. Two years later, William had been shot down in front of a movie theater, trying to shield his girlfriend from the bullets of four Proud Pistol boys, the gang who helped chase Vernon into the marines.

"Vernon! Vernon! Vernon!"

He tasted not Eileen's lips, but blood from his bitten tongue when he'd leaned over the dying Lee Tillman. He tasted the prunes and grits served at the city jail. He remembered the solid grip of his hands around the fat guard's throat, the bald head banging into the cell's steel bars, the sting of Mace in his eyes, and the thud of nightsticks against his head and arms.

"Vernon! Oh, Vernon! Oh, Vernon!"

"Say my name like that, baby. Yeah! Say my name!"

Mason reached into Terry T.'s jacket pocket and brought out a straight razor. A length of tape had been wrapped around the slot so the blade couldn't fall back into its groove.

"This is a dangerous weapon," Mason said. "Where'd you get this dangerous weapon, man?" His breath came in short bursts and his voice was heavy with sarcasm. He held the blade in front of Terry's wide eyes and open mouth.

"I go to barber college, Mason, you motherfucker!"

Joe twisted the cuffs tighter. They clicked three times and Terry screamed curses.

"Barber college, huh? That's funny, man. That's very good."

"What you bustin' me for?" The muscles in Terry's jaws flexed with strain and anger. "Man, what you busting me for? What'd we do, you pig?"

"Pig bastard!" One of Terry's partners spit. He was short, but built solidly, with a scruffy goatee. "He's nothin but a pig. Likes to get down on niggers, the fuckin', lousy, PIG motha—"

"You shut your mouth," Mason said to the jerking goatee. "You shut up or I'll shoot you in the kneecap. I'll make you a cripple who has to sell pencils!"

Goatee's mouth clamped tight, but his eyes continued the speech. Mason motioned to Allen Jones and the rookie moved a few steps closer.

"Up against that window," Mason told goatee. "Both of you! Spread it out! Get the legs out, fellas ... that's it! Lovely! Very good!"

The door to the Chicken Palace opened again as Mason and Jones dragged Logan over and placed him with his partners. A small chocolate face looked in, saw what was happening, and vanished back into the cold. Mason laughed again and Jones looked at him.

"That kid," Mason explained. "The one who peeped in. Didn't you see that kid, Al? Didn't you see his face?"

"You're nuts," Jones said matter-of-factly and searched all three men while Mason covered him. Fat Mac stood trembling and smiling behind his counter, and Mason kept turning to wink at him. The three girls leaned through the slot, their elbows on the wooden shelf, like watching a TV show. The radio announced the days's astrological forecast.

Jones handed Mason another razor, a small German-made .22 caliber pistol, and a length of bicycle chain.

"Another barber college student," Mason said, and slipped the second razor into his pocket. He unloaded the small revolver. "A Saturday-night special." He looped the bicycle chain into a ball and handed it back to Jones. "And a Hell's Angel shoelace. All of you dudes are busted. Read them their rights, Al."

Joe leaned against the counter, facing the suspects as

his partner pulled a white card from his wallet and began reading the Miranda Rulings of the United States Supreme Court. Real cool, Mason thought, not listening to Jones's words. I was real cool. He felt Mac close at his back. He heard the three cooks moving away from the shelf toward the rows of powdered chicken and pans of boiling grease.

"These the ones, Mac?"

"The one you hit. The other two I just seen around."

"They weren't with him when he tried to shake you down?"

"No, man. It was just him and another dude." The fat man's voice was unsteady. "Joe, why you figure they come in here with your police car parked right outside?"

"Didn't think you'd drop a dime on them." Mason hefted the .22 revolver. "They got more balls than they got brains."

"You got on that one dude pretty rough."

"Didn't have much to bust them on. But now we got a CCW charge on all of them. Carrying Concealed Weapons." He laughed. He knew he was too worked up and that this was what brought the laughter out. He tried to stop it, but couldn't.

"Maybe I should've kept my mouth shut," Mac said. "These dudes get out, they're gonna come here and see me first thing."

"You were a heavyweight contender," Mason said, flipping the revolver's cylinder in and out—click-snap, click-snap. "Don't you remember?"

"Yeah," Mac said mournfully, "I remember."

"Hey, T.!" Mason shouted. "Look at me, punk!"

Logan's eyes lifted to meet Mason's.

"Why'd you jump in my face, pig?"

"You listen to me, man. Anything happen to this Chicken Palace, I'll hunt you down and waste you. You understand, bad man? This here Chicken Palace is our favorite place to eat, you understand? We don't want nothing happening to it. Okay? Else I'm going to find you, Terrible Terry, and cut off your career for good."

Silence. Logan's eyes stared at the floor. His chest heaved and the veins in his neck stood out.

"You hear me, T.?"

"I hear you."

Mason turned and grinned at the owner's wide eyes.

"How's that, Mac?"

"Joe, I'm glad you are on this beat, man. I am glad you're here. But I don't think you've got a long and happy life ahead of you. No, sir."

"Doesn't bother me." Joe was still trying to wipe the grin from his face. He tapped the counter's cracked formica with the .22's barrel. He thought of what Terry's razor or the pistol could have done to him. "Did you hear what that punk said about barber college, Mac? That tore me up. That was really funny."

Jones finished reading the Miranda and looked at his partner. His young eyes were worried.

"You okay?"

"I'm fine," Mason said.

"You sure?"

"Sure, I'm sure. It was just funny, is all."

Jones sighed.

"What do we do now, Joe?"

"Give the station a call. Get a wagon down here."

"Why not take 'em back in our car?"

"No." Mason stuck the empty pistol into his belt, feeling it press against his belly. "I want the paddy wagon. I want everyone on this block to see these badass militants loaded into a wagon like meat. I want them to see these shakedown artists looking bad."

"I want you to leave go of Chuck," Walker said to Eileen. "I want you to let him loose."

"Do you really feel that way?" She stood close to him, wrapped in a dark-blue robe with yellow Japanese characters. Her hair was pulled back. Her face looked clean and scrubbed. She was healthy and fresh, miles away from what she had been an hour before on the bed tossing beneath her favorite Huey Newton poster.

"I really feel that way, little All-American Coke Girl."

Eileen's green eyes grew suddenly fearful.

"Is something the matter, Vernon?"

"Yes," he answered and snorted bitter laughter. The laugh frightened her even more. She stepped back. Her soft white hands clutched together in front of her breasts. He saw her body move under the robe. "You are what's wrong, baby. You're white, and that makes you wrong, and you're a phony white liberal and that makes you double wrong. You're wrong for me, wrong for Chuck, wrong for any black man."

"It's not my fault if I'm not bla—" She fell back and her head thumped into the wall from the force of his slap. He stepped close to her and ripped open the front of her robe. Her breasts swayed with the violent motion of his hands on her body.

"You think it's cute to hop in the sack with a black man," he said through grated teeth. "You eat your birth-control pills and spread your legs, and scream how unprejudiced you are! But you wouldn't if you thought you were going to have a nigger kid, would you? You're just a phony white bitch. You and your fucking posters."

"Vernon! You're—don't, Vernon! You're hurt—"

"I come here ready to accept you if you were real. If you really gave a damn about Chuck, I wouldn't have taken anything more than a beer and then split. But you—you're not real." He gripped her wrists. His face was only inches from hers and the scent of her fear washed over him. "I don't want you to tell Chuck nothing. You hear? I just want you away from him. I don't want you messing with my people."

She nodded, and tried to wipe the tears streaking her face, but his hands still held her wrists.

"Vernon—"

"Shut up! Listen. You put your white ass somewhere else," he said, speaking slowly, and so low-pitched that she raised her face to see his mouth. "I am telling you to leave, and never come back here, or I'll have you wasted. You go look for black men some-

110

where else, somewhere I don't reach, where I can't see you castrating them."

"For God's sake, Vernon—"

"God?" he asked, and laughed again.

"But you're not serious. Where will I go? What'll I say to Chuck?"

"You say nothing, slut. After I walk out of your little museum to Black Power, you pack and get the fuck out. Go home to Mommy and Daddy in Ladue, or Webster Groves, or wherever you learned to bullshit. But you get gone!"

He released her arms and she slumped down against the wall. He turned and opened the door. Eileen lay just inside, weeping, as his heavy footsteps sounded to the first floor and out into the cold.

It was turning darker. The sky was cloudy and the streetlights gleamed bright and white in the winter gloom.

Vernon stood for a moment, then hurried down the sidewalk. What would you really have done, he asked himself, if she'd been what Chuck wished her to be? Would you have drunk your beer and left?

It doesn't matter.

I knew what she was before she opened the door. I know what's best for my men.

Chapter Nine

ALL THE lights were on in the main room of Walker's headquarters when he returned. The harsh fluorescent bulbs flickered in their black-plastic brackets and Walker sensed at once that something was wrong. The smoky atmosphere was charged with fear, urgency, and rumbling anger. He could smell it as he shut the street door behind him and watched their heads turn.

"Vernon! Man, where you been?"

"It's the chief!"

"Hey, President Walker, man, listen."

Most of his men were gathered in the room, and, surveying their bright eyes, Walker knew he hadn't been mistaken. He pulled off his beret and turned to Spider's hunched figure.

"What's happened?"

"Terry T., Dirk Everson, and Bobby Clemens were busted. The T. wasn't out three days and that fucking Mason busted him again. Mason and his nigger partner."

Chuck Williams pushed through the circle of men. He faced Walker with his narrow shoulders thrown back. Chuck was sweating, and Walker felt shame clutch his throat.

"What were they arrested for, PM?"

"They were all carrying a weapon, Vernon. They went back to the Chicken Palace. Mason was there. Fat Mac must have let him know that Terry'd tried to shake him down the day before."

Walker nodded grimly.

"They disobeyed orders. We were going to give it a

week. The fools got what was coming to them." He pushed past Chuck and Big Chino and stamped to the center of the room. He set clenched fists on his hips and felt his stomach churn with rage.

Little Bit said, "Chief, we all did like you said, but Terry was blowing about how he had to keep on Fat Mac or he'd get his balls together and tell the cops."

"He talked Dirk and Bobby to slide over with him," said Chuck, coming over to stand next to Stanton.

"And what the fuck were you doing, PM, when those assholes decided to slide over there?" Walker stared at his second in command. "Didn't you try and stop them?"

"Only a gun could've stopped Terry, Vernon. You know that, man. You want me to use a gun on a member?" Chuck's eyes glittered wetly, his face tense and skull-like with worry. "On a member?"

"We are not the fucking Fraternal Order of Elks, goddammit! Yes! Kill the bastards if you had to!" He felt himself yelling, but Vernon couldn't stop the anger. "If you have to, man, then I want you to use a gun or a club or whatever you have to use to maintain some motherfuckin' discipline!" He swept an angry hand at the others. "You've all been laughing about how dumb the cops are—how dumb guys like Mason are! Well they aren't so goddamned dumb, are they? They've been on top for a long time! Joe Mason's head is like a roster of wanted dudes. He keeps that stuff in his brain and he knows everyone in this room. He sees you on the street and he'll remember an old wanted on you or he'll throw a bum rap on your back. He wants us off these streets! He wants us out of his damned district and he will do anything to get that thing done!"

"Let's stop the Pig Mason then!" Spider glared at Walker's strained face. "Let's stop the pig with a gun! If he comes around me, I'll kill him. Simple as that, man! 'Cause they ain't locking me up again—not without going to hands, guns, knives—*every motherfuckin' thing!*"

Walker shoved his way through the men in front of

Washington. "You ain't going to spit unless I give you the order!" He stepped close to Spider's quivering chest. "You can go back to being a pledge if you want, motorcycle man. Now shut your mouth. I don't want to hear about what you are going to do. You try and kill Mason he'd shoot both your black eyes out before you could aim in! You wouldn't make a pimple on Mason's white ass!"

The others in the room were clearly on Walker's side and, staring from one face to the other, Spider's expression twisted into a mask of wild hatred. He whirled around and started for the door, but Walker's voice stopped him.

"Motorcycle man!"

Spider threw a look over his shoulder and hesitated.

"What?"

"You leaving us, motorcycle man?"

"I don't see anybody here to stop me!"

Walker started for him and Spider threw himself up and waited. He sucked in air. He stared at the others, but they all looked through him. And Walker came closer, moving slow and easy, his hands loose at his side, his square face beaded with sweat. Spider shouted at him: "Stay away from me! You, man—you with your big stuff! Man, just stay back from me!"

Walker watched Spider's hands dance indecisively in front of his sleeveless denim jacket, and then jumped the last few feet to the other man in a single leap. His hands shoved against Spider's broad chest. The new man staggered back and fell down hard. His head smacked the floor and Walker kneeled on his chest and jerked out a .38 revolver from the man's waistband. With the gun in his hand, Walker stood up and stepped back a pace.

"Down dude," he said. "Stay down on that floor."

Spider sat up, shaking his head. Fear and uncertainty moved the muscles of his face. Chino, Williams, Little Bit, and the others behind Walker had not said a word. The silence was an affirmation of anything Walker had in mind and Spider realized this. His eyes darted back and forth, pleading one minute and raging the next, and at last staring, wondering what to expect.

Vernon motioned to Chuck. "Check him."

Williams jumped to Spider's side and pushed him into the cigarette butts and dust, grinning at the other man's discomfort and fear, anxious to make up for his blunder with Terry T. He found a long clasp knife in Spider's rear pocket.

"That it?" Walker asked. Chuck nodded. The PM stood up alongside his president. Spider stayed on his back, jaw muscles bunching. He stared at the ceiling, beyond anything now but fear and shame.

Walker looked down at the prone man, fully aware of the watching group. He stood, pointing the .38 at the ugly black face, and began to speak. Spider answered with barely any movement to his clenched jaw. His voice was hollow, devoid of its usual bravado.

"All the time the big man," he said. "Pushing."

"You want out of the Party?" Vernon asked.

"Yeah. Fuckin' militants. Shit."

"You want to leave us, man?"

"Yeah."

"You want to take our guns with you, too, do you?"

"The .38's my heat."

"Nothing is yours anymore. You won't submit to discipline. You won't follow orders. My orders, or the PM's. You just can't get yourself into working on teamwork and organization, can you, Spider?"

"This ain't the marines. Nobody is tellin' this man to do anything anymore."

"Don't worry. Nobody's going to try." Walker clicked back the hammer on the pistol. The sound was like a cannon in the quiet room. "Roll on your face, traitor."

Spider stared up at Walker with wide-eyed disbelief. The rage drained from his face and his throat worked hard.

"What you mean, 'turn on my face'? What you talking, Vernon?"

"Turn." Walker's voice was barely controlled. His arm and hand quivered. The pistol danced like a steel cobra in front of Spider's staring eyes. "Turn over, or I waste you watching it come. You want to see it coming, Spider?"

Little Bit breathed out a sharp curse, and Walleye suddenly giggled with nervous hysteria choking his laughter. Chino rumbled at them to shut up and the room plunged back to silence. They were still with Walker, and Washington felt the full force of their collective resolve. He knew that if Walker killed him they would all be willing to share in the execution. They were all eager to exhibit to Walker that his word was their only law. Like a freezing cold hand reaching into his chest, Spider saw that he'd gone too far. That it was now too late. He mumbled something and Walker squatted next to him. The pistol was pointed, cocked, and ready. Spider stared at the gun's muzzle with stark terror.

"What you saying?" Walker asked. "Are you praying, Spiderman? Do you want to pray before I waste you for good and ever?"

"Vernon. God, listen. Don't, Vernon. I'm sick, man. Don't be killing me, man. I must be sick to say the things I say. Don't. For God's sake, Vernon. Please!"

"Too little—too late, dude," Walker said. "You have been judged and found guilty and this gun's going to—"

Spider screamed.

His voice bounced up and echoed in the room and made all of them, including Vernon, start with its harsh, animal fear. Walker stood back, disgusted and wishing it hadn't been necessary to bring it to this point, but knowing the impression it would leave on the new man's soul. And the others, too, he thought. It'll show them the kind of things we have to do to win.

Spider's shout had fallen back to a throat-tearing cough, as if he wanted to bring his entire stomach out of his gaping mouth. A stain spread on the dusty linoleum beneath his spread legs, and Walker told himself, It's enough. End it. And he bent down again and grabbed Washington roughly by the front of his denims.

"Look at me!" Still aiming the pistol, pressing it under Spider's madly bouncing beard. "Look at me, motorcycle man!"

Washington's clenched eyes opened and blinked tears. The sweat poured down his face. Walker laid the pistol down on the heaving chest, smelling fear roll off the man like a wave. He let the pistol's hammer down carefully, and released the gun so it rested, untouched, on Spider's chest. Then Walker stood up. His knees hurt and his eyes were blurred with his own sweat. He wiped them clear and waved Chuck back as the PM started forward.

"Get up, bad man," he said. "You get up and bring that heat up with you."

Spider lay still for a moment, then fumbled with the pistol and staggered to his feet. He held the gun loosely, at his side, and kept his face averted from the stares of the other men in the room.

"Watch it, Chief," Chino said, his deep voice a whisper of warning, but Walker shook his head.

"No. Spider's got to see the way it is." He directed his voice at the slumped figure, feeling the same intoxicating sense of power in him as when he'd forced Eileen to betray Chuck, forced her to acknowledge his strength and power.

"This is a family, bad man," he said. "You wanted to leave, maybe kill us all. But I'm giving you a chance to come back or just to kill me." The power was in him now, all the way, and Walker could taste it and smell it. "Com' on, bad man. You got your chance. Com' on and stick that heat in me. Com' on. Waste the only dude in the fuckin' world who can make you what you want to be!"

Vernon moved closer to Spider, approaching like a matador closing in on a winded bull. He reached out and placed his hand on Spider's shoulder. He lifted the man's right hand, the hand gripping the pistol, and pressed the .38 into his own stomach. He felt the cold nose of the revolver through his sweater. "SHOOT!"

His face was only inches from Washington's face. "Shoot, you bad-ass loner! You want out of this family, then do it! Pull that motherfuckin' trigger!"

Spider lifted his head and stared at Walker. Anger still hovered in his face, but the black eyes filled with tears. The thud of the pistol dropped on the floor reached Walker's ears, but he was staring at the new man and laughing. Head back and laughing. Roaring. And the sound of it startled the others, as Spider's wailing scream had startled them before. But now Walker had his arm around Spider and hugged him hard.

I felt all of it, he thought, and knew himself deeper than at any other time in his life. He felt Spider's hand pound him on the back.

"Pissed in my pants, Chief!" he roared, and they were both laughing, and Walker knew that the spirit was still there, but controlled now, and directed only by himself.

"The family!" Walker shouted, and grabbed Washington around the neck. He felt the slick sweat drying on the black skin and knew he had a weapon more dangerous than a hundred rifles in Spider's new loyalty. He remembered reading *Call of the Wild* when he was a young boy. A scene from from that book had stuck with him for a long time, and now Walker remembered it clearly once again. A man is in a pen with a wild dog; the dog attacks the man, but the man has a club behind his back and hits the dog on the head. The dog backs off, surprised and hurt, then attacks again. The man beats him down again. This goes on until the dog is crazy with anger. He charges one last time and the man clubs him into unconsciousness. When the dog awakes he sees the man standing over him, ready to either begin it all over again, or accept the dog's obedience. The dog licks his hand.

"The family!" Spider yelled, and the men pushed up close to them, laughing now, loud and full of relief. They pushed forward and touched both men, Spider and Walker, as if the two had just returned from a walk into hades, returned to tell about brimstone and fire.

Outside the sandbagged window a siren wailed its way through the traffic on Delmar Boulevard.

Mason questioned Bobby Clemens first, while Everson and Terry T. Logan waited downstairs in the holdover cells. Clemens was eighteen and this was his first arrest as an adult. He was nervous and kept picking at his chin where a sparse goatee grew. The thin beard was black against Clemens's light-brown skin. His moist eyes avoided Mason's stare as the two of them sat facing each other over two school desks in the platoon assembly room. Allen Jones sat a few rows behind them, alternately listening and writing his report of the arrest.

"Look at me, Bobby," Mason said, his voice very soft and the words purring from his throat with an unnatural silkiness. But Clemens kept staring over Mason's shoulder at the ceiling, at the floor, until Joe's hand shot out and touched the boy's face. Just a touch.

"Look at me, fool! Aren't you a man?"

"I'm a man . . . po-lice. You the pig." And for a second Clemens stared directly at him and Mason felt a quiver run through his chest at the young man's naked hate. But then Clemens looked away.

"You had your rights read to you," Mason said.

"I heard 'em."

"You know what you're under arrest for?"

"The pistol."

"That's right. The pistol. What were you doing with that piece, Bobby? Were you going to kill someone with that itty-bitty piece?"

"I'll get another one and kill you, Mason."

"Will you?" Mason mused. "You know, Bobby, that would be something, if you did that—'cause I've never known a nigger yet who could shoot his way out of a wet paper bag."

Mason leaned back and saw the steel tension begin to straighten Clemens's slump. He heard Jones's hiss of anger behind him and prayed that Allen wouldn't blow his stack and ruin what he was attempting. He leaned forward and rested his elbows on his knees. "No burrhead mother's going to kill me, Bobby. *I* might kill you, but you won't be killing any Joe Masons in your lifetime. I can tell you that true, lad. Not if all you can get your black hands on is some punk-ass .22 cap pistol!" Mason lifted his thick eyebrows and then laughed loudly at the rage in Clemens's eyes, at the skinny body bending toward him, at the quivering voice.

"I will waste you personally, Mason. Pig Mason!"

"Oink," Joe said slowly, pronouncing the noise carefully and distinctly, and grinning at Clemens. "Oink. Oink. You're going to miss, if all you pop at me with is a lousy .22. You better get about six inches from my head, lad, or you're going to miss."

"I'll kill you!" Clemens said through gritted teeth and trembling lips.

"Wuff tickets," Mason said distainfully, and hoped again that his partner would keep his cool at his next words. "Just selling wuff tickets on yourself, Bobby. As long as we got the real weapons, and you niggers keep pulling punk-ass .22's, then I'm not worried about any of you killing me!"

Clemens's snarl turned to a secret grin of triumphantly held knowledge and Mason knew he was beginning to get to the boy's guts, knew that his insults were slamming Clemens's young pride. "What's funny, Bobby?"

"You, pig. You're funny." Clemens's handcuffed hands reached up and his fingers smoothed down the thin goatee. "I'm wondering if you ever seen the track of a BAR. You ever see something like that, Pig?"

"A Browning Automatic Rifle? Yeah. I've seen it working before."

"You are going to *feel* it the next time!"

"More wuff tickets. I'm not impressed."

"You will be, Pig Mason!" Clemens hunched over in the school desk and moved his linked hands with each word that jumped from his mouth. He was trying to make Mason see it, but without saying too much, and it was hard.

"It—it's coming, Pig."

"What's coming?"

"You'll be feeling it *real soon*."

Mason shook his head. He lit a cigarette and blew smoke in the prisoner's eyes. He grinned and used the word again, the hated word, to cut away more of Clemens's control. "You niggers are all the time talking about revolution, but you don't have the guns or the balls for letting it all go down. You nig—"

"Knock it off, Joe!" Jones said loudly, and Mason closed his eyes. Allen didn't understand. He's going to blow it. Mason cursed himself for not briefing the rookie before the interrogation began. He was about to turn around and ask his partner to leave the room, when Clemens aimed his rage at the black officer.

"You think that word bothers me, you oreo? You black-on-the-outside, white-on-the-inside, Uncle Tom mother? It don't! It runs off me! It only bothers you, Tom, 'cause you are a nigger!" Clemens was half out of his desk and Mason stared at him with lazy, disinterested eyes.

"Sit, Bobby. Sit the fuck down."

"He better sit down," Jones said, "or I'll bust his stinking head!" The rookie had his nightstick up and was standing away from the desk he'd been writing on. Mason nearly laughed aloud at the sudden reversal in roles.

"Both of you, sit down!" he shouted, then swiveled to face Allen. "Hey, man. Go on out and finish up the property cards on those weapons we seized."

"You all right, here?" Jones looked somewhat abashed, but still angry. The nightstick was ready to strike. He nodded at Clemens. "This—"

"I'm okay, Al."

"You sure?"

"Positive, man."

Jones gathered up his clipboard and pens and papers

121

and stomped from the assembly room, slamming the door behind him. Mason stared at Bobby Clemens.

"You seem pretty uptight, Bobby. You shooting up?"

"I don't shoot nothing," Clemens said, and stared at Mason's calm face. "Nothing but pigs!"

"That pig stuff don't bother me, Bobby. Just like I know the nigger stuff don't bother you, right? Like you told my partner, isn't that right?"

Clemens stiffened and Mason could amost feel him will his lanky body to relax. "Right. It don't bother me."

"Runs off your back, huh?"

"Sure. Like I told the Tom."

"Good. Then we both know where we stand, don't we?"

"I know."

"And I know, too, Bobby."

"Yeah...."

Mason drew in on his cigarette and offered the pack to Clemens. The young black man shook his head and turned to stare at the blackboard with its chalked burglary statistics, and the long bulletin board filled with wanted posters.

(The VC prisoner was short and heavily muscled. His face was very flat, and his eyes were determined. He stared up at Mason and Walker and the rest of Mason's squad with no fear in his dark eyes. The prisoner's lack of fear was probably what started it at first, but then it was like trying to kill a large rabbit with a BB gun. You became frantic after a while, trying to end it with something that just wasn't deadly enough, and what starts as torture ends in butchery. And it was all terribly pointless and stupid and the prisoner finally began screaming wildly and Walker had stuffed a handful of leaves in the man's mouth. There was no meaning to any of it, except that they discovered the murderer in each other that day and had no illusions about their own natures from that moment on.)

Mason smoked his cigarette and wished for a clean way to do what he had to do, but he knew that wishing was ridiculous. He ground the cigarette out with his boot and looked up at Clemens's roaming eyes.

"Vernon's got himself some BARs now, right, Bobby? He's got some BARs and maybe some carbines, and some other things, right?"

"Go to hell."

"You already told me about the BARs. If he's got Browning Automatics, then he's got more. He's making an army out of you dudes, ain't he?"

"When you find that one out, Mason, you'll have dirt in your mouth!"

Joe stood up wearily and lifted a set of jangling keys.

"Come on," he said, and Clemens stared up at him, then shrugged and lifted himself to his feet. He walked ahead of Mason with casual indifference, out of the assembly room, past an ancient coke machine and coffee dispenser, and down a short flight of stairs to a long, dimly lit passageway. At the end of the narrow hall was another door that opened into the damp room which housed the four holdover cells. The cells were used to keep prisoners until warrants were issued and they could be transferred to the main city jail.

Terry T. and Dirk Everson stood at the bars and glared at Mason as he pushed Clemens up to the door of their cell and inserted the big key. He knew he was taking a chance with all three men momentarily able to jump him and perhaps get his gun, but Mason decided it was a small risk. He knew that the three black men, and especially Terry T., believed that he craved an excuse to kill them and they would be wary of a trap.

"Back from the door, girls," he said, and Everson and Logan stepped away from the bars and stood against the far steel wall. They stood rigidly next to the commode and washbasin.

Mason opened the door, sliding it back on its track, and motioned Clemens inside. The young man hesitated.

"Go on, Bobby."

Clemens stalked past him and into the cell. Mason pointed at Dirk Everson, the door still wide open and his hand on his pistol butt. "You next. I want to hear what you got to say, Everson. I hope it's as helpful as Clemens's story." And closed the door behind Dirk's back. "This way," he said, and started away from the cell, but suddenly turned back and smiled at Bobby Clemens.

"Thanks, Bobby. We can make a deal now, I think."

"You shit!" Clemens screamed, rushing up and gripping the bars, shouting at Dirk Everson's blank face. "Don't listen to him, Brother Dirk! I didn't tell the pig nothing! Don't listen to this pig motherfucker!"

Mason looked sorrowful. He held his left hand to his forehead.

"Damn, Bobby. Man, I am sorry!" He shook his head. "Wasn't supposed to open my big stupid mouth, was I? Shit, I'm really sorry, lad."

"I didn't tell him nothing, Dirk! Terry, man! I didn't tell this pig-ass motherfucker nothing!"

Mason kept shaking his head sadly. He moved Everson ahead of him, and allowed his voice to float back to where Terry T. and Clemens heard him clearly.

"Don't take it out on Bobby, Dirk. He's just a kid and it wasn't his fault he let it slip about Walker's BARs, and those carbines you dudes got. He's just a kid. Damn, it sure makes me feel like shit. Me opening my big, stupid, honky mouth like that. You guys won't take it out on Bobby, will you?"

He heard Clemens screaming curses at him all the way into the outer hallway, but Mason was staring at the back of Everson's head and wondering where he was going to take it from here. Maybe he should punch Everson a few times, mark him up, then send him back. What would Terry T. think then? Clemens comes back without a scratch and Dirk comes back with a fucked-up face. What would ol' Terry think if—?

Mason could still hear Clemens cursing him as he slammed the door to the hall.

Chapter Ten

WALKER TOOK Chuck Williams aside, out of the press of members, away from the shrill talk and shouted arguments, hell frozen over and Spider changing his jeans.

Walker led Chuck to the office-bedroom and told him to sit down. The PM nodded and sat tensely on the edge of the cot. It was too much like that morning, when they'd argued. It was like setting the scene all over again. Goddamned too bad, Walker thought, and rubbed hard at his aching head and tight neck. His body ached, too, as if he'd been in a terrible fight, and his head felt thick.

Chuck waited for his president to speak first, knowing Vernon well enough to realize that something bad was bothering him, something probably connected with what they'd argued about, something about Eileen or Terry T.'s arrest or Spider's moment of rebellion.

Vernon lit a Kool and handed the pack to Chuck, who lit up with him. They stared at each other and Walker asked himself, What would I do without Chuck? He offered a slight grin and Williams grinned back. But Eileen's white face slipped in past Walker's defenses and the smile was gone. Had he made a mistake doing what he'd done? No, he didn't think so. It was something he knew he had to gamble on, throw craps with the whole thing, with Chuck and himself. And wasn't that all of what this was about, anyway? Just a big game of craps, all the time, everyday. A hope that anything would be an improvement on the way a black man had to live.

He knew how Lee Tillman would answer that one. Work through their system, Vernon, and beat them politically and economically. Show them how good a black lawyer is, or a black doctor, or—all crap! They had killed Tillman for believing in that and they'd killed the others, too. Even Bobby Kennedy, who was the only white man Vernon would ever have voted for.

He sat up straight on a folding chair and faced the PM of his Party. Chuck returned the look with nervous expectancy.

"How long we known each other, Chuck?"

"Shit. Don't know for sure, Chief. Long time, though. Since we were kids in the projects. I don't know—a long time."

Walker found his smile once more.

"Through a lot, right?"

"Everything but Nam."

"But blood, man—we've been through some blood."

"I've never bullshitted you. Never have."

"That's true. You and me, Vernon, we blow up—like this morning. You know, we holler, we beef . . . that's the way we always been, but we're tight."

"The thing is," Walker said, "you're my right arm here. You're the PM. My main man. I'm depending on you in this more than you think."

"I'm with you all the way, Vernon. When the stuff goes down I'll be there. Last night, when I wasn't here, was something that—"

Walker held up his hand.

"Listen, Chuck. If it goes down too hard you might have to be the one to pick up the pieces. Like I had to pick up after Lee was wasted."

"Don't worry about that, Vernon."

"I don't . . . really."

They grinned at each other. They reached and gripped arms. Walker felt that he'd been right in everything. He knew Chuck's loyalty, felt it gripping his wrists and hands, now—this minute. He settled back in the chair. He was more relaxed now than at any time since he'd returned to the headquarters. The arrest of Terry T., Everson, and Clemens seemed a minor blow.

"Have you thought about what I said this morning, PM?"

Chuck's face changed immediately. His eyes became guarded and his mouth thinned with suppressed feeling. Vernon felt his own mood alter as abruptly. He sensed danger.

"Vernon, man," Chuck began, searching for the right words, "I told you straight how I felt about that. Maybe you're right about Eileen, but I got to make up my own mind on it at my own speed. You start pressing me ... and I don't know. You understand how I am about being told to do something." He made an attempt at laughter, but swallowed the sound before it had a chance to break out of him. "You put a sign up on your lawn to keep off the grass and there I'll be—on your lawn. You know I'm like that."

Chuck, Vernon thought, you look like a kid. You sound like a kid. You're all lit up on that phony, All-American Coke girl. I got to her just in time, brother. It's why you let Terry T. and the others go out after Fat Mac today without trying to stop them. You are screwed up by this chick and you don't even like to think about *how* screwed up you are.

"Bullshit," Walker said out loud, but Chuck didn't hear him. He went on speaking.

"Think I'm strung out on her, Vernon. I don't know. Think maybe I love her, shit. But 'love,' man? Do I know what that's all about? Yet, man, I've never felt this way about no other woman."

"Motherfucker."

"Com' on, Vernon. She's more than what you think, man. She's really into the movement. She's been on marches and all. She was up at Ressurection City in Washington and...."

Vernon felt an anger seep into him that he'd only experienced once before—when Joe Mason refused to see what the Party was truly about, the truth of his, Walker's, position, and why the Party was so important to that truth.

Now, Chuck was being as blindly stupid. He was ignoring reality, holding to fantasy. Vernon knew that

Eileen would've killed his friend as surely as any bullet, but without the clean death a bullet can give a man. He knew he'd been right in what had happened with her, but there was no easy way to explain that to Chuck. The fact had to slap the PM in the teeth. Otherwise it would only be ignored again, or, worse, misunderstood.

"Wait a minute, PM."

Chuck stopped talking. His eyes met Walker's.

"Yeah, Chief?"

"Eileen has a small mole, like a lopsided star, between her belly button and pussy." Walker spoke the words carefully, and with calm deliberation, but Chuck jerked his back straight and his dark eyes widened.

"What did you say, man?"

"You heard it, PM, and you know what it means. She screams like a cat when she comes, and uses her nails the same way, like a cat. There's a poster of Huey Newton in the bedroom and the bed's an old brass four-poster." Walker felt his own icy purpose hold him stiffly straight. "I was there, Chuck. I was in that bed, and you're right about Eileen being into the movement. She's into it, all right, about as far as you can go."

"I don't believe you," Williams said, and his voice was hoarse with emotion. "You're jiving me. You wouldn't have done...."

"That's where you're wrong," Walker answered. "I would. And I did. For this Party—and for you to see how important we are to you and what a zero chick she is—I sure as hell did."

Williams lurched off the cot. He was clenched tight, face, body, fists like rock.

"Let her tell me that, you motherfucker, and I'll—"

"She won't be telling you nothing. She won't even be there when you arrive."

"What you saying?"

"I sent her ass away," Walker said, and lifted his pack of Kools from the desk. He lit a cigarette, but it was smacked out of his hand by Williams's swinging hand. The smoking cigarette hit the wall in a shower of sparks and Vernon stood up to face his PM. The anger was full-blown in both of them and burning the room with its heat as Vernon went on with his verbal attack. "A bigger, blacker, black militant could've had her after me, you fucking fool! That's all she's after. She's a fucking collector, Chuck! She just want balls to hang up on her stinking wall, next to her stinking posters of dead black men who got wasted fighting her kind!"

Williams swung at him then, but Vernon was expecting it and stepped away from the wild punch. He moved with the PM's movement and gripped his wrists. Using the force behind Chuck's swing he threw the man back onto the couch and slammed his knee into the struggling PM's chest. The air whooshed from Williams in a choking gasp and he doubled up in agony. Walker stood back, breathing hard and waiting.

The cot had crashed against the wall when Chuck fell back on it, and the sound vibrated throughout the building. Vernon's door was jerked open almost at once and faces crowded the opening. Spider, Chino, Ace Goins, Little Bit, Walleye, Beans—all of them—all shouting at once. "What's happening, Chief? What's going down, Vernon?"

He waved them back from the doorway.

"Go on back out, it's all right," he mumbled, and reached to push the door shut again. Spider stopped the movement with his boot.

"You sure, Boss?"

"No sweat. Go on." And Walker almost laughed at Washington's look of concern, remembering the scene they'd played less than an hour before. Today, he decided, has been a day for big scenes. And he turned back to his fallen Prime Minister.

Chuck sat up, head down and arms crossed over his stomach, taking deep, staggering breaths. His eyes pierced Walker's. "Don't look at me that way, main man. I did it all for you, not against you."

"I'll kill you, Vernon," Chuck said, "if it's the truth."

"It's true, PM. You know it's true, but you won't

kill me. You'll go home now and think about it and you will see why I did it, and who really loves you, Chuck. That's the important thing, man. Think about who really loves you."

Williams stood up, swaying, his face covered with cold sweat streaks. "You shouldn't have tried to play God with me, Vernon. I probably would've come around to your way of thinking. But you play God with other people's lives, man. You play fucking God."

"I don't hear you, Chuck. You're pissed now. I don't blame you for being pissed. But I don't hear you when you're this kind of mad, brother. Go home. Think some on it. We've been too tight, Brother Williams, for you—"

"Don't call me that," Chuck said, moaning. "Don't you ever call me your brother again. Nobody makes a puppet out of me, man. Nobody makes a fucking toy out of me! You don't do that to me and expect it all to keep going down the same motherfuckin' way as always!"

"Nothing's changed," Walker said, and bent to retrieve Chuck's fallen beret. He slapped it against his leg and handed it to the taller man. Chuck ignored the hat, brushed it aside, and started for the back door.

"Chuck," Vernon said, and the PM hesitated.

"You keep the beret, Vernon." His back turned and his shoulders slumped forward. "You keep everything."

"Nothing's changed, Chuck!" Vernon shouted the words, making them a command, but Chuck shook his head, his back still turned.

"Everything's changed," Chuck said, and sobs strangled his voice. "You shouldn't play God, Vernon. Ah, Vernon. You rotten motherfucker."

The steel door in the hallway slammed a moment later and Walker stared out the back window as Williams stalked down the alley, through a patch of overhead light, and then was swallowed by the dark.

Car 642 was back in service and cruising the dark alleys between tenements and crumbling warehouses. Rusting fire escapes were drawn black and dark against the walls to either side of Joe Mason and Allen Jones as the Plymouth's tires crunched over debris scattered in the alley.

"Someone," Jones murmured, as 642's headlights picked out a lone man walking in the alley. Mason nodded without speaking and they passed the man slowly.

"Hey, Oscar," Mason called through his open window, and lifted his left hand in a lazy wave. Oscar muttered, "Fuck you, cop!" The car moved on.

Joe smiled at the response and shivered, wanting to roll the window up, but knowing that he wouldn't be able to hear what was happening and hearing was as important as seeing. He resigned himself to having his left side frozen and glanced at Allen as he turned 642 left into another alley.

"See that dude?" he asked, and Jones nodded, his face unnaturally grim.

"Oscar Randall," Mason said, his eyes ahead, sweeping left to right and back again. He twisted around when he saw a kid step out of a rear apartment door carrying more trash for the alley to hold onto. "That dude, Oscar, he's a dope fiend. He's wired to the stuff and it's a rich habit. He looked okay tonight and I'm too tired to go through the jazz of checking him out. Still, he's good for boosting cars in the area or burglary or anything else. They call him 'Fella' on the block."

"Okay," Jones said, and Mason jerked the steering wheel over and stopped the car. The night settled around them, and the sounds of the neighborhood murmured and rattled in the darkness. A stereo blared James Brown; truck brakes hissed and squealed a block away; a crash and tinkle of broken glass sounded from the other direction.

In the summer, with the weather hot and the days long, the alleys and streets would be crowded with yelling, stickball-playing, tag-screaming kids. The winter, though, called the Hawk by the people of Joe's beat, spawned only ghosts like Oscar. For addicts, thieves, and hustlers there was no such thing as seasons, only good times and bad times.

"What we stopped for?" Jones asked. "That glass breaking?"

"No, man. I am just getting tired of talking to myself since we left the station."

The radio interrupted Allen's reply.

"FRANK SIX, LINCOLN SIX, AND SIXTY-NINE TO SUPERVISE AT FORD AND REINGOLD, A HOLDUP AT THE LIQUOR STORE. SUBJECTS LAST SEEN GOING WEST ON REINGOLD IN A 62 CHEVROLET. SUBJECTS DESCRIBED AS TWO NEGRO MALES, EIGHTEEN TO TWENTY. NUMBER ONE SUBJECT WEARING A BLUE WINDBREAKER AND DARK TROUSERS. NUMBER TWO NO CLOTHING DESCRIPTION. BOTH SUBJECTS ARMED...."

Over the buzz of answering cars, Mason said; "Too far out of our district to assist."

"Always Negro males, Negro males!" Snapping the volume of the radio down, Jones bit off an angry curse and said, "I'm going to faint when they put out a wanted on a white dude!"

"You get wanteds on white guys further west," Mason said. "Most of your pro burglars are white."

"That's even worse!" Jones exploded. "Makes black thieves look like punks. Can't plan a good job or nothing. Like that dude last week smashed into the jewelry store. Middle of the lunch hour, people all over the street, the beat man half a block away, and bam—right through the window!"

"That was an addict," Mason said, lighting a cigarette and blowing smoke through his open window. Far to the west he could just make out a patch of clear star-dotted blackness in the sky between the tall city courts building and a new high-rise apartment complex. "You can't judge black criminals on what dope fiends do. White criminals are the same way when it comes to junk. There's a lot of good black criminals."

As he spoke, Joe wondered how in the hell there

could be such a thing as a "good" criminal? Was Vernon Walker a criminal? He laughed. The only thing he could compare Vernon and his group to were the Viet Cong, and before he'd left Vietnam he had arrived at the conclusion that there were no stronger patriots in the country than the VC. So, using that analogy, Vernon Walker was a kind of patriot. If Vernon was a patriot then what the fuck was Joe Mason, cop, supposed to be?

"What's funny?" Jones wanted to know, his face looking hurt and angry with the hot-sheet light illuminating his nose and strong chin from below.

"Take it easy, Rookie," Mason said. "I'm not laughing at you. I was thinking about Vernon and his gang, at what that little army of his is going to be called by the history writers."

Jones grunted and settled back on the seat. He let out an exasperated sigh.

"About the crack I made when you were talking to Clemens, Joe—"

"Forget it." Mason flicked his half-smoked butt out the window. It left a trail of orange then vanished behind a brick trash pit. "You didn't know what I was trying to do. I don't blame you for getting pissed. I should've let you in on my ways of getting to an asshole like Clemens. I keep forgetting you're cherry to all of this shit."

"Cherry? Thanks a lot, buddy." But Jones flashed a smile and Mason let the tension wash out of him.

"Listen, Al. You'll work at this job for twenty years and you still won't know all you could about people. It's like being a doctor, man. You have to keep learning new stuff as you go along."

"I can dig that."

"It's a bitch sometimes. I think about quitting at least once a week. For real. I really think about just fucking quitting."

"But you don't."

"No." Mason grinned ruefully and examined his fingernails. "The wore-out line that old-time cops use is still my favorite, I guess. They're always calling the beat, 'the Whore,' and saying that the Whore's got them by the balls. This beat—any beat—and the people ... you know? All the jive you read in books. I can't put it into words. And when I start talking about it I sound like the worse kind of dope fiend, myself. Let me talk about the beat and I'm just the same kind of freak."

"I don't feel that way yet," Jones admitted. "But I'll tell you one thing. This is the only job I've ever had where I'm anxious to get to work each day. I mean, I really dig coming into work. You know? Not being able to predict what's going to happen, every day something different...."

"You're getting there," Mason said, laughing. "And don't worry about what happened with Clemens. We all blow our cool sometimes. Ten years ago we'd have been beating the shit out of Bobby Clemens, but today we screw with his brains. Just a different way of operating."

"I wasn't as mad at what you said as I was at the way it got to me. I thought I'd got way past that shit about 'nigger,' but you never do get past it, do you?"

"No, you don't, man. But you can't let the street bums know it gets to you or they'll eat you for dinner."

Jones was still smiling and Mason decided that the kid had worked it all out the right way. *If he can laugh at it, he'll be all right.*

"The professional police officer," Mason intoned, "lets insults, and all other forms of oral abuse, roll off him like water off a duck's ass!"

"Amen," said Jones, and his grin was open and white in the gloom of the front seat.

The radio hummed out their call sign: "NORA THIRTEEN. NORA THIRTEEN."

Mason picked up the mike. "Nora Thirteen, go."

"NORA THIRTEEN, AT SPARKS AND HOBART PLACE. SEVENTEEN O FOUR HOBART. A REPORTED PURSE SNATCHING. SEE THE VICTIM THAT LOCATION. NO DESCRIPTION OF SUSPECT AT THIS TIME."

"Nora thirteen's clear and en route."

He set the microphone down and pulled the car in gear.

"Off to see the wizard!" he sang, and Jones giggled as they moved down the alley and slid past a young black man and girl, locked passionately together in the walkway of a hulking building. The girl's skirt was hiked up around her hips and as the prowl car's lights struck the couple the girl made no move to pull her dress down. Her lover didn't even bother to look up, but only shuffled his woman further back into the darkness without breaking the embrace.

"Get on her, man!" Mason yelled, and Jones continued coughing out his high-pitched giggles.

"Dude's going to catch cold in this weather," the rookie said.

"A runny nose, for sure."

"A drip, anyway you look at it."

"Clap clap!"

And Car 642 was gulped down by the night, its brake lights gleaming as it slowed once to turn onto Rosebud.

Frank's Fireball Lounge was barely half full. The jukebox blared as usual, but now a slow Nancy Wilson number spun on the turntable. Chuck Williams made his way to the bar. He eased down on the stool slowly, using his arms and hands to lever himself into position, then looked groggily toward the few patrons on either side of him. His mind kept seeing Eileen's empty apartment—no posters, no stuffed animals, her clothes gone from the closet, and only the scent of her remaining on the bed—the bed where Vernon said he'd made it with her. Seeing it all, Chuck knew it was true.

Mona, working behind the bar tonight, recognized Williams. He wasn't a regular at the Fireball, but most of the people in the district knew him as Vernon Walker's chief lieutenant. Mona was surprised to see him and especially surprised that he was so obviously strung out. She'd been thinking of Mason, and his drunken lovemaking the night before, of the confrontation between him and Walker that Mason believed was inevitable. And, now, here was a part of what moved Joe into a pattern that Mona was truly beginning to fear.

"What's happening?" she asked, and centered herself in front of Chuck's bobbing head. The young man looked at her, but his eyes didn't seem to focus. With an obvious effort of will he made his lips move.

"Scotch. . . ."

"Okay," she said, but still did not move. She stared at him. She knew she was looking good. She'd dressed carefully, applied a tiny bit of makeup that only accented her big eyes, and had chosen a one-piece mini-dress that exposed a lot of her fine brown skin. "Anything else you want, Prime Minister Williams?"

His eyes cleared a little. He said: "You that Mona. You the sister. . . ." But his voice trailed off as Nancy Wilson's ballad finished and a rip-thumping Miles Davis instrumental replaced the soft sound in the dark room.

"I know you, too." Mona bent to the side and poured a dash of Scotch in a shot glass and added water. Williams didn't seem up to more liquor and she didn't want him to pass out. She wanted him to talk. And she wanted to know why he was in the Fireball, how he knew who she was, and much more. Her curiosity, coupled with a need to protect Mason, decided Mona on a course of action.

". . . not the Prime Minister of anything," Chuck was saying, and Mona slid the glass in front of him.

"No? What're you now, baby?"

"Nothing."

"You look like something to me."

"Nothing anymore. Back in the gutter."

"What's the matter?" she asked. "You been kicked out of Walker's roost?"

"Flew out myself." He made an ugly face and tossed off the dilluted Scotch. "Walker, that motherfucker."

"Vernon Walker?" Mona's eyes widened at Williams's hatred. "You talking about Vernon Walker?"

"The motherfucker," he repeated. "A motherfucking Jody. A back-stabbing bastard, trimming my woman. Did her and run her out and—fuck it."

Williams gestured with a loose hand, as if trying to clear spider webs, and Mona was glad she'd watered his drink down. He was far gone. She was also very glad that Frank Brown would be out the rest of the night and had put her in charge. Frank would love to get Williams in a talking mood, to pry out something he could use against Mason.

A sticky thought wedged in Mona's brain and it required careful consideration. What will you use this black man for? She asked herself. And just what is Joe Mason to you, anyway? Is he worth sticking your neck that far out for?

"Got to go," Williams mumbled, and Mona found her decision made for her. Her hand snaked out and grabbed at his wrist, holding him in place.

"Maybe you need a woman," she whispered, "to help you forget another woman." Her fingers played against the hard skin of his forearm and Chuck stared back at her. He grinned suddenly. His eyes were only inches from her face; he smelled her soft perfume.

"Maybe," he said.

"I like you." Mona smiled. "It won't be for any money. You're the kind of man I need."

"Goddamn that Mason," Walker said, standing in front of his office-bedroom's single window. "We could use Terry and those other two assholes, now." He watched the alley, morbidly fascinated by it since he'd last seen Chuck hurrying down its littered cobblestones. Behind Walker, seated and nervous at their president's restive anger, Spider Washington and Chino and Little Bit exchanged looks.

"Like you said, Vernon—the dude's just one white cop." Spider lit a cigarette and passed the pack to Chino and Stanton. Smoke rose up over their bent heads. "He's just a dumb cop."

"No, he's smart. He knows what's happening." Vernon tore his gaze from the alley and sat down on the cot. It had been over four hours since Chuck had stormed out of the office and the argument with the PM was beginning to eat away at Walker's confidence. "You get ahold of him, yet, Little Bit?"

"No, Chief. The PM's mother says she ain't seen him in over a week."

"What about that apartment?"

"Freddy checked it out. No one there. Door was open, though, like I told you. No one there."

"Check the bars."

"But, Chief," Chino protested, "the PM isn't into the kind of jive. Take us all the rest of the night to—"

"Get Walleye and four other members. Split them up. Have them do the best they can. Stick to this district."

"I'll go," said Spider, and Vernon shifted his stare to the motorcycle man."

"All right. Try hard and find him. Hit as many places as you can. We've got to get a line on him."

"Is it trouble?" Spider asked. "Is it about what you two were hassling about in here? How important is it, Chief?"

Walker lay back on the bunk. He looked up at the ceiling and thought of how much damage Williams could do with what he knew about the Party. He had been sure, four hours earlier, that Chuck would cool down and return. They'd patch things up. Now, though, he wasn't sure. He wasn't sure at all.

"It's important," he said, and Spider stood up, barrel chest swelling out and square-black face tight with determination.

"I'll find him, Vernon."

"You do that. No rough stuff, though. Just talk him back here."

"And what if he don't want to be talked anywhere?"

"I was ready to blow you away, Spider. Do you believe that? Do you think I would've wasted you?"

Little Bit and Chino stared up at Washington, who nodded.

"The only thing I can't believe is that I pissed in my jeans, Chief. But since I did have to change 'em, and I felt 'em soaked with my own chicken piss, well, I guess I'm a true fucking believer, now."

Spider managed a short, barking laugh, and they laughed with him, trying to ease the embarrassment that must have been eating into his huge pride. And Vernon wondered why it had been so easy to change Spider, yet so much of a battle to just attempt to make Chuck see things the way they were. Here was the motorcycle man, wanting to help. Needing to help, if only to work his way back into Walker's confidence. And where the hell was Chuck? Could the PM be trusted any longer with the information he carried around?

"Okay," Vernon said, speaking to Spider. "You're a believer. You know I meant what I said when I told you I'd kill anyone who'd try and hurt the Party. That's why I said it's important that Chuck comes in until he cools. He may do something stupid. I don't think so, but he just possibly could do something stupid."

"Can I have my heat back, Vernon?" Spider asked, and Walker hesitated.

Then he said to Little Bit: "Give the motorcycle man his gun back." He swung his legs off the cot. He couldn't afford to rest. Not now. Things might be moving faster than he'd first expected. He held up his hand at Chino's questioning face. "Hold tight, man. You and I've got some figuring to do. Some things that can't be left waiting any longer."

Spider and Little Bit left the room. There were still many members in the front room. Vernon saw and heard them as the door opened and then closed.

"Okay," Chino said, his eyes watchful as Vernon climbed off the cot and stood up to stretch.

The Party President rubbed the back of his neck, massaged his face and eyes, feeling the scratch of his stubbly beard on the palms of his hands, smelling the cigarette smoke smell of himself.

"Let's just hope, Chino," he said, "that everything still is okay."

It was 11:45 P.M. and the Thirteenth District Station House was changing watch for the third and final time that day. Officers strolled out from the assembly room and through the side door to the lot. Radio operators called in cars in a rotating sequence, so that there would always be units available during changeover. And the now-relieved men of the afternoon watch gathered in small groups in front of coffee and Coke machines. They stood in the long hall that ran from the main front rooms of the station to the assembly room and detective offices, chatting with grave-yard-shift dicks who wanted to know how the streets were shaping up before they began their own cruising. They discussed their hunting trips, bowling leagues, and bitching wives. They chattered about interoffice politics. About the sergeant's exam. About who was screwing whom.

Sergeant Baker detached himself from one of these groups as he spotted Mason and Jones coming in through the front double doors.

"You get those PDO's passed out?" he asked Mason.

"All of them signed, sealed, and delivered."

"Here's the plates, Sergeant." Jones held up three dirty Missouri license plates.

"Anyone give you trouble?" Baker's eyes were sly, and Mason stared at the heavyset police sergeant.

"Be serious, Baker," he said. "Me and my partner here can handle that petty stuff without calling the whole department in on it."

"The captain's got a phone complaint from a"—Baker checked a small notepad—"Mr. Stinson. One of those plates his?"

Mason nodded, and pulled out his own notepad.

"Stinson, 5960 Easton Avenue. Beaucoup verbal abuse—directed mostly at my partner. Uncle Tom. That sort of shit. Laid of bunch of bad words on me, but I'm ultra-cool. But then the bastard touched me. Stuck his finger into my chest."

Jones grinned and Baker's face turned florid with anger. "What happened, Mason? Just tell me what happened, so I can tell the captain. And knock off the funny shit!"

"Nothing happened." Mason's face was very serious, but his blue eyes were lively. "I simply informed Mr. Stinson that if he touched my person once more I would be forced to assume that he was assaulting a police officer in the line of duty. And that, of course, is a felony. He would then be arrested for that felony, and any force necessary to affect the arrest would be used—with pleasure—by my partner and myself. That's about it."

"What'dya mean, that's about it?"

"He turned over his plates and driver's license," said Jones. "And we told him that he should invest in automobile insurance, or else refrain from getting into accidents where he'd have to prove he's covered, post a bond with the state, or get his plates confiscated."

"Nothing to it," Mason said. "Very routine."

"You didn't threaten him?" Baker wanted to know. "You didn't use profanity, and tell him you were going to break his"—Baker consulted his notepad again—"fucking arm?"

"Never." Jones stood almost at attention and Mason played along, enjoying himself, and lifting his chin indignantly.

"Never in a million years, Sergeant Baker."

Baker stared at both of them. He shook his head. He took off his eight-pointed cap and mopped at a balding head.

"I'll tell the captain that what Mr. Stinson said is probably the truth, but that you and Jones have your own way of telling it."

His voice sounded weary, and Mason said, "It was bullshit, Baker. Nothing to get uptight about."

Baker stared up at him and replaced his hat.

"See Cramer at the desk. He's got a number for you to call, Mason."

Chapter Eleven

SPIDER WASHINGTON parked his chopped-down Harley at the curb in front of the Fireball Lounge. A group of four men and two women pushed through the door and out to the sidewalk. Spider got off his bike and stripped free of gloves and helmet. He rubbed his hands together and nodded to a tall black man in the group who lifted a clenched fist at him.

"Might as well crank that hog up again, brother. They're closing up for the night."

"It's not even twelve-thirty yet," Spider said. The man shrugged, gesturing at the closed door. He and his friends headed for a parked Olds in the lot next to the lounge.

Washington hung his helmet from the bike's handlebars and lit a cigarette. He approached the front door and tried it. It was closed tight. He knocked, and waited, listening. There was no answer, and he stepped back out to the sidewalk, looking up at the row of windows on the second floor, just above the flickering neon sign.

FIREBALL FIREBALL FIREBALL FIRE—

What's going down here? Spider wondered. He went up to the door again. He knocked a second time, much harder, and stood waiting, the cigarette clamped between his teeth. It was cold and he put his gloves back on, just as the door opened a crack.

"We're closed up," the girl said, her face barely showing behind two short chains.

"It's not one-thirty yet." Spider took the stub of cigarette from his mouth and flicked it away. "Sure is early to be closing."

"Not enough business tonight," she said, but Spider barely heard her. He was trying to make his brain work, trying to put together pieces that floated away and eluded him. There was something about the Fireball and Mason. Something Vernon had laughed about. And—

He sucked in a breath of freezing air.

"Your name Mona, girl?"

The phone rang behind her and the door began shutting in Spider's face. He jammed a gloved hand against it. "Wait a fucking minute!" But the door was shut tight, and all he could hear was the sound of the phone and the quick footsteps of the running girl. "Goddamn!"

Mason decided that he would wait for one more ring and then hang up. He couldn't understand what was wrong. Why, at just twelve-fifteen, was there no answer at the Fireball? He wouldn't call again, but he'd try and get hold of Mona at her apartment or else go on over to the lounge and see what—

"Hello!" the voice panted in his ear. Mason tensed at the sound of Mona's fear. It flooded into the receiver and he knew his instincts had been right again.

"Mona, what's happening?"

"Chuck Williams is upstairs sleeping off a drunk," she said, and stopped to get her breath. "Frank's not here, and I've closed the place up. But now I got me some bad-ass company."

"Slow down. What're you talking about?"

"What I'm talking about, Mason, is that some big mother from Walker's gang is outside on a motorcycle wanting to know why I'm closed." She hesitated. "Wait a minute, Joe." He heard the sound of the phone being set down on the bar.

"Son of a bitch!" he hissed, and glanced at Jones, who stood to the right of him at the booking counter. Allen's brow crinkled into a row of frown lines.

"What's going on, Joe?" he asked worriedly, but Mason didn't answer. He could hear the roar of a motorcycle, dim over the phone, and then the click-clack of her high heels returning.

"He's gone," Mona breathed. "He just drove up Olive."

"Okay," Mason said. "Get yourself together. Tell me exactly what's happened."

Officers came and went at the booking counter, said hello to Jones, and nodded at Mason. But Joe wasn't seeing them. He was bent over, the phone glued to his ear, eyes narrowed, chewing fiercely on his lower lip. Jones stayed close, hearing the unintelligible tinny buzz of the girl's voice, just barely audible over the sounds from the radio room and the main center of the station: the computer clicking, teletype rattling, hiss and buzz of messages going out, coming in, and phones ringing.

From Mason, all Jones heard were grunted replies, but he knew it was about Walker; he knew that something had broken Joe's way. His partner was excited, twitching with the nervous joy that Jones had seen so many times in just the few weeks of riding with him.

Allen scribbled a note on the back of a report form, reading, "I'M GOING TO LOCK UP OUR GEAR. BE RIGHT BACK."

He slid it in front of Mason. Joe glanced up and nodded. Jones gathered up their briefcases, clipboards, and pushed through the hall door. He made his way past the scattered desks in the assembly room and into the locker room just above the holdover cells below. The room was musty from years of old sweat and dust. Jones opened his locker and stowed their gear inside. He was locking the door when Joe hurried into the room, vaulted a bench, sat down on another, and began unlacing his boots.

"You changing into street clothes?" Allen called down the aisle, the lockers on both sides like buildings along an empty street. "Hey, Joe?"

"Yes!" Joe shouted, throwing the boots down and ripping off his jacket, shirt, and trousers.

Jones reopened his locker. He rushed now to catch

up with his partner. He tore his own uniform off just as fast.

"What the fuck are you doing?" Mason stood in his stocking feet, in his underwear, and Jones grinned at him. The rookie didn't slow down, but spoke in staccato bursts.

"Going with—you! Get—in—on—the fuckin'—fun!"

Mason stormed over to the young black man's side. He glared at the rookie.

"You ain't going nowhere, buddy! This is my own game and I don't want no innocent bystanders around who don't have to be there!"

"I ain't exactly an innocent fuckin' bystander, Joe." Jones stood to reach inside his locker for a brightly colored sport shirt. "I don't even know what's happening. But I do know it's got to be something to do with what you've told me about Walker. And that's enough for me to want to be in on the action."

"Wait a minute, Al!" Mason grabbed the other man's well-muscled arm. The kid is okay, he thought, and it pleased him that Jones wanted to come along. He tried to temper his pleasure with caution, but caution had never been one of Joe Mason's strong points. He knew he did too many things, said too many things, too quickly—jumped in where only an idiot would leap. This time he must force himself to be cool. He had to outthink Vernon, as well as the men in his department who would try to stop him. And afterward, he'd need enough heat to beat Walker to the end.

"I don't think it'd be good for you to...."

"What?" Jones asked, flashing his ready-for-anything smile. "Joe. I am coming with you, man."

Mason stood very still, in his jockey shorts and black socks, and told Allen what Mona had passed on and what they might run into. When he finished, Jones nodded. "So? I'm still in. If we can get Williams out of there, we may be able to dig up enough stuff so that Slater will go for a full-scale raid and search on Walker's headquarters."

"That's what I'm figuring," Mason said.

"Well, goddamn, man! You ain't going to do that alone! What if some dudes are already there? You're going to need a partner."

"I don't know, Al." Responsibility slumped Joe's shoulders. He saw thirteen faces gathered together to be photographed in An Hoa, Vietnam. He stared down at his feet. "Christ, my dogs stink. I can smell them from way up here."

"Listen, Joe." Allen Jones was already into his shirt and sliding his long legs into a pair of brown bell-bottom trousers. "Walker and his punks are the kind of bastards that give me and my own a bad name. Shaking down dudes like Fat Mac. Want to start a war that'll do nothing but hurt their own kind. Shit! I don't usually come on like a preacher. But it's guys like Walker who seem to want the hate to go on and on. It's like they live on it. Shit, you know what I mean?"

Mason nodded. He thought, Hate? I know about hate. That's what ties Walker and me together. What would Al say if he knew that neither you nor Vernon *really* gives a rat's ass for the street. It's us. It's him and me. So where do you stand on the question of hate, Mason? What do you know about living on hate?

"Okay," he said, "you tag along. But you do just what I say, okay?"

"You're still the senior man in the car."

"That's right. Get a move on now, Al. Mona's down there with Williams, and Christ knows what's been going on while we've been flapping our teeth!"

Jones, fully dressed, stared at Mason, still in his shorts and tee shirt. "I'm ready, Joe. You're the dude in his fuckin' drawers."

The big Harley Davidson was heavy with its engine shut down and despite the cold, Spider Washington sweated as he pushed the bike down the alley. He had driven two blocks up Olive, made a looping circle of two more blocks, returning the way he'd come, and then shut his bike down and pushed it to where he was now. He stopped, his boots scraping on the gravel-strewn cement, and held the Harley up next to him. To his right was the small parking lot of Frank's Fireball Lounge. He backed the motorcycle up between two stone garages. A dog barked twice, then was quiet. Cars moved by on Lovett to his left and Olive in front. Spider was satisfied with his position. He had a good view of the side door and front entrance into the Fireball and he'd wait for an hour before he moved. It'd be cold, but he had the feeling that a long wait wasn't in the cards. Maybe, he thought, I should've tried to call Vernon. But he threw the idea away. Wasn't time for that. Something was going to pop loose. It had to do with that Mona chick, and Mason ... Washington could feel it in his bones.

"And maybe our PM," he whispered to the bike, letting his hand caress the shiny gas tank, and leaning back against the surface of the wall behind him. He jammed his gloved hands beneath his armpits, feeling the solidness of his pistol there, stuck into his belt. Steam puffed out in front of his thick lips. "Our ex-PM...."

The basement, under Party headquarters, was damp and chilly, despite the big furnace rattling and clanking in a far corner. It was to this ancient coal burner that Walker led Chino Poole. The two men squatted down next to the half-empty rifle crates and the four smaller crates of ammunition.

"Let me show you something." Vernon took a screwdriver from his back pocket. He dug at some loose mortar around a brick and then pulled the brick easily from its setting in the wall. Black space showed behind the red-brick frame; Vernon slowly removed eight bricks from either side of the first hole. Chino moved closer and helped. Soon a square, tunnel-like opening appeared, big enough for a man to crawl into.

"You bring the flash?" Walker wiped at a trickle of sweat on his forehead and Chino flicked on the light. It pierced the darkness of the hole and showed a shaft running out from the wall and ahead a good twenty feet. The sides of the shaft were shored up with scrap lumber.

"Jesus!" Chino breathed. "Look at this shit."

"It goes about to the alley, right now," Vernon said. "But it ain't worth a damn until we can get it at least to the other side."

"When did this happen, Chief?"

"The PM and me chewed this motherfucker out when we first rented the upstairs. It beat our ass, too, Brother Chino. I can tell you that."

"Looks like a lot of work."

"There it is." Vernon sat back against the wall next to the opening. He lit a cigarette and held his match for Chino. He jerked his thumb into the tunnel as the other man puffed a Kool into life. "This is going to be a way out for us if the shit drops down too hard. I want you to get some members from upstairs, starting tonight, and continue where your leader left off." He grinned and Chino grinned back.

"This reminds me of the VC in Nam, Chief. All the guns and tunnels and shit."

"That's the idea."

"Tonight? You want us to start tonight?"

"That's right." Vernon blew smoke in a gentle trickle through his nostrils. He liked the damp smell of earth down here. It brought back the feelings he wanted to remember about Vietnam—the nights on watch in the bunkers with the sky lit by far-off falling flares, or the sky black with monsoon clouds, or the wide-open skies spread over with more stars than he'd ever seen before or since. The basement smell and the incompleted tunnel brought back, too, a silent-movie picture of him and Chuck chopping, digging, hauling. . . .

He drew on the cigarette and felt his shoulder muscles relax. Maybe he was jumping the gun. Maybe Chuck was okay and wouldn't go running off half-nuts and maybe—no! Too many damned "maybes." It's better to be safe, ready for the worst.

"There're more shovels and lumber back of the coalbin," he said to the silent Chino. "Call any members who aren't here already. If they can't make it in tonight, make sure they get in by tomorrow. Set it up in twenty-four-hour shifts. Have ten members here all the time for a while, at least until we're sure we can relax."

"Am I getting promoted or something, Chief?" Chino met Vernon's look with his own steady gaze.

"If Chuck isn't back before tomorrow morning, with his head on straight"—Vernon rested his hand on Chino's leather-jacketed shoulder—"then you're the new PM."

The '57 Chevy roared down Olive with Mason behind the wheel and Jones in the passenger seat. Both men were in civies with heavy jackets concealing their off-duty weapons. Neither spoke, but occasionally they glanced at each other and grinned.

As they approached the Fireball, Joe unbuttoned his jacket and Allen did the same.

"What's this Mona like?" he asked, wetting his lips. The Chevy turned left and bounced into the parking lot next to Frank's. Mason turned the engine off. He looked at Jones's tense face.

"You'll like her. She's real."

"You like her?"

"I don't even know her," Mason said, opening the door. "Stay in the shadows."

They got out of the car and headed for the side door. It opened just as they reached it. Without hesitating, Mason entered with Jones right behind him. The door shut and Joe whirled to find Mona flattened against his chest. He held on to her for a moment, and then she pulled away and said: "I don't dig all this cops-and-robbers shit. I don't dig it at all, Mason."

"The calvary's here, now. This is my partner, Allen Jones. Allen, this is Mona—the hooker with a heart of gold. Where's Williams, baby?"

"Allen," Mona said, and took Jones's hand. The rookie looked embarrassed and Mona smiled for the first time. The smile softened the fear in her eyes and eased the shadows in her face. "He's still upstairs," she said to Mason. "He was sleeping a few minutes ago. He's really bummed out about the stuff I told you."

"It sure don't sound like Walker's style," Mason said. "But this is all too fucking elaborate to be a trap—I hope. Al, you stay here and watch the door. Mona, you guide me and we'll rap to the PM. What about Brown? When's he expected?"

"He called after I talked to you. He's wired up with some woman tonight. I told him I closed early. He didn't much give a damn. He's feeling good."

"Fine." Mason was eager to climb the stairs and get moving. He touched Jones's arm. "Al, you hear me call, come running. Otherwise, stay put and watch the lot."

"Roger." Allen made a mock bow to Mona. "And pleased to meet you, ma'am."

Mona smiled, but looked away and hurried after Mason when she saw the young police officer draw his revolver and turn to watch out the single pane of glass in the side door.

The pig, Mason, Spider thought, feeling his shivering cease as the door closed behind the white cop and his black partner. The pig Mason and his Uncle Tom pig buddy. But perhaps it didn't have anything to do with the missing Chuck Williams. Maybe pig Mason was just sharing some of Sister Mona with Uncle Tom pig? But if that was it, why close the joint early? Bars don't close up on drinking customers unless something's more important than the regulars business.

"No, Spider baby," he whispered to himself, "you are on the track of the cat, all right. You are Tarzan of the apes, Captain Midnight, Superman, Dick Fuckin' Tracy, and all on the track of the cat." He chuckled, wondering if he should try now to get to a phone. But once again, he decided against it. They could be back out any second, or something might happen that he shouldn't miss.

He hoisted his jacket and took out the pistol. It wasn't much of a heat. Just a .38 caliber. But it would waste a dude. He knew it would waste a dude. He'd rather have one of them magnums, like Dirty Harry or something, but all that mattered in the end was whether the dude was dead, not how big was the fucking hole that killed him.

Once a man believes, Spider thought, there ain't nothing can touch him again. Vernon made me believe. It was the hundredth time he'd repeated the phrase in his mind, and it wouldn't leave him. It helped him accept what had happened. The endless moments on that dusty floor, Walker kneeling next to him shoving that heat—this heat—in his face, his own urine soaking him, the fear like a beast in his stomach. All of it kept flashing through Spider's mind.

Vernon made me believe . . . Vernon made me believe.

And he gripped the pistol tighter.

He waited.

"Williams!" Mason said, and shook the sleeping man's shoulder once more. "Chuck! Wake up, man! Com' on, wake up!"

"He's really under," Mona said softly, standing at his shoulder in the dark room. "I think he was dropping some reds with the booze. He's really oiled, Mason."

Joe nodded and bit at his lower lip. He sat down on the edge of the bed, the bed where he'd made love to Mona for the first time, and kept his hand on Chuck's arm. "Light a match, baby," he said, and lifted the PM's eyelid as Mona held the lit match close. Chuck's eyeball rolled up and back.

"He's not under that bad. Get a wet rag."

"Motherfuckin' Vernon—" Williams's slurred. "Motherfuckin' Vernon—"

"That's the way, Chuck," Mason said softly, and bent to grab up Williams's hand. He pressed at the base of the man's fingernail with his own thumbnail—pressed as hard as he could, and felt Williams jerk. He pressed in again, and sensed the other's pain. Mona came back and handed him a wet washcloth. Mason wiped the sweat from Williams's face and neck, almost tenderly trying to soothe the drunkenness away. "Com' on, Chuck. Com' on, man."

Williams opened his eyes slowly. He stared at Mason and Mona, crouching over him, then tried to roll over onto his side. He was still mumbling, and Mason held him on his back.

"Chuck, this is Joe Mason. The cop, Chuck. I hear you want to talk to me."

"Go to hell!"

"I hear you want to talk to me."

"All of you can . . . want to talk to Vernon."

"So do I, Chuck. I want to get him, too."

"Get him?"

"Get him, Chuck! For what he did to you. We'll help each other, man."

"Your ass. You're Mason."

"That's right. And you know me, don't you? You've seen me."

Williams nodded. His tongue probed the insides of his mouth. "Feel like shit. Total shit."

"You ought to. Can you walk out of here?"

"Where?"

"Station, my place, anywhere you want. But they're looking for you, Chuck. This place isn't any good."

"Who? Who's looking for me?"

"A dude on a motorcycle."

"Spider," Williams mumbled. "It would be that fuckin' Spider."

"You know what they want from you, man?"

"Leave me be."

"They want your ass, now, Chuck. They don't think you'll keep your mouth shut. It's your ass they want now, buddy."

"Are they outside?" Williams's eyes were suddenly bright with fear. "Spider?"

"I don't know," Mason admitted. "But we'll help you get somewhere safe."

"What do you want, Mason? What?"

"Walker's ass."

"Okay."

With Mona's help, Mason got the tall young man off

the bed and halfway down the stairs before Jones heard them and came up to help. Mona got her coat and opened the side door. Jones and Mason, their arms around Chuck's waist, and his arms draped around their necks, stumbled out into the harsh night air.

Mason dragged to a stop as Mona locked the door behind them. He stared up at the dark sky. The clouds were gone and the stars were faintly visible through a thin haze of pollution like tiny cold fires.

Chuck stirred. He felt the strangeness of the men next to him. They weren't his brothers. They were cops, pigs he'd sworn to destroy, but here they were holding him up, protecting him (though he didn't kid himself about why) and his friends were after him. He heard Mason's black partner say, "Looks like it's clearing up, Joe. Looks like a good night after all." And then Williams saw a black shadow move among the shadows across from the parking lot. The shadow bent low, looked like an animal. He shook his head and groaned.

"You all right?" Mason asked, and Williams lifted his head again, his eyes wide and pleading.

"Joe?" Allen said. "You want to get the car door, and I'll hold—"

"Spider!" Williams croaked, and the shadow materialized into a thickset man running full speed at them, body low and bowed legs pistoning.

Mason felt Mona's hand clawing into his back. He jerked away from Williams and pushed him and the girl back and down in front of the parked Chevy. Jones leaped in front of him as he grabbed for his holstered automatic. The night flashed into leaping crimson flares as the charging Spider fired twice. Jones went down on his knees, moaning, and Spider veered to the left, his face clear now in the street light. Mason had the .45 out, holding it before him in both hands, pointing straight ahead, but Washington had leaped to the other side of the Chevy.

"Mona!" Mason shouted. "On this side! Over here!" He reached and grabbed her outstretched hand, pulling her down next to the slumping Jones. He saw

Jones's pistol lying gleaming on the cement. He saw his partner's back jerking and shuddering, and rage filled his head as he dragged Williams over and dumped him down next to Mona.

"Spider! You motherfucker! You're dead! You're going—"

A sudden crack cut off his yelling and a searing hot pain burned across his neck as Washington leaped up and fired over the hood of the Chevy. A scream broke from Mason's lips. He jerked the trigger of the .45, and the automatic boomed. Orange flame speared out a foot in front of the pistol's muzzle. The shot went wide and Spider fired again—both men standing and shooting over the car's hood like duelists—the .45 roaring, the .38 crack-snapping in the cold air.

Then Washington lurched backward, sliding five feet on his leather-jacketed back, screaming, "Christ! Christ!" Feeling the whole of his right shoulder crushed and numb and the blood pouring out of him. Eyes spinning, teeth rattling over the taste of death. Hurt. Hurt. "Ah. . . ."

Mason, crouched down muttering to himself, and duck-walked around the front of his car. The automatic was still clutched in front of him. He spotted Washington, on his back, moaning and slobbering with pain and Mason stood up.

"I see you Pig Mason! I see you!"

"And I see you—" Joe walked toward the wounded man, a wild laugh breaking from him as Spider tried to lift his pistol with a shattered shoulder.

"I believe, pig! You can't kill me! I believe!"

Mason said nothing. He closed the gap and Spider began sliding backward, tears streaking his face, a pool of dark blood leaving a path under his dragging legs. The side wall of the Fireball stopped his movement finally, and weeping and cursing he tried to transfer the .38 from his dead right hand to his left. He did it at last and pointed the shaking weapon at Mason. He jerked the trigger. The hammer snapped. He jerked the trigger again, and once more the hammer clicked. "I'm a believer! You can't kill me, Pig!"

Mason stopped, watching the man carefully, and lifted his own pistol. He took one more step forward until he was only a few feet from Spider's outstretched boots. He aimed over the top of the .45's small, slit-sight and saw Spider's mouth gaping open, screaming: "Vernon! Vernon!"

For a tormented moment, he almost let Spider live. But then Mason remembered Jones, slumped on his face on the other side of the Chevy, his pistol unfired. Mason pulled the trigger.

The shot echoed, boomed off the wall, each reverberation sounding higher than the last, until there were no more sounds. Chuck asked, "What? What—?" And Allen Jones said "uh" one last time.

(The village crackled and smoked as it burned slowly, crumbling hesitantly to the ground. The small group of marines stood near the well at the far side of the village, where the heat from the burning huts was not so bad. They surrounded a small young man dressed in filthy white pajamalike trousers and shirt. The man's lips were split and bleeding and his left eye was swollen shut. A purple wound marked him from the bridge of his nose to his cheekbone.

Sergeant Mason pointed a finger at his wide eyes.
"You VC!"

The young man gripped a bent ID card and tried, for the sixth time, to give it to Mason. "No, VC! No. No, VC, mahrine!"

Corporal Walker's black hand sliced down on the Vietnamese wrist. The extended hand fell back to the young man's side. "You're a VC," Walker said, with his mouth almost touching the man's ear. "You are a motherfuckin' Gook VC!"

Claude Benson reached between Mason and Walker and slapped the man's face, twice, as hard as he could. His elbow bumped into Walker's neck as he swung, but Vernon never took his eyes off the prisoner's face. "You're a VC all right. Where are your buddies, gook? Victor Charlie. Huh? VC Ah Dow?"

"Vietnam!" the man screamed, and thrust the ID

card—once again—at Mason. Joe grabbed the card and threw it into the well. The man hurled himself at Walker and pushed to the edge of the well, staring down and shouting in Vietnamese, until Walker dragged him back and stood him with his back to the wall.

"Hagerstrom's dead," Benson said, his eyes screwed up against the village's flaming end.

"And Riley," Pfc. Moss croaked, and spit to the side.

"Vietnam!" the man shouted again, looking at all of them, staring from one to the other, at their bearded faces, haggard eyes, and tight mouths. "No, VC! Vietnam!"

"You want your ID so fuckin' bad?" Sergeant Mason asked, and his voice turned to a dull monotone as his eyes met Walker's.

"Vietnam!" the man shouted.

And they lifted him up and tumbled him over and into the well and he fell, scrabbling at the rough sides, and hit the water and bobbed to the surface, holding onto the sides and staring up at their faces looking down at him.

He continued to howl in Vietnamese, desperate to convince them, pleading—but they weren't listening. They could hear Lieutenant Stamper's bullhorn voice calling for the platoon to reform! Goddammit! And they were each busy pulling the pins from one M-26 fragmentation grenade apiece. Reform! Reform! They dropped the grenades in the well—into the man's screams—and walked slowly away.

"Fire in the fucking hole," Mason said, and they all laughed at that, even Walker. That was a good one, boy. They'd remember ol' Sergeant Mason saying that.

And the four grenades exploded, lifting a black geyser of water and mud and blood high into the smoke-choked air.

A ripple of earth, like a rug being flipped, ran under their boot soles and was still.)

Chapter Twelve

THE AMBULANCE rocketed through stoplights, flashing its own revolving lights, whooping out its electronic siren wail, passing pulled-over motorists and clumps of people halted at corners. In the front seat with the driver, Mona sat twisted around, staring at Mason, who was bent over the stretcher. The ambulance attendant next to him held a rubber oxygen mask over Allen's mouth and nose.

Mason was talking to Jones, but his voice was lost in the sound of the siren, the hissing of the oxygen tanks. Jones was unconscious, unable to hear what was being said to him. But Mason talked anyhow, feeling the bandage on his neck, a stiffening pain when he moved his head, and fear.

"Al, you dumb bastard, you're going to make it and you can bet your ass on that, man, there ain't no way you are not fuckin' going to make it, Al, and am I pissed off at you, Rookie, getting in the way like that, boy were you dumb, like I haven't been training you all this month or something. But still, shit, don't sweat the petty shit, man, you're going to be all right, 'cause I know, Al, and my instincts are always right on the button, my instincts are always—"

The ambulance took a hard corner and threw Mason into the attendant. The black-rubber oxygen mask slipped off Jones's face. A red trickle of blood and saliva ran from the rookie's nose and mouth. Mason grabbed the mask from the startled attendant and quickly replaced it on Allen's face. Cover it, he thought. Give him air. He'll make it. And he bent closer. He shouted into his partner's ear, "I know you ain't dead, Al, so com' on quit playing on me that way, asshole, no punk-ass militant's going to kill you, man, listen up, Al! You're going to fuckin' make it! You can hear me, man, I know you can fuckin' hear me, Al!"

Flashbulbs illuminated Spider Washington's body. He was hurled up against the brick wall as if trying to dig his way into the solid stone.

Police officers kept the crowds of curious citizens back and the emergency light of the waiting paddy wagon painted the wall over what was left of Spider's head—red, black, red, black, red, black.

Sam Oakland, clipboard in hand, strolled over to Sergeant Lou Capello, one of the night watch supervisors. Oakland chewed an unlit cigar with disgusted anger and nudged Capello.

"Mason would have to kill this fucker on my watch."

"This piece of dog shit"—Capello gestured to where Spider's body was being lifted onto a stained stretcher—"shot a cop. I don't give a fuck whose watch he got killed on as long as the worthless son of a bitch got killed. Period. I'm tickled pink Mason blew the dog away."

"So? A nigger shoots a nigger."

"What makes you such an asshole, Oakland?"

"Jones was a—"

"Don't say it, Oakland. I know you. I remember assholes like you from when I was a kid. Behind my back you talk about wops. I know you. Jesus, you're just a stupid fucker."

"Yeah, Sarge," Oakland grudgingly agreed, but still chewed the dead cigar with a vengeance. "I'm a stupid fucker or I wouldn't be here, now, doing this. You're right. I damn well agree. Now, what about him?" He nodded at Chuck Williams, who sat cuffed and dull-eyed in the back of Oakland's radio car.

"You heard Mason." Capello popped a Tums into his mouth. His full lips sucked reflectively. "He goes in and gets booked protective custody. Christ, my stomach's killing me. Assholes like you don't do my stomach any fuckin' good."

"Why do I have to be all these assholes?" Oakland wanted to know. "Hell, I don't have to take this kind of abuse. Are you abusing me, Sarge?"

"Shit, yes."

"See? I should've been a plumber like my old man. What kind of trouble did he have being a plumber? None. That's what kind: none. No fuckin' trouble. Did he have to fight niggers day and night? Negative. Shit, Sarge, you worry too much. That'll get your stomach every time."

"You get my stomach." Capello looked at Oakland carefully, as if inspecting the other cop. "If you weren't good at what you do, I'd recommend. . . . No. Shit. No, I wouldn't."

They were silent for a moment. The crowd surged too close once and Oakland charged over to assist the other officers in pushing them back to the sidewalk. They tried to make the onlookers go home, but despite the freezing night the people stayed, even after Washington's body had been hidden from view in the wagon. They stayed to look at Chuck and at the wall. When Oakland rejoined Capello, the patrolman was red-faced from the cold and a building frustration. "This fuckin' report's going to be one stinking-ass bitch, Sarge!"

"Wait'll Joe gets back from the hospital. He can fill in most of it for you. He won't be there long from what I saw of Jones. The rookie's hit bad."

"What were they doing down here?"

"I don't know."

"Well, how'd they get in the middle of a shootout?"

"I don't know."

"They weren't working on anything?"

"Not that I know of."

"I mean no department time?"

"No."

"Christ."

"Yeah. . . ." Capello shivered. "If I could only burp I'd be all right. Just one fuckin' burp. You ever know these guys who can just burp whenever they fuckin' want to?"

"Sure," Oakland said. "I can." And he demonstrated.

"I knew you were one of those guys. Jesus."

"I can fart whenever I want, too."

"I knew it."

The paddy wagon pulled away and the crowd began to draw back slowly into the shadows. Oakland said, "We should've brought that black chick in, too."

"Mason'll bring her back with him."

"She's a hooker, isn't she?" Oakland asked, and Sergeant Capello, stomach rumbling, blowing on frozen fingertips, glared at him.

"She's a friend of Mason's is all I know."

"Well, fuck." Oakland spit the stub of cigar to the ground. "We ain't cops no more; we're just a bunch of goddamned social workers. A friend of Mason's. Shit!"

Washington's dead, Chuck thought, sitting so that his handcuffed wrists were between spread knees. The motorcycle man is wasted. And he felt too sick to care. He could sense the Scotch leaving him, the reds he'd dropped leaving him, and he felt his stomach clenched like a fist and his head banded with steel. He saw Eileen's apartment deserted, ravaged in the girl's haste. He saw Mona's face close to his, and then Mason's, and then the shadow sprinting at them. He heard, once again, the crack of Spider's heat aimed toward him, trying to stop the PM from talking, trying to close his mouth forever. And he was too fucking sick to care.

The bystanders were pushed up to the right side of the police car he sat in. Most of them were black. They bent and stared in at him. He lifted his eyes and tried to bring their faces into focus, tried to regain his old defiant glare, but had to swallow his desire to vomit. He could feel the sweat break out on his forehead and cheeks and run down his sides as one round bug-eyed face stared directly at him.

"Walleye," Chuck breathed, and the face seemed to

read his lips. The face nodded up and down. Yeah, it's me, Walleye, PM. Then it was gone in the crowd.

Chuck slumped back in the seat and brought his linked hands up to his head. He felt the cold handcuffs touch his nose and his eyes brimmed full of tears. And he searched, for the first time in years, for a way to pray.

"He died on the table, Officer Mason. The bullet that entered just below his shoulder was the bad one. It struck the shoulderbone itself and was deflected downward. Lodged to the right and just behind the heart. A very difficult and dangerous area to remove a foreign object of any kind. There was massive internal—"

"Did you—did he say anything?"

"No. He never regained consciousness."

Mason nodded to the small group of people standing at the far side of the emergency room's crowded floor.

"Those are his folks," he said. "The two police officers are from my station. They'll want to know, too."

He watched the tall, reed-thin doctor cross the room to the mother and father and younger sister of Allen Jones; he knew that he too should have some words for them. Their black faces. Their black hands clutching at each other. The sister wild with weeping—weeping since she and her family arrived.

I should go over there, he thought, but he was too full of something else, now. Full and empty at once. Something he'd once grown used to, but had not expected to feel again.

(The bodies of the three marines lay side by side in the sand of Viem Dong on a spread shelter-half, ponchos covering each man. The three men had been the first fireteam of Sergeant Hank Barber's third squad, second platoon. Their names, part of Mason's and Walker's memory, were especially and most sharply burned into the mind of Hank Barber himself. They were his people. He was responsible for them. He saw to it that they received their mail. He passed out their C-rations and their ammunition. He kept them as dry and as safe as he possibly could.

When they were killed, all together, manning Observation Post West (OP West, you bitch!) it was Barber who took it the hardest of anyone. He sat down in the sand, next to his bunker, and wept until he couldn't weep anymore, then raged and cursed and tried to charge out of the perimeter. The men restrained him and he sat again, and stared, until he finally fell asleep two days later.)

Mona touched Mason's arm. He blinked down at her haggard face.

"What a miserable scene," she said, and he nodded.

"We've got to go," he said, and guided her to the glass door and outside. He lit her cigarette and asked her if she were going to cry.

"Hell, no."

"Good girl." He pushed back a lock of stiff black hair from her forehead. "I hardly knew Al that good, but I liked what I thought he was going to be. The thing is, though, that I should've taken care of him better."

"It was too fast. It wasn't your fault."

"Doesn't really matter, now," he said. "What matters is what I owe."

"Jesus," she said, "this is turning into some terrible shit. Look at my goddamned hand. My goddamned hand is shaking like a leaf."

Captain Alex Starvos, the thirteenth district's internal affairs officer, came out of the sliding glass doors and stopped next to Mason and Mona. "Give you both a lift to the station?"

"That's where we're going, Captain," Mason said, and guided Mona to the unmarked car with a gentle hand in the small of her back. "Com' on, baby. You've been a hero so far. Now's when it gets a little tough. You okay?"

"I'm fine," she said, and tossed the cigarette away,

still staring at her hands as if they'd betrayed her. "Can you believe my shaking like this?"

When Walleye had finished talking, Vernon jerked open a drawer in his small desk and took out a pint of Johnny Walker. He unscrewed the cap and handed the bottle to the fat man sitting opposite him. Walleye took the bottle and drank without another word. He closed his eyes and his throat moved and a bubble rose into the upside-down bottle.

"Save some, fat man," Chino said, and caught Vernon's eyes. Walker shook his head and Chino shrugged. When Walleye finally set the bottle down, Vernon leaned forward again, hands clenched into tight fists on the desk's littered top.

"Williams was in the police car?"

"In the back seat," Walleye said. "He looked right at me. He saw me. He was cuffed."

"And you're sure Spider was wasted?"

"Chief, he didn't have a head left!"

"Okay. Keep cool. Was Mason there?"

"Not by the time I made the scene. But he did the shooting on Spider. I heard the pigs talking to each other. He was hit, too, from what they said. But not bad."

"And his partner—this black cop—was hit?"

"Bad. Spider got him good. Can I have another drink?"

"Not yet, fat man. Go on downstairs and give Little Bit and the others a hand with the tunnel." Vernon grabbed at Walleye's shoulder as the big man stood up. "Better still, brother, why don't you slide home and get some Z's? Com' on back first thing tomorrow. You've done your night's work."

Walleye shook his head.

"What do I got at the crib, Chief? I'd rather stay here, if you don't mind?"

"I don't mind. Go on and give them a hand, then, and thanks for bringing the word. When the shit gets tight you've always come through. You got heart."

Walleye grinned and lumbered to the office door,

closing it behind him without another word. Walker paced the small area in front of the cot, while Chino sat silently behind him. Below their feet they could hear the muffled sound of tools clinking and men's muttered voices.

One down on both sides, Walker was thinking. An eye for an eye. The motorcycle man tried to do too much alone. Yet, it was probably the only play he could've made. But now what about Chuck? Is blood going to show or will he snitch?

And he thought of their conversation, him and the PM, before Williams had been swallowed by the alley, before Eileen had dropped down between them for good. They had talked about growing up, about Nam, about what the Party meant to both of them, about how Chuck would be all right when it counted. When it counted, huh? Well, it counts now, Chuck, old bro. What will you do?

Reading his president's mind, Chino asked, "Should we move everything out of here, Vernon?"

"You're my new PM, Chino." Walker stopped his pacing. "What do you say?"

"Make our bird. Get the fuck out of here. Set up somewhere else. Or, at least, get the heat out of here."

Walker nodded, but the nod wasn't to agree with what Chino suggested. The head, moving up and down slowly, was saying yes to Joe Mason, an affirmation of all that Vernon Walker knew about Joe Mason.

Sarge, you'd love to see us slink away from here, wouldn't you? It'd be a real feather in your cap. Maybe even something to make you feel better about me humping your ass out of that rice paddy? But it isn't going down that way, Mr. Squad Leader. No way. I don't run away after the first skirmish.

"We don't make our bird, Chino," he said. "We don't run out and the guns stay. We've had a bad break, but we haven't begun to put anything together yet. On the streets, where it counts, we'll do all right."

"And the PM?"

"You're the new Prime Minister."

"Chuck. . . ."

"He's blood brother to all of us. We have to trust the blood in him to do right," Vernon said softly, and wondered, But can we trust the man in him? It was the man I hurt.

To cover doubt, he had to act. He had to do something to smother the fear of impending ruin.

"How far are we on the tunnel, PM?"

Chuck stood up alongside Vernon, rubbing the palms of his hands against his jeans. He cleared his throat. "We got that bitch all the way past them pipes and past the middle of the alley. I just hope no big-ass trucks go over while we're digging."

"There should be enough dirt and rock between the alley and the hole, but make sure it's shored up good."

"I will do that, Vernon."

"Do something else, Chino, man." Walker draped his arm around the lanky new PM's broad shoulders. "Will you do something else?"

"Speak, Chief."

"Get me one of the good carbines up here. A clean one and a thirty-round magazine." Vernon laughed. "I want to have a decent hello ready if Mason comes around again looking for another cup of coffee."

"A good carbine."

"Right."

And Chino moved quickly to the door and out, leaving Walker with his jumping, disturbing thoughts.

I need a woman. If I call Marcy, what will she say? Will she tell me to go to hell or ask me over? She'd tell me to go to hell. Don't blame her. Never sees me. Barely knows me. Who knows me? *I* know me. Mason. Ol' Joe Mason. . . .

Chino reappeared with the rifle and magazine. Walker hefted the weapon and inserted the magazine, but did not chamber a bullet. He looked at Chino.

"Thank you, Brother Poole."

"Anything, Chief. Just speak."

Walker nodded at the half-empty bottle of Johnny Walker. "Pour us a sip of Scotch, and then settle down to listen." He picked up the volumes of Mao and Giap, the North Vietnamese general. "If you're the new PM, you've got to know what I know."

Chino handed him a paper cup of Scotch.

"I'm not much on books, Chief."

"You will be." Walker set the carbine down, leaning it against the cot. He sat down by the side of the window where he couldn't be seen and motioned Chino to move his own chair. He lit a cigarette and opened the red-bound book first. He looked up at Chino's intent face. "Just imagine the police as a tiger, Chi, man, and we're the wolves, a pack of hungry wolves."

Chapter Thirteen

HENRY LEHR woke to the sound of the phone ringing and, after the first twinge of annoyance, was suddenly very frightened. He thought he had no reason to be afraid, but he was afraid; his hand trembled as he reached across to the nightstand. His wife, Eunice, in the twin bed across from his own, mumbled a fashionable profanity and sat up as he lifted the phone to his ear. He answered and heard Vernon Walker on the other end. Though the bedroom was cool and dark, Henry felt sweat pop out on his body and run like icy blood from his armpits.

"Are you getting all of this, Lehr?" Vernon asked, and Henry nodded, staring at his wife's shape in the gloom.

"Yes. You want me to try and talk to him."

"That's right. Maybe Mason hasn't got to him yet. If not, you're the man to convince Chuck to keep his lip tight. We need this kind of insurance right now, Lehr. It'll give us some breathing room."

"Breathing room for what, Vernon?"

"I'm asking you to go over to that station now. I know it's late, but go now. You're his lawyer. They won't argue with your seeing him."

"Asking me, Vernon?" Lehr suppressed a laugh. "My God, Vernon. Politeness becomes you even less than bravery becomes me."

"There was a shooting tonight, man. Some things may be going down because of it. It's something that you should know about."

"Then tell me, Vernon. Let the attorney know."

Vernon explained and Henry knew that his first premonition of danger had not been a false alarm.

"Vernon, this will blow it all wide open."

"It won't blow nothing. If we handle it right, it will be all smoothed over in a week. You've done it before. You can do it again."

"I don't know." Lehr turned away from his wife's eyes and dragged the phone to the other side of the bed, sitting with his back to her, hunched over and mumbling. "Perhaps you should move out of that place. They could use this for a search warrant."

"I'm betting that you can stop them at the pass."

"Williams?"

"Talk to him. Tell him that Spider played his own game. He wasn't told to try and get him. Tell him he's still a member in good standing."

"What's this going to do to your backing, though, Vernon. The people who—"

"Fuck them, Lehr. Money always comes into this kind of thing. It's always there and you know it."

"All right. Calm down. There's no reason to be upset with me. I was only mentioning the obvious."

"Do it, Henry." Walker's voice hardened. "Just go down to that station and talk to him."

The phone clicked in his ear and Lehr hung up slowly, sick and tired and afraid. He thought of his house, this house, and its ten handsome rooms, of the paneled den he'd just had finished. He thought of his daughter in college, his son almost graduated from high school. He felt his wife, breathing hard behind him, beauty parlors, the country club.

He stood up, ignoring what she was saying. He went to the wall-sized closet and dressed quickly. Eunice chattered on and on. Henry was thinking, Vernon's right. Money always comes into this kind of thing and money is where I'm at. Money buys my safety, and I'm the champion of the underdog. That's what they call me in the *Post*. Of course in the *Globe*, I'm that rabble-saving son of a bitch who returns killers to our streets.

"What is it, Henry? Who was it on the phone? Where are you going?"

He grunted something noncommittal, but his mind answered, It's trouble, Eunice, my dear, my wife, my checkbook.

Is it Tuesday, or still Monday, Mason wondered?

He decided to call it Tuesday, but still the past few raging days would not fall into any sensible sequence. He gave it up. It's just early morning of some day; and it's not important.

He opened the car door after Captain Starvos had parked the unmarked Plymouth, and helped Mona out, thinking, If she can't be protected then she'll have to be secondary to getting Vernon. If Allen can die for it, she can die for it.

And he hated himself, but thought it nonetheless.

"You all right?" he asked, and she nodded.

Captain Starvos gave Mason and the girl a sad grin. "Good for you," he said to Mona, without any sarcasm, the first words the swarthy captain had spoken during the entire drive from the hospital.

Mason was thankful for Starvos's tact. He liked the dark little man whose sense of humor and street sense made him a favorite with the station's patrolmen. Starvos did a good job with internal affairs and was a born human-relations man, but Joe and many others would rather have had the officer as a platoon commander instead of a paper pusher. Starvos himself had voiced a similar wish. Above everything else, though, Alex Starvos had no phony diplomacy. He'd tell you if he thought you were wrong. So he stayed where he was, helpful but not powerful.

And so, Mason thought, instead of Starvos we've got Mother Bruener.

Captain Eric Bruener, the boss of Mason's platoon, appeared in the front foyer of the station, just beyond the closed glass doors.

"Son of a bitch!" Mason hissed. Starvos flashed his sad grin once again.

"A hell of a night, all right."

"What's he doing here?" They climbed the steps to the front doors. "He's not on duty."

"Must've got a call to come in."

"Can you divert the bastard for a minute so I can get down and talk to Williams, Captain Starvos?"

The IA captain shook his head and pushed the door open.

"Sorry, Joe. You know I can't interfere with platoon business. Wish I could get him off your scent for a bit, but I can't do that."

Mason held the door for Mona and shook his head.

"Son-of-a-bitching motherfuckin' goddamned—"

"Joe," Mona said, "please keep cool."

"Remember," he muttered, as Captain Bruener came lumbering down the hall at them, "I told you the rough part was yet to come? Well, kid, here it is."

Bruener was a huge man, over six feet four, with enormous hairy hands. But his heart was a small, weak thing. Bruener was the worrier of all worriers. He was afraid of almost everything that could affect his position and yearned only for the day when he could retire and get the hell away from trouble forever.

"Jesus, Jesus, Joe!" Bruener bellowed. "What the hell went on out there tonight? Goddamn, Joe. You were off-duty. Both you and Jones—and Allen Jones dead! We couldn't believe it. A call came in a few minutes ago. It's terrible! Jesus Christ, Joe!"

"This is Mona, Captain."

"Jesus Christ, Joe! What kind of thing were you two involved in? Who is this Charles Lemay Williams that Capello's got booked on protective? And Jones, Joe! He's only been on the crew for a month, for God's sake!"

He followed them all the way past the desk to their right, to the battered coffee machine.

"I want the whole story, Mason! We'll use an office in the back here. Goddammit, Mason, I'm talking to you!"

Mason stopped and faced his watch commander.

"I have to talk to Chuck Williams first, sir."

"You—shit! You'll talk to me first. I want the whole

story, now! I'm the one who's going to have to explain all this to the boss, not you!"

Mason looked for Starvos, but the IA captain was heading for the stairs that led up to his second-floor office. Joe turned back to Bruener. "Let me have just a few minutes, Captain. Just give me a few minutes before the guy gets a chance to start clamming up."

Bruener hesitated and Mona stepped in front of Mason. She smiled up at the tall, gray-haired Bruener.

"I can fill the captain in on what happened at the Fireball, Joe. You can give him the rest in just a few minutes. Wouldn't that be okay, Captain?"

"You're...."

"Mona," she said, holding her hand out to be engulfed by Bruener's massive fist. "And I'm pleased to meet you. I've heard about you."

Mother Bruener smiled for the first time that night, and Mason—if he hadn't been so tired, so sick with anger, so hungry for a hot meal—would've hugged her. You've got him by his big balls, he thought, as Bruener nodded, holding onto Mona's hand for just a fraction too long and obviously intrigued by this tiny bundle of dark-brown ass, proud breasts, and bright eyes.

"Very well, Joe," Bruener said. "Talk to your pet prisoner. Protective custody. My God, what next? Now, Mona. We can talk in here. This is where the thirteenth's narcotics squad works out of, and...."

Mona threw Mason a piercing, weary, lovely wink, and Joe inclined his head just an inch, murmuring at Bruener's departing back: "Thanks for small favors—you mother."

"Let's keep that motherhumpin' dirt coming!" Chino yelled into the tunnel mouth and was answered by a chorus of disgusted curses. He crouched away from the yawning hole in the wall and stared at the two members slumped against the scarred brick.

BabyJames Wilson and Lee Simms ignored him and passed a tall can of Schlitz back and forth. Both their faces were coated by a layer of the yellow-brown dust and the smell of beer and sweat lifted from their bodies. Their mouths were slack around burning cigarettes.

"Why ain't you two in there?" he asked them, and Simms peeled his cigarette from his lower lip.

"No room, new PM. Not with Walleye's fat ass wedged in that fucker."

"Little Bit's up at point," BabyJames added. "He digging and passing dirt back to the fat man, and ol' Walleye just spraying it behind him like a dog digging for a motherfuckin' bone."

"We're just waiting," said Simms, "until he comes up for air, then we'll clean some more out."

"Digging like a real-ass dog," said BabyJames.

"A fat hound."

Chino nodded, apparently satisfied. He took the beer can from Simms. He tilted it and finished the remaining beer. Simms loved that. He was very happy about that. His dirty face twisted and he glowered angrily at Chino's bland, innocent eyes.

"That there was the last fucking can, man."

"And I'm not the new anything. I *am* the PM."

Simms's expression changed from anger to delight. He barked out a short laugh. The laugh echoed around the clink-clank sound of Little Bit and Walleye, far up the tunnel and hacking away at raw earth. Simms shook his head and held out the smoking butt of his cigarette.

"Might as well finish this too, then, Prime Minister!"

Poole laughed with them, but his head was upstairs with Vernon Walker—stretched out on his cot, carbine propped next to him, eyes closed, but, Chino was sure, not sleeping.

The assembly room was empty, but for Sam Oakland, sitting at the front of the room, and Chuck Williams, handcuffed to a desk. Mason pushed the door open.

Sam looked up from the sheaf of papers he was laboring over.

"Well, goddamn," he said. "If it ain't Dirty Harry

himself. In the flesh. Bandage on his neck and all. The red fuckin' badge of courage."

"Go fuck yourself," Mason said, and nodded at Williams. "What's he doing here? He should be in one of the holdover cells."

"I had some questions to ask him." Oakland lit a fresh cigar. "How's the kid doing?"

"He isn't," Mason murmured. "He didn't make it."

"What? Speak up, Dirty Harry."

"He's dead."

Oakland studied the tip of his smoldering cigar.

"That's too bad. I didn't know him, really. New kid and all, right out of the academy. Plus which we didn't really have too much in common." He clamped the stogie between stained teeth and gathered his papers. He stood up and grabbed his hat. "You want to talk to this dude, Mason? Go ahead. I'll slip into the dick's room. Slater's here, by the way. He got called in on this shitting shootout of yours—this little Gunfight at the OK-fuckin'-Corral. Bang. Bang. Terrific."

Mason said nothing. He stood very still and stared down at Chuck Williams. Chuck stared back at first, but then lowered his eyes as Oakland stepped around the front desk and brushed past them.

"I never liked you, Mason," Oakland said, stopping there with his arms full and the cigar moving up and down with each of his clipped words. "I was glad when they transferred you off our crew. You were bound to get some cop killed sooner or later. You're a razzle-dazzle boy, Mason."

"I don't give a happy fuck if you like me, Oakland." Mason was still looking at Williams.

"Yeah? Well, I wanted to tell you, anyway."

"I respect you for that," Mason said. "Thanks for what you've done on this."

"Don't mention it, Dirty Harry." Oakland opened the assembly room door and walked out.

Mason sat down at the desk across from Williams. He lit two cigarettes and handed one across to the handcuffed man, then remembered the cuffs and bent to unlock them. He threw the cuffs to one side of the room. They smashed and jangled against the wall and Williams massaged his wrists. He accepted the proffered cigarette and both men were silent for a few minutes that felt like a very long time. They smoked and watched the smoke curl up and flatten out and tremble in the heated air.

"Your partner's really dead?" Chuck broke the silence first. "That other cop dead?"

"He's dead."

"You sound very cool about it, man."

"I'm hot inside. I try to keep the outside cool."

Williams understood that. He nodded.

"Your partner—that other cop—he was a brother."

"He was a police officer."

"Spider got him. Those first shots?"

"That's right."

"Spider was crazy. He was a wired-up crazy dude."

"He's nothing, now. He's dead. And I loved killing his black ass."

Chuck's eyes had been wandering. They swung back now and locked, once again, on Mason's face.

"You and Vernon were in Nam together, weren't you?"

"We were in the same squad."

"Vernon says he saved your ass."

"He did. I was hit in the legs, out in a paddy all night. There was another guy there, but he didn't live long. He died before it got light. His name was Johnson. He was black. He was from Albany, Georgia. Vernon spotted us and came out and got me out of there. He carried me a couple of miles."

"There was a guy in my platoon from Georgia. But he was a white dude. A real redneck named Schuyler."

"You were in Nam?"

"Sure. In the army. I was drafted."

"Who were you with?"

"One hundred and first Airborne."

"A good outfit." Mason drew hard on his cigarette.

"Hue City was a bear," Williams said. "That was a motherfucker."

"That's right." Mason offered a tiny grin, the barest

uptwisting of his lips. His grin said, You were in Nam, huh? That's a bond between us. You understand a little more than most guys.

"Why?" he asked suddenly, while Chuck's eyes were relaxed and sleepy. "Did Vernon do it to your chick? That doesn't sound like Walker. That was a real bitch of a thing for a dude to do to his rap. Why'd he do that, Chuck?"

"Shut up, you—"

"Calling me names isn't going to change it."

Chuck's eyes widened until they showed white all the way around. His pupils were dilated and sweat showed on his thin mustache.

"I'd like to go to the john."

Mason didn't argue. He stood up with Williams and the black man said, "I talked too fuckin' much to that Mona broad, didn't I?"

"You were strung out bad," Mason said. "You were oiled up good, man."

"But I said too fuckin' much."

"Yeah," Mason admitted, "you did say too much." And he turned his back on Williams and led the way to the rest room in the dully lighted hallway. Chuck followed docilely.

The projects in St. Louis are the same as in any big American city; holes chopped into doors so that the doors have to be changed to heavy metal; shit in the elevators and garbage on back stairways; gangs of youths forming to protect each other from other gangs; social workers handing out welfare to pay for babies as long as fathers aren't in the home. The fathers lay up in pool halls or unpaid-for Lincolns and visit wives like rapists slinking through the dark.

The world there, in the projects, has a special kind of stink and there's no hope but for another day to pass and roll into a week and the seasons are either terrible heat or terrible cold. Young men look up to criminals and the criminals swagger like Old West gunfighters. A kid grows up thinking that having heart is as important as having air or food or money.

And me and Chuck, Vernon thought, half-asleep and sinking deeper, me and Chuck and basketball in the sweating evenings. Loud radios always carried everywhere, and the sounds of cars so familiar that if there were a sudden silence, project people would go mad.

And hate, always hate. Real wars on the streets to prime you for an Asian war that didn't really come close to the fear of a battle with auto antennas and knives and sawed-off shotguns. Dank alley wars filled with screams, curses, and shouts. Blood splattered on white tee shirts. Blood drops becoming red spiders on black faces. The welcome sounds of police sirens, screeching tires, and tennis-shoe-slapping retreats.

Sleep crowded him. It moved against his mind, blurring his thinking.

I remember my father as a runner, too. I remember his sad eyes and the way his lips were purple red from too much Sweet Suzy Wine. I smell his beaten breath now, and see his eyes, and feel the touch of his horny hands. I see him slouched over the table when my brother William was shot down, my mother screaming down at him, and the radio screaming in the hall, and my sister wailing almost as loud, and man—I'm tired of remembering all that shit! I wish there were some way to cut memories like that out of me. I want to be born today, to have no past; only a future of hurting back and paying back and . . .

But sleep was on him, smothering and warm.

The sound of digging drifted up from the basement and pattered into the deep-breathing silence.

Once, a few hours before dawn, Chino opened the door and looked in and then shut the door, cutting off the spear of light that had shot into the dark room like a spotlight.

"Thank you, lady," Mason said to Mona, seated next to him in the Chevy, as they drove away from the station. "You came to the rescue with Mother Bruener."

Mona nodded, but could not manage a smile. She

leaned her head on his shoulder, her cigarette loose between two grasping fingers with long, shiny, red nails.

"How'd it go with Williams?"

"We only talked for a few minutes. His lawyer came in and started quoting state and federal statutes pertaining to certain violation of protective-custody laws."

"He wanted him out?"

"There it is, baby."

"This was the chubby white-eyes with the flashy suit."

"Lehr's his name. Walker's long-haired protector."

"Did he make his point?" Mona looked up at him as they stopped for a red light. A few cars were on the street. It was chilly early morning, with sunlight creeping hard over the eastern skyline of the City. "I know by the way Bruener was talking—"

"If Williams hadn't wanted to stay locked up, Lehr would have got what he wanted." Mason gunned the Chevy as the light changed. "That fuckin', chickenshit Mother Bruener!"

Mona grinned coyly.

"The captain was very nice," she said. "He sho' know how to treat us nigras, nice!"

"He's a spineless—"

"Joe—"

"I just hate to see a good man like Jones get zapped for worthless pieces of shit like—"

"Mason!" she said loudly, covering the sound of his curse. "Stop it, please, for Christ's sake, man! Stop it!"

He took a stuttering breath and nodded. You're right, baby, he thought. It won't help Al now to holler and moan, but I keep seeing the kid on his hands and knees, head down, trying to gulp some air that won't come. His Italian-leather shoes scruffing on that concrete, and Spider's two slugs in him.

"Where we going, Mason?" Mona asked, and she looked away from him, staring out the passenger window and letting her cigarette burn into its filter. "I've got plenty of food at my crib and they don't know where I live."

"You don't know that," he said. "We'll go to my place." And she mumbled something and slumped back in the seat, not caring where they went, and they didn't say another word until Joe pulled the Chevy to the curb across from his apartment.

Mason told her to stay in the car and he got out and checked the street, but it was daylight by then and nothing moved except traffic. He opened the car door and motioned her out. They ran across the street, and Mason thought, Really a damned war, now, buddy. All the bad nerves. All the sweat. All the watching your rear. All the ass-breaking hours of watching for something that comes only when you're not watching.

He unlocked the door and went inside first. He climbed the stairs and checked each of the rooms, then called Mona up to join him.

"Is all that jazz necessary?" she asked.

"No," Mason said, and stripped off his jacket. "But it makes me feel better. You want chow or sleep?"

"Sleep," she said, and headed for the bedroom. She stopped at the door when she saw he wasn't following, but was stretching out on the overstuffed couch, the big .45 laid out on the cocktail table next to him.

"You going to sleep there, Mason?"

"I'm going to lay down here," he said. "Go on. I'll give you about four hours." He turned his head and looked at her exhausted eyes, slumped shoulders, and hanging arms. "Negative. I'll let you Z-out for six."

She entered the bedroom without answering him and lay down with all her clothes on and was asleep in just a few minutes.

(There were many long nights when you had to stay awake and couldn't even think of sleep, because thinking about it brought it on, and it wasn't long before you were saying to yourself that a few seconds of resting the old eyes wouldn't hurt. But the few seconds always snuck up on you, when you're like that it takes death himself to wake you for the split second of awareness before you die.)

The holdover cells were constructed of heavy-gauge steel painted sick green. The paint had peeled many times and more paint had been slopped on, so the bars and walls were bumpy with ridges and whorls of piled-on paint. There were two bunks in each cell. The bunks were also steel and were bracketed to the wall with no other support. They sagged. The springs on the bunks were bare and without mattresses because prisoners had managed to smuggle in matches and set them on fire. There was a combination washstand-toilet against the rear wall and when it flushed it made a noise like a launching torpedo. Pipes clanked and banged noisily, so once they'd tried the flusher out many prisoners got a kick out of continually flushing the toilet, or stuffing toilet tissue into its mouth which flooded the floor with spilled out feces and gray water.

On the walls, also steel, prisoners had left many a mark: J.H. WAS HERE. FUCK THE PIGS. UP WITH THE PEOPLE. JESUS SAVES—IF YOU'RE WHITE. BORN TO RAISE HELL, etc.

The slogans had been made in various ways, some with the black rubber heel of a shoe, some by scratching away the green paint to the bare steel below, others by holding illegal matches up to the painted walls and burning the words in. But all of the words—scribbled, rubbed on, burned into green—echoed the hollow bravado of men trapped, only stooping to graffiti because of the scars time was slashing into their minds.

Chuck Williams sat on a bare bunk, the flat springs etching creases into his trousers, and watched the tiny hairs on the backs of his hands. He never once looked up at Henry Lehr, who stood outside the cell.

"Chuck, listen to me, please. All you have to do is say the word and I'll have you out of here in five minutes."

"I don't want out of here just yet. I enjoy it like it was my own crib."

"I don't believe that."

"Do I give a rat's ass what the fuck you believe, Lehr? Ask me. Do I give a rat's ass?"

179

"I'm trying to help you, Chuck."

"You're sweating your hide is what you're doing."

"Vernon told me to tell you that you're still a member in good standing."

"You tell that back-stabbing bastard to shove it."

"I don't understand why you—"

"Vernon understands."

"He sent me here to help you."

"Like Spider tried to help me? You do know he wasn't aiming at that black cop he wasted, don't you?"

"That was not by Vernon's orders, Chuck."

"How do I know that, Lehr? Get the hell out of here. You make this stinking place stink worse. I'm tired. I don't want to listen to your shit." He lay back on the hard springs and draped a heavy forearm over his eyes to block out the light that always burned. Lehr shifted from one foot to the other.

"Have you given them any statement yet, Chuck?"

"Leave, man. I am tired of hearing you."

Chapter Fourteen

A BRIGHT cold day. A Tuesday in the week that's rolled itself into an avalanche, stretching two men out dead. And now this day, Vernon Walker thought. Another fat question mark.

He propped himself up on one elbow, stretched out on the cot, and watched the outside alley. He wondered briefly about Eileen, whether she was really as vanished as she seemed to be, seeing her humping, naked form again and tasting the scent of her as if she were next to him now. Once more, as he'd done often since that evening, he examined his motives, sorted them out, withdrew the tiny light of lust, and felt that he was right. He was right. Why couldn't Chuck have seen it the way he did?

Yet, even as he asked, he was ready with an answer. Chuck had really loved her. That was where he'd miscalculated. Vernon Walker, smart guy, had screwed things up.

He found the top of a cluster of bare trees growing up between brick walls, bravely finding some nourishment in the narrow strip of rocky soil they grew from and into which they'd sunk twisted roots. He watched the naked branches move slightly, touched by a vagrant wind. Small sparrows sat upon the telephone wires crisscrossing the pale sky above the trees. Vernon stared at the birds, not really seeing them. His breath came slowly. Squeezing his eyes shut he rubbed at the three-day growth of beard on his chin and upper lip. He listened for the sound of digging, but could no longer hear it. He shook himself and stood up, booted feet bumping the rifle.

Good morning, Mr. Carbine. Did you have a good night?

The rifle gleamed with oil, mute and deadly.

He laughed and shuffled out of the room into the front office. Members lay in huddled bunches, wrapped in blankets or rolled up in surplus sleeping bags.

A real bivouac. Look at them. Camped out inside.

Wilson and Redman Moore and Freddy Brown. Chino snored with his back to the front door, another carbine across his stretched-out legs. Lee Simms.

"Love all you mothers," Walker murmured, and made his way through the sleeping forms to the basement door.

The cellar was very cold and Vernon checked the furnace and found its fire-core smothered in burnt-out coal. Clinkers, we called them when I was a kid, he thought, and grabbed a long steel pole and broke the clinkers up, then lifted them out with a tool like giant tweezers. There were five members in the basement, too tired to do more than open bleary eyes at the noise Walker was making, and then fall back to sleep.

"Love you all, you hard-working mothers." He set aside the tools and grinned as the furnace started clanking and pulsing with heat. He stooped over to the tunnel's mouth and crawled up to where Little Bit and Walleye had stopped their digging.

The two friends were curled up, back to back in the gloom. A hoarse, rattling snore was crackling from the fat man's open mouth. Little Bit slept on, oblivious to the rumbling roar.

"Wake up, you two assholes," Walker said grunting, trying to pry his way around Walleye, but unable to squeeze past. He felt the rough lumber pressed into the tunnel's walls. The wood scraped against his trousers as he gave Walleye a hard shove. "Wake up!"

The two sleepers came awake with violent curses and Little Bit groped in the dark and found a shovel and tried to turn it to face the opening. Vernon, crouched over and half leaning back against the wall, burst into laughter. He choked on it, spit, and felt tears crowding his clenched eyes.

"Vernon?" asked Walleye. "Is that you, Chief?"

"Who are you, motherfucker?" Little Bit yelped, and started poking the shovel blade down the tunnel as Walleye flicked on a muddy flashlight.

Little Bit blew air through thick lips.

"Chief. Jesus, man, you scared the shit out of me!"

"What are you," asked Walleye, "the only dude in here? He scared shit out of me, too."

"I can see that for myself you jive-ass tank."

Vernon controlled his laughter and straightened up into the middle of the dark hole, so that he was once again on his hands and knees. "Com' on, Walleye. Get that fucking light out of my eyes."

"What? Oh, sorry."

"Shine it down that way. Let me see how far we're getting on the great escape."

"We got it measured off, Boss, and I think we just have to go up, now."

"Up?"

"Straight up," said Little Bit. "And we're out."

Vernon took the light from Walleye and the beam stabbed forward to where the tunnel ended in a sloping hill of mud. "You been burrowing up already."

"Right. Few more strokes and—"

"Well, shit." Vernon grabbed the shovel from Stanton and crawled over Walleye's legs. "What are we waiting for?"

He felt eight years old. The sweat soaked through his shirt. The smell of earth and the presence of friends inspired him. He laughed again and started shoving the small spade upward at an angle from the horizontal tunnel. Little Bit wedged himself in next to Walker and they attacked the vertical shaft with their hands, the spade, and a multitude of curses. The hole widened. Mud fell in a storm of crumbling clods into their hair and faces. Walleye handed them short pieces of wood to pound into the shaft. He also held the flashlight, but its beam was soon drowned in a sudden rush of daylight streaming down into the tunnel.

"We're out, Chief!"

"Light of the world!"

"Look at that, man! Vernon, we did it!"

"Bunch of fucking rats, man."

"Moles—bunch of fucking black moles."

"See where we are, Little Bit. You're the smallest."

Vernon helped Stanton wiggle up into the shaft and held onto his knees as the muffled voice floated down to him.

"We're next to a telephone pole—and a brick pit—we got the vacant lot in front and a garage to the left ... there's weeds and shit all around."

"Perfect. Motherhumpin' perfect."

Little Bit dropped back down and grinned whitely at Walker. They were all nodding and grinning at each other.

"Let's get some coffee cooking," Vernon said, "and some life into our brothers. Com' on, we'll finish shoring up that hole later."

"I'll run down to the bakery, Chief," Walleye said, scooting backward in front of Vernon's retreating figure. "Take me a sack and heist a big-ass bunch of donuts and stuff right off their fuckin' trucks. Do it all the time when I need a snack."

"You do that, fat man." Vernon stood up outside the tunnel mouth. He brushed at the dirt on his corduroys and hands. He rubbed at his thick hair, then he looked at Walleye and Stanton and laughed again. They were both completely covered with dirt from head to foot, clown-faced with dust and grime.

"Just like Chino said," Vernon mumbled, his laughter dying. "This is getting to be just like Nam. You two dudes look like Nam."

Neither Little Bit nor Walleye had been in the service, but they nodded with their president, a little worried, perhaps, as his sudden change of mood transformed his face into rigid planes, but eager to agree with him. The five members in the basement were waking up and grumbling as they lit cigarettes and spoke their first questions of the new day. What was happening? What's going down? And Vernon stared long and sadly at their expectant faces.

"This is the way Nam was, huh, Vernon?" Little Bit prompted, and Walker nodded slowly.

"Exactly."

The phone rang and Joe lurched off the couch, stepped into the kitchen, and grabbed it off its hook on the wall. He looked back through the living room to the bedroom. He could see only Mona's feet on the light-blue bedspread. She hadn't stirred.

"Yeah?" he said into the black-plastic receiver. "Mason here."

It was Ellen. She was at work. He could hear the sound of typewriters and the buzzing of phones, the high-pitched background voices of a busy office. She had read the morning newspapers. She had heard the reports on the radio.

"Are you all right, Joe? They said you were shot, for God's sake!"

"A scratch on the neck. Nothing to worry about."

"Nothing to worry about? Joe, I'm not insensitive. I care about you."

"Okay," he said, but thought, Insensitive? Jesus Rap Brown Christ!

"It's terrible about that young officer. Did I ever meet him? Was he married?"

"No to both questions. You didn't meet him. He was after us."

"It's just terrible." Her voice trembled, and Mason tried to analyze this, but was just too tired to give a damn. He felt the weariness, the hunger of it all, deep in his bones.

"The papers," she said, "have it all on the front pages. You shot a man—killed him."

"Yes, I did."

"The papers—"

"I haven't seen them yet. Did they spell my name right?"

"Joe! I'm not calling to—"

"How about Jones's name? Did they spell his name right? That's Jones. J-O-N-E-S. First name, Allen, a black man, twenty-one, single, lived with his folks, had a 71 Dodge Charger he creamed in his pants over, and about six different girls who affected him the same way. J-O-N-E-S. Are you sure they got it all down correctly? My name they can misspell, but not Jones. When you get zapped to get in the papers, you don't want them misspelling your goddamn name."

"I don't deserve your hatred, Joe," she said, then lapsed into sudden silence. The sounds of the office took her place. He knew she was crying.

"I don't hate you, Ellen," he said. "But I'm a cop, remember? Cops sometimes have to shoot people and people sometimes shoot cops. You had three years of it, Ellen. You should know all about it by now."

"And I begged you to—"

"I've got the job I want to have," he said, and let the air loose from tight lungs. "I know you begged me, but this is what I want to do."

Another silence, then: "Mark is just talking like crazy, now, Joe. You should come over more often. Maybe this weekend you could take him to the zoo or something. I don't think it'll be too cold, and—"

She put together a few more staggering sentences, then realized that he wasn't going to be drawn into a conversation, that he was somewhere she couldn't reach on this morning. She asked him for the second time if he were all right. He said he was fine, it was just a scratch. She hung up and he hung up. He stood barefooted on the cold linoleum of his kitchen, his clothes rumpled and smelling of fear, sweat, and tobacco. He stared at the small table next to the sofa, at the .45 on it. It was dark and heavy. Deadly. "I'm crazy 'bout you, ol' gun," he said harshly. Then a braying sound ripped out of him. The sound woke Mona and brought her to the bedroom door.

"What is it, Joe?"

"My ex-wife is what it is." He glanced at his wristwatch. "Go on back and hit the sack. You still got two hours left for Z's."

"Too damned tired to sleep."

"Then take a shower. I got seconds. I'm filthy and I

stink. I'm a dirty pig cop, and I stink." He held out his hands. "See that? Blood. My partner's blood."

"What'd she want?"

"Who?"

"Wife. The ex-wife."

"My balls," he said, and when she started across the living room to him, he motioned her back. "Take a damned shower or go back to sleep!"

Mona halted, startled at his crazy bright eyes and flushed face. She forced her lips to smile at his twisted image.

"I'll take a shower. Okay? Then I'll fix something to eat. You'll feel better when you eat."

But he wasn't listening. He sat back down on the couch and stared at the .45.

What was Spider's first name? he wondered. What was his real first name, before he became Spider, before he fell for a bike and cut-off denim jacket and guns and hatred? It doesn't matter, really. It doesn't make any difference if his name was George or James or Bill or Bob or goddamned Maximilian. I zapped the Spider, and no one else. I zapped him because he killed a friend of mine and I would've zapped the bastard even if he hadn't shot Jones. I enjoyed zapping him and it wasn't bullshit when I told Williams how much I liked doing it.

The phone rang again. Mason cursed and went to it.

"Yeah? Mason here."

"Captain Starvos, Joe."

"A friendly voice from the darkness."

"Maybe. Like the man said, I've got some good news and some bad news. What'd you want first?"

"Lay the bad on me, Captain."

"Okay. Jones is going to be laid out tomorrow and the next day at Ralston's Funeral Home. We've split the honor guard up with the three platoons. You're down for tomorrow morning at ten. That's two hours with Zackowski. You're also down for pallbearer, too. Joe—Allen's dad wanted that. You on the pallbearer thing."

"Okay." He let up on his grip and changed hands

with the phone, moving it from right to left. "All right."

"Also, Joe, the guys from the papers are here. I've put them off as long as I can. They want to talk to you and the major's cleared it. You've got about an hour before you have to be in for work. Why don't you come in a little early? Get this crap out of the way, all right?"

"Fucking vultures."

"I know, but you don't have to say anything about the extenuating circumstances, Joe. That can wait for the coroner's inquest. I'll be there with you. I can try and steer a few bombs off-target."

"That'll help." Mason resigned himself to facing the reporters he'd always mistrusted. "Where are they burying Allen, Captain?"

"Where? Hell, I really don't know, Joe. Calvary, I think. Does it make a difference?"

"No, I suppose it doesn't. I just wondered where he'll be."

"The funeral itself's Friday morning."

"A pallbearer, huh?"

"His dad, Joe. If you'd rather not, I can—"

"No, it's okay. I want to do it." Mason thought of what was happening to Allen's body—what had to be done before the young cop could be displayed at the wake. He swallowed hard and felt his throat muscles tighten. "I'll be in right away, Captain Starvos."

"Hold on, Joe! You forgot the good news."

"I've been voted police officer of the year."

"No," Starvos said, and when he went on his voice was more heavily accented than usual with his native Brooklynese. "Chuck Williams says he wants to see you. He won't say anything more to Slater and his boys. He wants you and you alone. I think he's ready to snitch on his friends. Is that better than cop of the year?"

"It'll have to do," Mason said, and they both tried to laugh. But it didn't work like it should have.

"Sit down, Henry. You look stuck together with spit."

188

"I ... don't feel well at all, Vernon. I've been up since you called last night. I was able to see Chuck—"

"All right. Wait a minute." Walker turned to the open door. "Hey, Walleye! Tell Chino I want to see him."

"Right, Chief!" Lehr's eyes fell on the carbine, now lying on the crumbled blankets of Walker's cot.

"Chino?"

"The new Prime Minister."

"Chuck's out for sure, then?"

"He's not with you, is he? I've already got the word he's not under arrest for anything."

"Protective Custody," Lehr said, and his large brown eyes looked even more hound-dog than ever. "Listen, Vernon, Chuck's much worse than you said. His attitude is—"

"You want a cup of coffee? A roll?"

"No, thank you, Vernon. Now, as I was—" The attorney looked up as Chino entered the room and toed the door shut behind him, then leaned against the far wall and nodded at Walker. The new PM's curiously flat eyes studied Lehr, who perched on the end of a folding chair, his briefcase on the floor beside his polished shoes. The lawyer's soft hands were intertwining, weaving, clasping, opening.

"This is Prime Minister Chino Poole, Mr. Lehr." Vernon's voice was sarcastically formal, and Henry winced.

"I think we've met," he said. "I've seen you before, haven't I? How are you?"

"I'm fine, Mr. Lehr," Chino answered, playing Vernon's game. "And how are you, sir?"

"Fine." Lehr coughed nervously.

"You don't look fine, Mr. Lehr."

Henry had started rising to shake Chino's hand, but now he sat back down on the metal chair and forced himself to ignore the PM's cold smile.

"You know what I have to tell you, then?" He spoke to Walker and the Party leader nodded.

"Sure. But it was something I wanted to try. I had hopes that he'd believe you."

"I'm talking to you about seriousness now, Vernon. This is very serious."

"You don't have to tell me what is serious, Lehr. I'm a serious man. That's one of the reasons you crawled out of the sack in the middle of the night to do me this favor."

The lawyer's eyes wandered back to the rifle on Vernon's cot. He'd played with this kind of thing for years now, but for the first time he felt he was with men who really did not care whether they lived or died. It terrified him, and steeled his sagging courage at the same time.

"I'm taking myself off this case, Vernon," he said. "And, as a matter of fact, I'm resigning as your attorney, also. For any further legal services you require, I'd suggest a call to Legal Aid."

Walker stared at him without blinking and Henry had to lower his eyes from that steady gaze. He stood, pulling his overcoat tight around him, as Chino straightened from the wall and glared at him. Violence, the smell of it, permeated the small room. Walker waved his PM back.

"There's only one reason you'll walk out of here on your own two feet, Lehr." Walker lit a cigarette and leaned back on the rear legs of his chair. "And that's because we don't need you anymore. In just a few short days events have pushed us ahead of schedule, way past needing anything like you—anymore. You understand what I'm talking about, don't you, Counselor?"

Lehr nodded silently. He stared down at the rifle, then back to Walker's hard-set face, and nodded again.

"That's right, Mr. Lehr. It's hot now, isn't it? The fire is lit and the buildings are starting to burn. And the rats have our permission to leave. So—leave."

Lehr turned toward the door, but Walker's almost cheerfully pleasant voice stopped him.

"And there won't be anything you want to say to anyone, will there, Mr. Lehr?"

"I have a family, Vernon," Henry croaked, and behind his back Chino's shark's smile broadened.

"That's right," Vernon said. "You have a family. They live in Ladue. We have the address. And what's going to happen won't bother them. Not yet, at least. Not today, or this week, or next month. Not yet."

And Henry Lehr opened the door. He stepped into the hall and unlocked the steel door that opened to the alley. He hurried to his car and, after unlocking the door, looked up at the window not six feet away. Vernon and Chino, side by side, were smiling and waving at him.

Mason, standing, sipped at the mug of coffee. He was in uniform, ready to go, and very conscious of the starched blue shirt and dark-blue jacket, the trousers with white stripe, the heavy silver badge on his jacket, the weight of his revolver lying in its holster against his hip.

"You won't eat?" Mona asked.

"We're always eating fuckin' breakfast. Did you ever notice that? I grab you when I'm drunk, we go to your place, or come here, we ball, we sleep, and the next morning we're sitting there eating breakfast. We've never eaten lunch or supper together. One of these days I'm going to take you out to dinner."

"Sure, but if you don't eat now you'll—"

"The coffee's enough."

"Okay, get skinnier, motherfucker."

"Such a hard woman."

"Your damned right, Mr. Po-lice."

"It's a good thing we're not in love or this could develop into a fight."

"It's a good thing is right."

"Listen," he said, moving to the head of the stairs with the cup of coffee still in his hand and his hat in the other, "you stick around here today. I'll tell the guy who drives this beat to check up on you every hour or so. If you need anything, you call me at the station. If I'm in the car they'll give the message to me and I'll call you right back. *Don't go out.* Call Brown and tell him you're down with a dose of clap or something. Okay?"

"Sure." She stood with her arms crossed. Her small breasts were hidden beneath his old shirt. "Don't go out. Listen and wait. Call you if they start breaking down the door. Got it."

"That's it. You're a real hero. I mean that."

"A heroine, asshole."

"Whatever." He handed her the empty cup. "And, Mona, if my ex-old lady should call back—"

"I pretend like I'm the maid?"

"No." He smiled. It felt like an honest-to-God genuine smile. "Just tell her I'll get in touch in a day or so."

"For real?" Her dark eyes were serious.

"For my son. I think maybe I'll take him to the zoo if it isn't too cold. Want to come?"

"Go to work, Mason," she said. "Go fight your stupid war."

He held her by the arms, his fingers very gentle and pressing slightly into her elbows.

"You ever hear of Achilles, baby?"

"Runs numbers out of a pawnship by the stadium."

"That's the guy." He gave her a quick kiss on the tip of her nose. "Seems the gods asked him if he'd rather have a long boring life or a short glorious one. He chose war and glory."

"And he got a fucking arrow in the heel, too. I've read a few books, Mason. You ain't the only one's read books. But tell me one thing."

"What's that?" He had turned and was halfway down the stairs.

"Did Allen Jones go out with trumpets blowing? If he did then I missed it."

He stood without speaking for several moments, hands on his hips and head down, and then looked up at her and smiled again. The smile made her want to turn and run and never stop.

"I'll see you tonight," he said, and started down the stairs again, taking them two at a time.

"Joe! Hey, Joe—I'm sorry I—"

But he was out of the door and gone.

Chapter Fifteen

THE REPORTER from the *Post* lifted his hand a bare fraction of an inch from the arm of his chair in Captain Alex Starvos's office. "Officer Mason, did you know Reginald Washington? Had you ever met, or seen him, or had contact with him before last night's—uh—incident?"

Reginald Washington, thought Joe, and tried very hard to suppress a grin. Or maybe they called you Reggie? Is that what they called you? Is that why you got mean and ugly and turned killer and changed it to Spider?

"I knew of him," Mason answered, and leaned forward, resting his elbows on Captain Starvos's desktop. The IA officer sat just behind him and to the right, puffing out clouds of blue smoke from a battered pipe, as Mason added: "But I never actually knew him."

"I've been told you'd arrested him before on at least two occasions."

"Your information's wrong, sir."

Starvos grinned around his pipestem and lifted dark eyebrows at the *Post* reporter, who smiled back but without much conviction. He was a round man, round-shouldered, roundly bald, with a thin fringe of hair in a circlet about his skull, and a round belly protruding from his very expensively tailored sport coat.

The two other reporters in the office, representing the *Globe Democrat* and Channel 5 TV News, started to ask questions at the same time, but the *Post* reporter headed them off in a much louder voice. The voice was the only thing about the man which was not round. The voice was pointed and sharp, and, much of the time, drew blood.

193

"Reginald Washington," the reporter said, "belonged to a militant group whose president is a man named Vernon Walker. Do you know Vernon Walker, Officer Mason?"

"I know him."

"Weren't you in the marine corps with Walker?"

"I was in the marine corps. Yes."

"With Walker?"

Captain Starvos interrupted the question with a dry cough. "Bob, you said you wanted this interview so you could find out more details about last night's shooting death of a police officer. Let's stick to that, all right? This isn't a trial and Officer Mason is not required to give you any more information than he feels is necessary."

A smug smile lifted the edges of Roundboy's pursed lips. "Then I'll just have to write a story based on other people's information."

"If you do, Bob," Captain Starvos said quietly, "be damned sure you have proof to back up every word."

"I'm not in the habit of leaving myself open to libel suits, Alex. I have the makings of a real story here, and I want"—he hesitated—"I would like Officer Mason to give me his side of it. And the crux of the story really, Alex—Officer Mason—is this: What exactly was, or is, your relationship with Vernon Walker?"

Mason sat without speaking while voices buzzed around him. He looked over the three reporters' heads, past their moving mouths and gesturing hands, and saw himself as a seventeen-year-old recruit at Parris Island, South Carolina, a squad leader in Southeast Asia, a new husband, a rookie cop, a father. But that was past. When he looked ahead he couldn't see beyond this day. He couldn't imagine a future and that stunned him. He thought of his son's future, and it was the same with Ellen, Mona, Captain Starvos— all of them. But where are you, Mason? he asked himself.

"I don't have," he said loudly, and the voices stopped. The reporters stared at him and Captain Starvos started forward from his chair as Mason stood up.

"I don't have," Joe repeated, "anything else to say. Officer Jones and I were working on a case. We were attacked by a subject known as Reginald 'Spider' Washington. The subject fired at us. Officer Jones was struck and died later at City Hospital. I returned Washington's fire and the subject died of gunshot wounds from my weapon. That's it. I've got work to do. I'm very busy. And I don't have anything else to say."

Mason sidestepped around the big desk, moved past the grinning *Post* reporter, and slammed the door of the office as he hurried out into the hallway.

The big room of Party headquarters was littered with crumpled sandwich wrappers, beer cans, cigarette butts, and the scattered bedrolls of the members now gathered in a nervous group around Vernon Walker. Outside and through the piled sandbags, Delmar was jammed with four-to-six-o'clock traffic. Horns blared, and the busy street hummed with its own peculiar mechanical growl. Walker spread out a much-used city map indicated a red-inked intersection with his long black finger.

"The district station," Little Bit said, squeezed in between Lee Simms and Walleye. "That's the thirteenth."

"Give the little soldier a prize," Vernon said, and his men laughed softly. Everything seemed soft, easy, in delicate balance. Vernon felt that if he raised his voice the roof would crumble and crush them all. He made a pistol out of his hand and aimed at the red X on the soiled map. "Pow!" he said, and the laughter this time was louder. It loosened them all, and Walker went on with his briefing.

"At eight on the nose, Walleye and Wilson make their phone calls. Now, remember, when you two call you'll be getting the switchboard at Central. They'll ask you if it's an emergency and you say yes—it fuckin' well is and start hollering for the thirteenth district. When they connect you, tell whoever answers what you have to report what we've gone over already. But don't tell it to Central, though. Scream and yell to be connected to thirteenth. Okay, you got that wired on?"

"There's nothing to it," murmured the fat man, and Wilson nodded. "Nothing to it."

"Okay," Walker said, and lit the first cigarette of his second pack of the day. "Chino, Simms, and Brown are waiting at the first location. Little Bit, Harry, Baby-James, and Fox have number two covered, right?"

They all nodded.

"If you have questions, let them out now, or forever hold your fuckin' peace." Walker puffed on the cigarette without tasting it and looked at the black, brown, and tan faces on either side of the table. They all met his stare. They were all together in what was going to go down.

"That's it, then. A half hour after squads one and two leave, we move out," Walker said, and grinned at the short, thickly built black man standing directly to his left. "Right, Beans?"

"That is right, Chief."

Beans Mundy got his nickname from a mean, mad girlfriend who'd poured a pot of boiling beans over his head during an argument. Mundy had slapped her to a babbling pulp, then run out of the apartment and dead into a group of friends. When they saw his wild eyes and the terrible burns on his face they rushed him to the hospital, all the time asking him what had happened. All Mundy could answer, along with violent oaths, was "Beans! Beans! Beans!" The name stuck, even after the burns had healed into thick patches of pink skin on his otherwise ebony face. Now, Beans Mundy tried to grin back at Walker, but his cheek muscles refused to cooperate and the smile turned into a masklike grimace of scar tissue and pinto skin.

"Then we going to do our thing, right, Chief?" he asked, and Walker draped an arm over his thick shoulders.

"That's right, Beans . . . our thing."

"I don't want you to tell me a damned thing, Chuck."

"And I don't know if I can, Mason. A lot of dudes that were like very tight with me would get pulled into this thing. There's some people who really were my brothers, man. I just wanted to find out what you want."

"Nothing."

"Is this that reverse—reverse—?"

"This isn't any reverse anything."

"You got a smoke?"

They both lit cigarettes. Mason was in the cell, standing up against the steel wall opposite the bunks. Chuck sat on the bottom bunk, hunched over his bent legs. A prisoner in the cell next to Williams screamed once, as loud as he could, then said in a neutral voice, "Cop? Get me to a hospital, cop. I am getting very sick, man. I am on the methadone program, cop. I'm on meth. And if you get me to a hospital they will give me a fuckin' shot and I won't be so fuckin' sick. Cop? Hey, cop?"

Mason told the man to shut his mouth, that he'd tell the dicks when he went back upstairs, and the man started to curse and scream again until harsh retching cut off his voice. The vomiting subsided after a while and Chuck said: "Bastard. The poor bastard."

Mason said: "I'll tell the dicks when I go back." Chuck nodded and the men stared at each other.

"I can't come in on them, Mason."

"I don't give a rat's ass."

"I can't be a fucking snitch, man!"

"Then you'll be a dead man and I don't give a rat's ass about that, either."

"What're you doing here, then? What you talking to me for, if you don't care?"

"I'd rather be with you, than with the slimes I have to—" Mason shook his head. "Forget it. Just tell me one thing."

"What?" Williams shifted his eyes and stared at the tip of his cigarette. He flicked ashes. "Ask."

"Why're you hanging on to that protective-custody crap? You can walk out of this cell right now if you want."

"I'm trying to figure out what to do," Williams said. "This place keeps me covered for a while, that's all. I can think here without looking over my shoulder."

"You won't be able to stay much longer. Maybe we can stretch another twenty hours, but not much more."

"It's all right."

"Sure."

"No. I'll know what I have to do by then."

Mason let himself slide down the steel wall, until he was crouched in front of Williams.

"Tell me about Eileen," he said. "You tell me about her and I'll tell you about my ex-wife. I don't have her anymore either, Chuck. She split because of what I do. But it wasn't really the same thing as your case, was it? I was luckier than you were. My boss didn't screw my woman. Didn't screw her, then tell me to stay away from her—or run her away—did he, Prime Minister?"

"Shut your pig's mouth, Mason." Low and dangerous, Williams's voice filled the cell and Mason was glad he'd left his pistol upstairs. And now the addict was moaning again. The man's voice came through the steel wall, a gagging growl of pain and sickness, as Mason cocked his head and regarded Williams with lazy indifference.

"It's eating at your gut, isn't it, Chuck?"

"I don't want to hear your pig voice anymore."

"Just like you were on junk, right? Vernon Walker. Your main rap. Your brother. He screwed your woman and what did he tell you, huh? I'll bet it was something good. I know Vernon and it had to be something perfect. What was it, Chuck? Did he tell you he balled your chick for the good of the Party? Or was it for your own good, man? Did he do it for you?"

A curse, half-scream and half-roar, broke from Williams's curled-back lips. He sprang from the bunk, past Mason's crouched figure, and slammed into the wall. He beat at the rivet-dotted barrier with both fists. "Stop your goddamned whining! You dope-fiend motherfucker!"

The moaning slowed for a heartbeat, then the addict's mechanical-man voice came again: "God's sake, cop, where are you? For the love of God and all that's holy, get me some meth—get me some, cop. I'm fuckin' dyin'."

"Die then!" Williams shouted and then sobbed out a tortured laugh. He glared down at Mason's head. "You know all the right buttons to push, don't you, pig?"

Joe rose slowly. He didn't answer. He slid the lead-weighted blackjack back into his rear pocket. He pulled open the cell door and closed it again, twisting the big brass key in the lock.

"You're not going to say anything else?" Williams was still laughing. "You don't have anything else to say to me, you motherfucker?" Chuck gripped the bars and very deliberately spit into Mason's face. The spittle ran down Joe's cheek. He took out a handkerchief and wiped his jaw clean and stepped to the cell next to Williams's where the addict lay weeping and rolling in his own vomit. The stench was incredible, but Mason hardly noticed.

"I'll let them know you're hurting, buddy," he said, and the emaciated black man rolled over and stared at him.

"For the love of God and all that's fuckin' holy, cop—"

"Mason!" Williams yelled, and Joe turned for a moment to stare at Chuck's fingers curled around the cell's bars. The fingers were all he could see of the other man, and the knuckles were bloody from the ex-PM's attack on the steel wall.

"What do you want, Chuck?"

"I want to talk," the voice said. "I want to, man. Just about Walker. I mean it, Mason!"

"Well," Joe murmured, "that's tough shit. I don't want to hear what you've got to say. I've changed my mind."

"You want Walker, don't you?" The black fingers curled, uncurled, and tightened on the bars again. "You want to get him, don't you, Mason?"

Joe stepped back in front of Williams's cell. He stared at the man behind the bars, the man who'd once been Walker's right hand, the man who'd once been so damned defiant and proud.

"Think about it, Chuck," Mason said. "You don't want to say anything now. You're pissed off, Chuck. So shut up. I don't want to hear you."

Williams's face flattened with surprise. His eyes were wide and disbelieving.

"What the fuck is it with you, Mason? What the fuck do you want? You wanted the word on Walker, didn't you? For shit's sake, you son of a bitch! Isn't that what you wanted?"

Mason spun around on his bootheel and walked away, down the row of cells and all the way to the door before Chuck's voice stopped him again.

"Mason!"

And Joe felt the other man behind him, without looking to see, felt him still hanging onto the bars, still spitting, felt his agony and his fear.

"Goddamnit, Mason!"

Joe thought of taking his son to the zoo. What would he say to the small boy when he showed him the predators prowling within their cages? What would he say to himself when he saw the lion's lethargic eyes, the fur falling off in ragged patches, the incessant pacing? He fumbled in his jacket pocket and lit a cigarette before pushing the door open and going through into the hallway. Williams shouted one last time before the door swung shut: "*Mason!*"

Roy Slater was waiting in the dimly lighted passageway. The chief of detectives seemed even paler than usual from the extra hours he'd put in during the last two days. A shadow beard showed on his jaw, cut through by the pale scar.

"Was that Williams?" he asked, and Mason shook his head.

"The junky in number two."

"What about Williams?"

"What about him?"

"Is he going to give you what you want?"

"Are you beginning to believe my fairy tale then, Captain?"

"None of us want shitbums like that on the street. Anything he can give us on Walker'll help."

"Well, I hope he don't give us a damned thing then," Joe said and walked as fast as he could down the hall, but Slater kept pace with him and grabbed his swinging arm.

"What's that crack supposed to mean?"

"Whatever you want it to mean."

"Mason! Goddammit!"

Joe jerked to a stop. He bit into the filtertip of his cigarette. He talked around it and ashes drifted down on his blue jacket front.

"I hope he don't snitch, Slater. I hope he don't let me bullshit him into thinking we can protect his ass or that he'll be doing something for the sake of the goddamned community!" The glowing tip of Mason's cigarette jerked up and down as he talked faster and louder. "All he has left is himself. His pride. His balls. What he thinks he believes in. I want him to cut off his balls, Slater, so I can get Walker and I'm getting a little damned tired of my own motives. I'm sick of letting some poor bastard think he's going to get a better shake if he turns evidence. And I'm sick of all the lousy politics when the shit starts flowing down from upstairs! You wouldn't go for a search warrant on what I told you, and neither would the DA, or any jerk-judge who's probably on the payroll of a half-dozen fences and thieves. But now—now, man—that a cop's dead and things are starting to go to shit—now you want some action. And it doesn't matter a fuck if I have to turn a good man into a Judas, just as long as we got a case—and I'm getting so I don't know whether to puke or laugh."

A muscle jumped in Captain Slater's cheek. He rubbed at his stubble of beard and his washed-out eyes blinked rapidly. His face reddened with anger as he jabbed a finger at Mason.

"All of a sudden, you got the corner on the sensitivity market, Joe. Is that right, huh? Shit! Where the hell do you get off, talking like that to me? And what's all this shit about Williams being a good man? Jesus! Just where do you get off talking like that?"

Mason dropped his cigarette and stamped it out on the tile floor. He took off his hat and wiped at the sweat on his forehead.

"You're full of shit, Captain. With all due respect— that is what I think right now. You and everything else, and maybe I'm losing my objectivity on this case—but I feel what Williams is feeling and it's fucking me up."

Slater shook his head. He managed a constricted grin.

"So, I'm full of shit, am I? Well, maybe I am. . . . It's been a long time since anyone under me had the guts to tell me that—so maybe you're right."

"Fuck. It ain't you, Captain."

"No. Don't hedge your bets, now, Mason. And don't let yourself get hooked on this feeling shit where Williams is involved. You can't do that and be a cop—not a good cop."

Mason nodded. He turned and walked down the hall with Slater at his side. They climbed the short flight of steel stairs, pushed through the upstairs door, and emerged into the front office and booking area of the station. Neither man said anything more until a young white patrolman approached them and spoke to Mason.

"Sergeant Baker says I'm supposed to go with you. They just transferred me here from the ninth. Had two months of vice before they let me get into uniform—and so here I am."

A hand stuck out to be shook. "My name's Rawlings." Gray eyes, open and trusting. Blond-brown hair showing beneath pulled-down cap. Leather shined. Brass shined. Choirboy face shined.

"I'm thrilled to make your acquaintance," Mason said, but ignored the boy's extended hand. After a moment of embarrassed silence, Rawlings let his arm fall back to his side. Mason's voice rasped. "But you can tell Sergeant Baker that nobody's—"

"Joe," Slater murmured, "knock it off."

Mason pressed his lips together.

"Okay, Rawlings. Go on out and find a car for us. I'll be with you in a minute."

The rookie grinned broadly and, his arms full of briefcase, cushion seat, lunchbox, nightstick, and clipboard, hurried out of the station. Joe glanced at his wristwatch, noting the time and the increasing activity of the booking counter and complaint phones. The radio board was alive with calls and the teletype clacked into the computer hookup behind the counter. "I'm about two hours late for the streets."

"The reserve cars will pick up on your calls," Slater said. "Now—what about Williams?"

"He's ripe." Mason lit another cigarette. He'd lost count of how many he'd smoked since the hurried cup of coffee with Mona. "He's ready to be plucked. Only it's not going to be me who puts the finishing touches on his young ass."

"Okay. But how have you handled it so far?"

"Very cool. Stay heavy on his chick, Eileen. Did you get the word on that? You know what went down with her and Walker?"

"I heard."

"That's what you stay on. That's what'll bust him open. He knows that he wouldn't have a very good chance alone against Walker, but he don't want to think he's snitching, either. He's not a snitch and he never will be. Let him think that he's getting back at Walker."

"I understand, Joe. Thanks."

"Don't mention it, Captain. For both our sakes, just don't ever mention it to me again."

Mason went to where his briefcase and gear were stacked behind the radio counter. He retrieved his service revolver from a small locker under the booking desk and returned the key to Slater. "Give that to Bruener will you, Captain. My new partner will be getting itchy pants."

"Have a good tour, Joe."

"Sure."

Chapter Sixteen

AT 7:30 P.M., Walker finished working on the bulky overcoat and tried it on. The coat was a size too big for him and was made from thick wool. The right sleeve was stuffed with newspaper and tucked into the coat's right pocket, giving the illusion that Walker had his right hand in that pocket. But Vernon's right arm and hand were free, under the coat, and gripped a sawed-off double-barreled shotgun hung on a coathanger-wire swivel stitched into the overcoat's lining. One front button was secured, and the scattergun was out of sight. All you saw coming toward you was a black man in a dark coat, wearing a wide-brimmed hat pulled down over his forehead.

The members around Walker expressed admiration. They slapped hands with each other. They crowed with laughter. They checked the coat and gun out again and said, Vernon, baby, you are the daddy of bad men. You are a motherfuckin' bad dude!

And Beans Mundy said, "Wait a minute! Dig on this!" and spread the raincoat he was wearing to expose three quart bottles—old Schlitz empties—full of gasoline and inserted into hidden pockets. Two bottles hung on his left side and one swung under his right arm. Beans grinned wildly, his scarred face a monster's visage.

"Do you all dig this shit! Whoomp! Whoomp!"

"That's enough jive," Walker said commandingly. "You are going to have plenty time for jive—later. Let's get moving to those positions, Little Bit, Chino."

"Going now, Chief."

"Grip my hand, President."

"Blood will tell."

"We will do it."

"Determination, man."

Hands formed into fists rapped on each other. Thumbs and forearms gripped. Bear hugs. Farewells. Curses and excited giggling. The back door open. The Hawk swooping in to sting their faces. The two squads moving out, their arms full of paper bags. Evening shoppers.

"Vernon and Beans—so long, dudes."

"Later!"

Walker and Mundy secured the steel door and Vernon hollered: "Walleye!"

"In here, Chief!" The fat man's voice came from the rear office-bedroom. Walker strolled carefully to the open door, trying not to let the heavy shotgun swing too much on its makeshift swivel. He grinned at Walleye, who was very seriously studying a "script" Walker had written out for him.

"You got it all down yet, Brother Chubs?"

"Almost, Chief." Walleye's mournful expression seemed to firm up with sudden resolution. "Let me run it down. 'This is an emergency. Please! You've got to get the police here! He's going to do something terrible if you don't get here right away! He's—'"

"That's real good," Walker interrupted. "You call at eight and Wilson'll be calling right behind you from the pay phone outside of the Star."

"We've got it down, Chief. I'll do it right."

"Even if you screw up they'll still send a car to check it out. I'd like to be there if they send Mason, but"—Walker stood back from the door—"me and Beans are going to be busy, too." He flipped open the button with his left hand and in the same fluid movement swung the shotgun up and through his flapping coat. The twin barrels pointed at Walleye for a split second and then Walker dropped the weapon back to its hiding place under the dark wool. Walleye giggled and shook his head. He waved at Beans as the scarred man and Walker walked out to the main room. The room was almost deserted. Only three members still worked on gear. They grinned at Vernon and he suddenly felt the need to move, to be busy—moving.

"Com' on, Mr. Beans. We'll walk right out the front door."

"How we getting there, Vernon?"

"The same way. We walk in, Beans. There isn't a cop in this district can catch us on foot. We don't want to be stuck with a car."

"Yeah, that's probably right, Chief," Beans said, as they nodded to the others and opened the front door to the icy night wind. "But I was kind of seeing it real fast, you know? Drive in and then burn rubber getting the fuck out!"

"Forget the movie shit, Beans. If we don't get out on our feet, we ain't getting out at all."

They started walking down Delmar and Mundy's teeth chattered. He huddled into the raincoat and was too damned cold to be nervous. He trusted Walker more than any dude he'd ever known. They'd do it and they'd get out and Walker would know the right way to move, where to go, and how to do all the things that had to be done.

In his trust and his willingness to obey, Mundy was the perfect soldier. But in another, very important way, he was not.

He doesn't realize what it's really about, Vernon decided. Or what it's for. The stakes aren't real to any of them as they are to me—and maybe to Chino and Little Bit. Chuck almost understood, but how do you tell men who've lived all their adult lives in a country where you open an icebox for food, open a purse for money, and watch pro-football on Sunday afternoons, that there must be an end to all of that? An end to build a new way. Maybe, Walker thought, that's one thing that Mason could be right about. A lot of blacks aren't going to want to sacrifice what they have in their hands for what might be in the bush.

"We have to make other bloods come in with us, Beans. Do you understand that, man?" Walker stared out from under his slouched hatbrim at the shorter man at his side. The scarred face was deep down between the raincoat's upturned collar. Vernon thought they looked like a couple of spies.

Mundy answered, "Sure, Pres, I can dig that."

"We have to make the pigs crazy paranoid," Vernon went on. "We have to make them start shooting niggers in their sleep. Can you see that, Beans? They'll be like some scared dude you keep teasing until he begins swinging at anything in front of him."

"Sure," Beans said. "My kid brother's like that."

They came to a corner and stood waiting for the light to change. Mundy took his hands out of his pockets and blew on his fingers. The bottles of gasoline, blasting caps sealed into the slim necks, clinked softly. "I'd mess with my kid brother and mess with him, you know? Just for kicks, and pretty soon—*wham!* He'd go off like a fuckin' bomb."

"That's what I mean," Walker said, as the electric light showed a neon-green man walking, and they started for the opposite sidewalk. "That's right man."

"I'm fuckin' freezing."

"We have to make the pigs go *wham*, like your kid—"

"It is too motherfuckin' cold to believe!"

"What?"

"Cold," Beans let his teeth chatter without trying to stop them. "Cold—as—a fuck-in'-witch's tit!"

"It'll be hot enough for you damned quick!" Walker sank back into himself, feeling anger well up into his throat. He wished, moving head down into the wind, that he could travel in time, that he could race back over the last days and alter everything that had happened.

Eileen and Chuck? he asked. And Vernon told himself, yes, he'd change even that. He'd find some other way to do the same thing. Someway that wouldn't have killed Spider and made the PM into a white man's lap dog, and forced me to start jumping the gun before we're really ready.

"Pres?" Beans's voice cut into his thinking, and Vernon grunted: "Wha'dyouwant, Beans?"

"You think he'll be there?"

"He'll be there."

"Maybe they moved him to city jail."

"He's not charged with anything, man. That's why he'll be there. And that's why we got to do this. He's just hiding out with the pigs. He's a traitor."

"I just thought—"

"Listen, man. Even if he's not there, he's just target one. Anything in blue can be target two, right?"

Mundy jerked his head up and down. He felt better now. He knew what they'd do if things didn't work out exactly as planned. Vernon could just say it like that, man, and it was so fucking clear. If target one wasn't there, they'd go after target two. Anything in blue.

"Right, Pres," Beans said, and they walked on into the freezing night with the city blinking on and off to each side, above and below them.

Boston 13 was the police unit assigned the first call that came through the station switchboard at 8:09 P.M. Boston 13 was a two-man car and the senior man in the vehicle was a tall blond veteran of six years on the street named J. D. Witt. His partner was Jack Ross, six inches shorter than Witt, but twice as outgoing with civilians and a very aggressive arresting cop. Ross, in his four years with the city, had been commended twice for bravery, and under investigation five times for charges ranging from conduct unbecoming a police officer to brutality. Of the five charges brought against him, he'd skated four and drawn a suspension for the brutality charge. His favorite expression when Witt tried to restrain him from thumping a prisoner was, "Screw the assholes and save the people!"

And at 8:09 P.M. in the rumbling front seat of Boston 13, on this particular night, it went like this: "Boston 13. A call for police at 5462 Rosemont. Alledged disturbance in progress."

"Boston clear." Ross scribbled the address on the notepad under the hot-sheet stand and hissed a curse.

"Just when we were getting ready to eat. 'Call for

208

Police.' Shit! It could be any goddamned thing. Could tie us up for an hour. Shit!"

Witt flipped on the red lights, but not the siren. He made a U-turn on Wayne and headed north toward Rosemont. He grinned at his partner's anger and shifted a wad of gum from one cheek to the other.

"No sweat, Jack. Cool thyself. We'll get this out of the way in a hurry and in a half hour we can be suffering from all the heartburn you'd ever want."

"You hope." Ross shifted in the seat to glance at the riot gun bracketed on the screen behind them. "To hell with the shotgun. This ain't no fuckin' holdup. I'll lay odds. Not in that neighborhood. A murder or suicide, a child beating, an overdose, but not a—"

"We'll soon find out." Witt reached to turn off the flashing red lights as they turned onto Rosemont Avenue. Walls, front porches, and crumbling sidewalks moved past on their left and right. Darkness settled around them as Witt turned off the headlights, and steered the Plymouth to the curb. He killed the engine and opened his door as Ross climbed out on the opposite side. Both men took their nightsticks and slipped them down through the metal rings on their wide leather belts. Ross aimed his flashlight to their immediate right and shook his head as J. D. stepped over the curb and stood at his side.

"This block is just about deserted." Ross spit to the side in disgust. "Most of these buildings are fucking condemned, J. D. Where the hell is 5462?"

"Might just be a crow call. What's this one?"

"Can't see the number. Probably doesn't even—"

But Jack Ross never finished the sentence. Snapping bright flashes of orange blossomed from above the two patrolmen and to their left and right. Ross was hurled backward, slammed into the car's fender, spun around and down to the space between the Plymouth's front wheel and the curb. Hit five times in the first burst, a sixth slug caught him in the neck as he was thrown back, killing him, and he was dead before he settled into the gutter.

J. D. Witt was hit in that first explosion of fire, hit in both legs, but he managed to draw his service revolver and dive down and under the bullets that cracked and spattered on the street, the sidewalk, and into the metal body of the parked car. He heard the windshield go and felt pieces of shattered plastic hit him as the two red lights disintegrated. He bit into his lip and tasted blood and decided, in an instant of the most terrible fear he'd ever experienced, not to fire back. He felt no pain in his riddled legs, but he knew he was hit there and he thought it must be bad. The legs were like sacks of wet sand dragging along behind him. He inched his way to the edge of the lawn rising up from the sidewalk. He breathed in the scent of cold earth and buried his face in brown grass and felt his bladder empty in sudden, helpless relief. The firing stopped and silence settled on the street like a falling ton.

The second call—this time a report of a purse snatching and injured victim—was received minutes after Boston 13 was dispatched to Rosemont. The call was given to a reserve unit in the district, one of three paddy-wagon cruisers, operated by an overweight corporal named Tom Croft (due to retire in six months after twenty years in the department).

Croft arrived on the scene of the alleged purse snatching and dismounted from his big white-and-black wagon, just as a citizen who lived in the 5400 block of Rosemont reported that two police officers had been gunned down. The citizen used Boston 13's radio—sitting on the glass-littered front seat of Ross and Witt's car—and babbled: "If anyone's listen'n out there, you got a couple cops here that's been shot, and you better send some fuckin' help, or somebody— 'cause these guys are really shot and I ain't jivin'—" But the citizen didn't release the mike button and the radio operator at the district station couldn't reply. Most of the radio cars in the area, though, had heard the caller use the street name—Rosemont—and were already speeding to the scene and unlocking shotguns on the way. Croft, the paddy wagon driver, also heard what had happened. Measuring a purse snatching to a shot cop, he leaped with what agility he could muster back into his cruiser and started jamming the old wagon into reverse. It saved his life, that hop into the front cab of the vehicle, because the storm of sniper rounds that struck the cruiser, smashed its windshield, punctured its tires, and drilled thirty-nine holes into its fenders, sides, and high roof failed to find Corporal Croft. The veteran was down and under the dash, radio mike in hand, screaming for assistance and only scratched by flying safety glass.

"Ambush!" Mason yelled, over the sound of the whooping electronic siren, and jammed on the brakes of his car as Tom Croft's voice crackled over the radio.

"Officer in need of aid under fire automatic weapons. Snipers at 4301 Laurel construction site next to apartment building. Don't come in from south—they're firing from that area—officer in need of aid—officer in need of aid—"

"Pop Croft, and Boston 13!" Mason shouted through clenched teeth and wheeled the car into a neck-wrenching U-turn. Rawlings hung onto the door handle and screamed back.

"Where you going, Joe? Croft, Boston 13—aren't we going to help them out?"

"It's a setup," Mason growled. "Shut the fuck up, kid, and get that gun down. We're heading back for the station!" He spun the wheel right and left, trying to thread his way through traffic, the siren madly whooping, barreling between cars, and seeing the curious and hostile black faces of men emerging from a poolroom, a gang of kids racing along the sidewalk trying to keep pace with the hurtling police car and pointing at Mason and Rawlings with broomstick guns, yelling. A window sliding up and a grizzled black face poking through a square of hard light, neon signs flashing, headlights jamming his vision, red taillights winking on all at once as cars tried to pull out of his way. The world rocketed past: Discount! Used cars!

Tony's Bar and Grill! The In Spot! Church of the Seventh Light!

Mason saw it all and felt the total blackness of the neighborhood, of his whole beat, and he suddenly felt like an intruder, an alien on the streets where he worked. And he knew, without any real evidence, that Vernon Walker was making an important first move in a chess game begun years before in Vietnam.

He grabbed the mike off the hot-sheet stand and tried to outshout the siren: "Nora thirteen to dispatcher! Nora thirteen! Nora thirteen to dispatcher!"

But the channels were jammed with other radio traffic: frantic cop voices asking, pleading, shouting, some distorted by distance, or slashed by car sirens. Mason switched to another frequency, cursing as he swung the car around a truck, using one hand for the wheel and the other for the mike. Rawlings gripped the dash and his choirboy face twisted with fear at Mason's maniacal driving. Joe threw him the mike, needing both hands to control the car.

"Get anyone you can, kid! Have 'em try and contact the station! Whirl that fuckin dial, but try and get the station! They're going to have company!"

There were three uniformed cops and two officers dressed in civilian clothes jammed into the small corner behind the district station's radio board when Vernon Walker and Beans calmly mounted the front steps, pushed through the glass door, and entered the front foyer.

Outside, in the cold night air, the harsh sound of sirens beat against the blaring croak of car radios. The teletype machine stuttered insanely as Detective John Cassiday said to Detective Captain Roy Slater: "Goddammit, Skipper, you got to let me take a car and get out there!"

"All the cars are out! Shut up, Cass, and work on that other channel! Where the hell is Captain Bruener?"

Officer Croft sent his voice into the crowded room as Walker approached the front counter.

"Officer in need of aid—officer in need—"

"Excuse me, Boss," Vernon said, staring into the lights toward the five policemen on the other side of the long, L-shaped counter. "Excuse us, Boss!" Slater wrenched his eyes from the radio console and turned to stare at a double-barreled shotgun pointed directly at his sweating forehead.

"Good Christ—"

"No," said Beans, standing slightly behind Walker, "it's just us niggers."

"Boss, grab the back of your fuckin' heads and put all your minds on me and this here scattergun!" Vernon waggled the shotgun at the five men and they each stood up slowly, locking their fingers at the backs of their necks. Walker grinned. "That's nice! Now, you!" he aimed the shotgun at Cassiday. "You with the devil-eyes. Tell me—don't show me, motherfucker—where the keys to your cages are."

"There ain't no keys," said the black officer who had been operating the radio, the radio which was still babbling in the many-tongued voices of patrolmen, Pop Croft, and the helpful citizen who continued to jam the channel. The black officer glanced at the insane radio and then met Walker's stare. "There's just cell keys. A key for each cell. Don't take no key to get into the main holdover area."

"I wasn't speaking to you, Tom," Walker said, and his voice started to crack with tension. He nodded at the radio. "Turn that fucker off. Off, Tom!" And the black cop flicked a switch.

The voices faded and were gone.

"Now," Walker said, feeling his chest and stomach settle into a hard lump, feeling his sweating hands grip the shotgun even tighter than before, feeling himself become cool and almost empty of thought, "we're going to transact a little business, pig people."

And he thought: this is it. The way it used to be and the way it should be. This kind of gut smoothness. This is the feeling that was lost, but now I've found it again and never—world, do you hear me?—never am I going to lose it again.

"Which door to this holdover area, Tom?" he asked, and knew his eyes didn't blink or his voice tremble. "Just point at it. Don't move. Just point."

The black officer hesitated. He looked at Captain Slater, who just barely nodded his head, and the black officer lifted his hand away from the back of his neck and pointed at the green-painted door between two empty desks. "That one."

Chapter Seventeen

CARS WERE jammed into the intersection. A truck with a long trailer was jackknifed from the edge of one corner to the corner across the street. Horns blared. People stood on the sidewalks and laughed, gestured, and cursed. And Joe Mason's car was wedged on the yellow-painted median line, with nowhere to move. He leaped out and cursed louder than his still-whooping siren. He crawled over automobile hoods. He ran down the line of traffic. He dragged drivers from the front seats of their cars. He moved them out of the way, as Rawlings helped up ahead, and while the eternal minutes crawled by a path was finally opened for them from the middle of the street to the sidewalk.

The truck driver rushed up to them as the two cops scrambled back into their car. The red lights flicked on the man's twisted face.

"I got a couple hundred cases of booze in that truck, Officer! Where the fuck are you going? You can't leave here! There's an accident! Where the—?" And stepped quickly back at the sight of Mason's revolver.

"Get the fuck out of the way," Joe screamed, "or I'll blow you away, asshole!" He stood up, half out of the car. He waved the pistol at the gaping crowd. "All of you fuckers, get out of our way!" He leaped back into the car, gripped the wheel, turned the siren up to full screaming volume, and jammed his boot down on the accelerator. Rawlings howled something that was caught up in the sound and whipped away as Joe piloted the car through the narrow path available in the street's traffic, over the curb, onto the sidewalk—scattering people right and left—and back onto the clear street on the other side. The new cop had a second to glance at Mason's face and was stunned into white-lipped silence by the soundless laughter twisting Joe's mouth. He's laughing, thought Rawlings. For Jesus Christ's sake, this fuckin' madman is fuckin' laughing!

Walker stared at the door and nodded at the black cop, whose name tag identified him as "Brown." He saw that the man was not wearing a pistol. "Where's your heat?"

"In the drawer."

"Leave it, Tom boy, and come around to this side, but keep your hands tight on the back of that nappy head. Beans!"

"Yeah, Prez!" Mundy's face was covered with gleaming sweat, and his eyes were lit. "I'm ready."

"Go around the corner and watch that oreo."

Mundy jerked his pistol loose from his belt and shuffled to the end of the counter, covering the radio operator as the officer pushed through a wooden gate to the booking area. Beans slowed his movement when the bottles in his raincoat rattled against each other. Walker hissed: "Careful, goddammit, Beans!" Just for an instant, he turned his head to glare at his man.

Cassiday bent forward, swinging his right arm back, reaching for the butt of the snubnosed .38 clipped to his belt. The two remaining uniformed patrolmen saw the detective make his move and one of them tried to imitate the action. The other shouted a warning to Slater and dove down behind a metal desk. The detective captain tried to jerk away from Cassiday and fell over a chair.

At the cop's shout Vernon jerked the twin triggers of the shotgun without aiming or looking around at the four men's dance of panic and anger. The roar of the weapon filled the big front room of the station and Cassiday's scream roared out at the same instant. Walker dropped down behind the counter and reloaded the smoking gun. He shouted for Beans, but the rattle of sudden shots cut his voice in half and he bounced up again, firing over the counter at the flashing picture of Roy Slater firing back from behind a desk. The officer next to him was trying to drag Cassiday from under the radio console.

Walker dropped down again. He cracked open the hot barrels and slipped in two more shells. A third shell dropped from his fumbling fingers and rolled across the floor. Walker stared at it, hearing Cassiday's moans and looking up to see Mundy crawling on his hands and knees around the end of the counter. Mundy held a quart bottle out to his Chief, and Walker dropped the shotgun, gripped the bottle by its neck and lobbed it over the counter. The breaking of glass and the crack of the detonator came at the same time, then a coughing WHOOOOOM! and a flash of flames.

"Fire in the hole!" Walker yelled and Beans grabbed at his arm. The stink of burning flesh, more screams— and a black hill of smoke pressed against the concrete roof of district thirteen's station house.

"What you say, Prez?"

"Nothing! Where's the Tom?"

"Had to waste him!" Beans was dropping bullets all over the floor as he tried to reload his pistol. "Motherfucker jumped me! Had to waste him!"

"Okay!" Walker lifted his chin at the doorway that the dead Officer Brown had pointed to.

"Let's go!"

Mundy's eyes widened in animal fear.

"Prez! Are you crazy, man! We got to get the fuck out of here! Pigs'll be crawling all over the joint!"

"We're here to get a traitor!"

"They are going to be in this fuckin' station in—"

"This is what you all were screaming for, isn't it?" Walker jerked his thumb at the sound of wounded men, men slapping feebly at burning clothes, the hiss and pop of gasoline eating at scattered sheaves of paper. "This, Beans, is what it's all about, you stupid bastard! What'd you think it was? What—?" But he couldn't shout any longer. His head and heart and soul were suddenly filled with stark pain like he'd never felt before. He shoved Mundy aside and crawled for the green doorway. His arm pushed Beans to the side and waved at the smoking air and his eyes rolled to the body of Officer Brown, curled up at the edge of one of the desks, and he heard the clatter of metal and looked down and saw Mundy's pistol sliding at him. Beans himself was staring at him, both of them crouched on hands and knees and staring, and then Beans leaped up and ran for the front entrance. The remaining two bottles of gasoline clinked in his raincoat and he was through the doors and gone.

Tears stinging his eyes, cutting through the smeared sweat and grime on his face, Walker grabbed the pistol and shotgun and lunged off the littered floor. He ran for the door through which he would find Chuck. He wept and cursed.

Weeping and cursing, Beans held his raincoat to him and tried to control the wildly swinging bottles. He felt the doors shut behind his broad back and took the first two high steps down—and then suddenly stopped. He stood stock-still. He swallowed convulsively "Vernon!" He half-turned around. His hands fluttered at his face, at his raincoat buttons. "Prez, man!" He started back the way he'd come, not hearing the screech of tires behind him, nor the slam of doors, nor the sound of shotgun and Colt .357 Python booming into the night.

Chapter Eighteen

A YELL split from Joe Mason's lips as the black man on the steps burst into bright flame and erupted like a blasted building, falling onto the top stair of the station steps. He let his service revolver come down to his side then, and ran around the front of the Plymouth. The rookie, Rawlings, was down on the sidewalk, puking his guts up in great heaving gasps. Mason jerked the boy to his feet, bending to retrieve the shotgun in the same swift movement. He smelled the sour odor of vomit as he shook Rawlings and yelled: "Knock it off! You'll see worse than that!"

"He's dead!"

"I hope to fuck he is!"

"We killed him—I—you—fired and I didn't even aim and he blew up!"

"Com' on! He isn't the only one! There's probably more inside, you asshole! Grab hold of your ass! I need you now, dammit! There's cops in there who need you, too!"

Rawlings wiped at his mouth. His eyes refocused. He pulled the shotgun from Mason. "Okay. Okay, now."

The two men stumbled up the stairs, past the smoking heap that had been Beans Mundy, and through the doors. The station was filled with smoke and Rawlings almost lost control again when they saw what lay behind the counter. But Mason dragged the rookie away and they kicked open Captain Bruener's office door, Mason going in first, pistol stabbing the air and his body crouched low. He stopped dead, seeing a pair of shined shoes sticking out from the back of Bruener's desk. They got Mother Bruener too, he thought, but then the feet moved and the captain's face lifted up and over the edge of stacked papers and fitness reports.

"Now, you're going to kill me, aren't you?" Bruener said, and his big hands were outstretched and pleading. "I heard you killing the others, and now you're here to kill me, aren't you? Well, I'm not going to fight you. You can kill me whenever you—"

"What's the fuckin' matter with him?" Rawlings asked, but Mason held the young officer back.

"Go ahead," Bruener said, his eyes staring and blank, his tongue sticking to dry lips with each word. "Go on and get it over with."

"Get on his phone," Mason told Rawlings. "Hold on to your stomach and get somebody down here! Don't worry about the captain. He's found his way out of this mess. Go on, kid. Do it!"

"Where are you going, Joe?"

"The holdover. Now, get on that fuckin' phone!" He turned to go, but grabbed the shotgun from Rawlings and took one final look at the babbling Bruener. He ran out of the office then, thinking of the four men behind the counter—dead? wounded badly?—burned and smoking in pools of splattered blood, and the body of Brown, almost at the Captain's door.

(The platoon was trapped and pinned down in the middle of the flooded rice paddy and Lieutenant Stamper was dead, alongside two others from second squad and four more from the strung-out column of marines.

Mason saw Johnson try to move forward. He saw the man get hit and knocked down.

And that was when he forgot, for the first time, that James R. Johnson was a black man, a Negro, a nigger. That was the first time he truly saw a black man as just a human being, his man, and one of his people. Sergeant Mason jumped up to help, but felt his legs twist out from under him. He spun around in slow motion. He clawed at the air and before he splashed back to the black mud and water he knew that he couldn't run, or walk, and that he would surely be dead before the day was finished.)

Walker heard the shots, outside the station, as he came to the bottom of the steel stairs. He stood still for a moment, trying to control his breathing, and peered ahead down the ill-lit hallway. He clutched the shotgun and jammed the pistol into his coat pocket. He pushed open a door and for a moment almost laughed. It was a bathroom, but with no sign on the door. When he backed out he tried the door to the bathroom's right, but that door was locked and for an instant he wondered if the black cop had lied about not needing a key to the holdover area. But then he heard a shout up ahead and recognized Chuck's voice. He ran to the sound.

The thud of running feet echoed above him and he knew the station was sealing him into its bowels. With a strange sense of relief, Walker accepted that fact, as if he'd always known it would happen this way, as if he were reliving an ancient dream.

He shoved through the last door and shouted, "I'm here, Chuck!" His eyes swept the coldly sterile room, took in the cells and the narrow lane in front of them. The door shut of its own accord and Vernon wished now that there were keys to lock it.

"Vernon!"

"I'm right at the door, Chuck!"

And the addict in number two caterwauled: "For the love of God—"

Walker straightened from his crouch and walked down the lane—wall to his left, cells to the right—and saw the addict sprawled on the cell's floor. He stopped in front of Williams's tall figure, standing just behind his barred front door.

"Hello, traitor."

"I haven't told them anything."

"I'm going to waste you, Brother."

"I know. Just don't call me that."

"What?"

"Brother. I'm tired of that."

"Blood's blood."

"Not anymore."

"You're the man who went against his raps," Vernon said. "You're the man ready to bury us all."

"I haven't said anything to them. Quit talking and do it, man. I got ears. I hear what's happening." His eyes rolled up toward the cell's ceiling. "I know what is going down up there. You're as dead as I am."

The sounds of boots banged down the hall. Walker smiled humorlessly. His voice was hollow in the barren steel room.

"Mason," he said. "I just know it's gung-ho Joe."

"You're as dead as me," Chuck repeated, and pressed his face to the bars. His lips moved between two green poles of crusted steel. "When it came down to it, Vernon, I was as dedicated as you always said we should be."

"I can't believe that, Chuck." Walker took the pistol from the overcoat pocket. "This is all I can believe in now."

Mason hit the door and dove to the floor, sliding forward on his elbows and chest, shotgun pointed ahead. He rolled to the right until his back pressed on the first cell in the holdover block. One shot banged out in the metallic stillness and then Mason heard Vernon Walker's voice, distorted, not sounding right, coming to him like the memory of the rice paddy and dead Johnson.

"Welcome aboard, Sergeant Mason!"

"I'm here, Vernon!"

"Oh—I can tell that you're here, Sarge. I knew it was you."

"You zap Chuck, Corporal Walker?"

"He is zapped," Walker's voice said, and once again Mason was struck by the toneless quality of the words.

"You shouldn't have, Vernon. He didn't snitch. He was a good man!" Knowing for sure now that Williams was dead, and seeing in his mind the lane in front of the cells, he knew exactly where Walker had to be.

"If he didn't," Walker intoned, "he would have."

"He didn't have much of a choice."

"None of us do."

Mason rose slowly to his knees.

"Corporal Walker," he said.

"Sergeant Mason, old squad leader."

"I should let you go, so we could keep the war hot!"

"It'll stay hot all by itself. Don't worry about that, Sarge. It'll stay burning, man."

"What's a little murder? Right, Vernon?"

"Just some more blood on the deck, Sarge."

"That's true. Are you hit?"

"Not a scratch. You?"

"I'm fine. You looking to carry me out again?"

"Not this time."

Mason laughed then, and Walker laughed with him.

"Some fancy work you did upstairs," Joe said. "It looks familiar."

"What we learned—right, Sarge? Just what we learned."

"There it is."

"There it fuckin' is," Walker repeated, and they both laughed again, and stood up, their view of each other blocked.

Joe was glad he'd left his cap in the car. He always hated wearing that goddamned hat, and he felt better without it binding his forehead. He thought, I should be seeing my whole life running past, now, but I'm not seeing anything.

What he really wanted was a cigarette; only he knew there wasn't time. He saw, in a second of sharp-focused photography, his son, his '57 Chevy, Ellen's face, Mona, and Allen Jones.

"I'll see you in hell, Mason." Walker's voice seemed to have gained strength and confidence. There was no hate in the words, not even anger.

"Wouldn't want to go to heaven," Mason said, and slid the safety off his riot gun. "All our friends are—"

He gripped the wooden stock tight under his right arm, against his chest. "You set, Corporal Walker?"

"All ready on the firing line, Sergeant Mason," Walker said, and lifted the double-barreled shotgun's muzzle just as Joe stepped around the corner, and into the narrow lane.

The booming echoes stirred the addict. His eyelids beat like insect wings against a screen door. His mouth opened and he groaned into the air that reeked of gunpowder, blood, and his own vomit.

"For the love of God . . . Somebody—"